DRAGON'S BLOOD

DRAGON'S GIFT: BOOK TWO

JASMINE WALT

DYNAMO PRESS

ONE

He wants the Dragon's Gift.

Those words echoed in Dareena's head, over and over again, as she sat by Lucyan's bedside. She gripped the dragon prince's hand tightly in hers while the healer helped him swallow a concoction to speed his recovery. Her heart ached to see him so battered—the cocky grin he always sported was gone, and his head and ribs were bound tightly with muslin bandages. The air in the room was as grim as the black and blue bruises on his face and chest, and not just because one of her beloveds was laid out in bed looking as though he'd been trampled by the horses.

No, they were all gathered here—Dareena, Lucyan, Drystan, Alistair, and Tariana—because the elves had them by the throat. They needed to figure out their next move.

"Thank you," Lucyan said hoarsely, waving the healer away. "Please, leave us for a moment." He sank back against the pillows, looking exhausted.

Every word he spoke seemed to pain him, and Dareena wished they could leave him alone to rest.

But time was not on their side, not when an envoy from the elven kingdom would be here any moment to collect her.

The healer bowed and left, shutting Lucyan's bedroom door behind her. Once she was out of earshot, Lucyan opened his eyes and pinned Drystan with a fierce stare.

"Tell me what happened."

Drystan sucked in a breath. "I shifted," he said, and he sounded as if he still couldn't quite believe it. "After Father threw you against that wall, I grew so angry, I just *changed*. The two of us crashed through the window in the throne room, and we briefly fought outside, but Father flew off after I wounded him in the eye. It would appear he's headed for the Black Mountains."

"Well, good riddance," Lucyan huffed. He squeezed Dareena's hand and gave her a fond look. "I'm glad you made it out of the throne room safely. In fact, all of you look remarkably well for having been in a fight with a dragon king. So why does it feel like we are about to go to someone's funeral?"

"Because Drystan may have won the battle against our father, but we have lost the war against the elves," Tariana said, her voice brittle. "Solara arrived with a message from Arolas, Elvenhame's crown prince and the new general. They have slaughtered or imprisoned over half our forces."

"Half?" What little blood remained in Lucyan's face drained completely. "How is that possible?"

"Apparently, the elves have managed to get their hands on some newfangled warlock spell," Tariana said bitterly. "They have a strange magic that forces us to change back into human form when we draw near and also greatly weakens the dragon born and prevents them from healing. They managed to kill three of our sisters by forcing them back into human form mid-flight, and laughed as they fell to the ground and split open their skulls. *Three* of them. And two more have been taken prisoner."

"Fuck," the brothers said in unison as Dareena stared at Tariana, frozen with shock and horror. Three dragons dead... over half their forces slaughtered or clapped in chains. Her stomach roiled, and she pulled in a slow, deep breath through her nose before she could become sick all over Lucyan's bed.

Pull yourself together, Dareena, she told herself. The last thing the brothers needed was for her to fall apart right now.

"Thankfully," Drystan said, his tone rife with sarcasm, "the elves have been magnanimous enough to hold off on wiping out the rest of our forces. Instead, they have agreed to release the prisoners in exchange for Dareena."

"What?" Lucyan roared, coming off the bed. His eyes blazed red with anger for a split second before they widened with pain and he collapsed on the bed again.

"Lucyan!" Dareena jumped up from her seat, pressing her hands into his shoulders. "Lucyan, please, don't tax yourself. You need to rest."

"Like hell I do," Lucyan snarled, his eyes bright with the same combination of anger and grief that roiled in Dareena's heart. "They can't take you from us. You're our *Dragon's Gift.*" He gripped her wrists, an agonized look on his handsome face.

Dareena sucked in a shaking breath, blinking back tears of her own. "I don't have a choice," she said softly, pulling back.

She met each of the brothers' gazes in turn, and her heart ached at the stricken looks on their faces. "If turning myself over to the elves means saving thousands of lives, I have to do it."

Drystan gave a deep sigh, while Alistair scraped a hand through his blond hair.

"As commendable as that is," Tariana said softly, "and as much as I don't want to lose half our army, you are the only thing that is standing between our line and certain extinction. You are far too valuable to be used as a pawn."

"Nevertheless, I must go," Dareena said, just as softly. "If I do not, they will wipe out the rest of our army and take the kingdom. At least this way they will only have one hostage, not thousands."

"If you are to go," Alistair growled, "you'll not go alone. I will accompany you."

Drystan and Lucyan both nodded their assent. "One of us needs to be by your side while the rest of us figure out how to clean up this bloody mess," Lucyan said.

Drystan opened his mouth to add something, but before he could, the door banged open. "I'm sorry to disturb you, Your Highnesses," Tarius Bellamin, the steward, said as he bowed hurriedly, "but an envoy from Elvenhame has arrived, and they demand to speak to the three of you immediately."

TWO

The next fifteen minutes were a mad rush to the throne room. Servants were called in to help Lucyan into something presentable, while the other two brothers hurried back to their rooms to change clothes. Dareena still looked fresh as a daisy in her white gown, but the brothers looked as though they'd been in a brawl, and the last thing they needed was to receive the elven envoy looking as though they'd all been dragged through the mud.

Finally, the five of them made their way to the throne room, which had been cleaned up some, though there was nothing to be done about the missing window behind the dais. Drystan sat on the throne, and two more chairs were brought in for his brothers, while Dareena and Tariana remained standing on either side. Lucyan had to be in excruciating pain, sitting on that stiff-backed golden chair, but he revealed nothing, his features schooled into casual indifference. She hoped the tonic the healer had given him was kicking in and that his dragon healing would have him back to normal soon.

"Send them in," Drystan commanded the steward, his deep voice echoing in the chamber.

The guards nodded and opened the double doors to admit the envoy. The steward entered, and directly behind him, a tall elven female with long, silver hair sailed in, her willowy frame draped in shimmering green and white fabric. Her jade eyes were arctic, her aristocratic features coldly beautiful, and she wore a cruel smile on her face as she glided toward the throne, flanked by two elven soldiers.

"Presenting the Duchess Lilani of House Valenhall," Tarius said, bowing low. The duchess inclined her head in the barest show of deference, and Dareena felt a brief flash of anger. From the way Drystan's jaw tightened, she knew he'd seen the slight as well. "Lady Valenhall, you stand before Princes Drystan, Lucyan, and Alistair, Princess and General Tariana, and the Dragon's Gift, Dareena."

"Charmed," the duchess drawled, her green eyes flicking over the princes dismissively before latching onto Dareena. "Though I can't say I'm particularly impressed at the dragon god's choice," she said, arching a pale blonde eyebrow. "Perhaps he, too, realizes how hopeless your situation is."

"Did you come here to speak to us, or are you here to bandy about insults?" Lucyan asked in an utterly bored voice before Dareena could voice the retort that was burning her lips. "If it is the latter, you have come a long way. A letter would have been perfectly sufficient."

The duchess bared her teeth in the semblance of a smile. "You are flippant for a man who is on the brink of losing his country," she said. "Although, whose country is it now? Our spies have already reported King Dragomir's abdication—I assume you are king now, since you are sitting on his throne?" she asked Drystan.

"I am," Drystan said, not missing a beat. It took everything Dareena had not to exchange glances with Lucyan and Alistair—if Drystan didn't want the duchess to know about their decision to rule jointly, there must be a good reason for it. "And as I understand it, you are here to take my wife hostage in exchange for the release of our prisoners."

"I am indeed." Lady Valenhall smirked. "In addition, both sides will call for an immediate cessation of hostilities, and the royal families will sit down together to negotiate a truce."

"Why not do that now?" Alistair demanded, speaking up for the first time. "Instead of wasting all this time bandying about with hostages, the king could have traveled here himself, and we could have something signed by the end of the day. We are not warmongers, Lady Valenhall—that was our father's way, and as you can see, he is gone."

"You'll forgive me if my king doesn't trust you at your word," the duchess said with a cold smile. "Given the history between our two races, it would be foolish for us to give up our bargaining chip. As you can imagine, holding thousands of soldiers prisoner is quite troublesome, not to mention expensive. We would much rather give them back to you and take your Dragon's Gift in their stead."

"And if we refuse?" Drystan asked.

"Then the prisoners will be executed immediately."

The princes stiffened, and Tariana's eyes blazed with hatred. Dareena felt numb all over—how could the elves sanction the murder of thousands? Were they really such an awful, bloodthirsty people? Surreptitiously, she fingered the stone on her right ring finger, wondering if she truly descended from the same race as the cruel woman who stood before them.

"Very well," Drystan said. "We agree to your terms, on one condition."

"You are hardly in a position to make demands."

"You will acquiesce to this one," Drystan said firmly. "The Dragon's Gift may be the future mother of my children, but she is still only human herself. I insist on sending Alistair, my brother, with her to Elvenhame for protection."

"Two hostages for the price of one?" Lady Valenhall said, sounding delighted. "Well, if you insist."

"You must also agree," Drystan said, "that neither my brother nor the Dragon's Gift will be harmed in any way, and that your king will keep them in his castle as guests, not prisoners."

"But of course," the duchess said. "We are not barbarians like you. Your family will be treated like royalty during their stay. I'll even sign an agreement stating such."

"When will the prisoners be released?" Lucyan demanded. "Are we merely to take your word that they will be allowed to return home?"

"They will be set free as soon as we cross over into Elvenhame's border and will be allowed to return unmolested. The two of you had best pack your bags," she said to Dareena, her lips curving into a devious smile, "and you may want to make your goodbyes to your husband. You may not be seeing him again for a good, long while."

THREE

Once the agreement was signed, Dareena and Alistair were whisked off to their rooms to pack. They were only allowed to bring a single trunk each, so Dareena had to be choosy about what she selected to take on the journey.

"I wish they allowed us to bring weapons," she said to Rona as her maid packed her underthings into her wooden trunk. Dareena was perched on the edge of her bed, tracing the hilt of her jade dagger, which she'd worn faithfully on her thigh ever since Drystan had given it to her. She remembered that day quite clearly, when he'd slid her skirts up to show her how to strap the holster on, and Dareena had thought she would combust from his sensual fingers on her bare skin.

Gods, how would she get through this? She'd lived her whole life without the prospect of a desirable mate, but now that she had three, she couldn't bear the idea of being parted from any of them. Drystan's fierce, protective embrace...

Lucyan's saucy smiles and laugh-out-loud jokes...she would miss them terribly.

At least I'll have Alistair with me, she thought, and was incredibly grateful for that. Her noble soldier with his heart of gold would hold her through the long nights ahead.

"Even if you did pack it, they would likely take it away when they searched your bag," Rona said ruefully. "Best to leave it so it will be here safe and sound when you come back." Her voice wobbled a little, and Dareena knew Rona was wondering *if* she would come back.

"Don't worry about me, Rona." She pushed herself off the bed and embraced her maid. "I will be perfectly fine. The duchess gave her word that I wouldn't be harmed."

"That's all well and good," Rona sniffed, pulling away, "but the duchess isn't the king, is she?"

Dareena bit her lip. The thought had crossed her mind, but as the duchess was an envoy, she represented the king. Her word was as good as if the king himself had come, and she *had* signed an agreement...

"Oh, what am I doing, making you worry like this?" Rona shook her head. "Of course the elves won't harm you. They aren't known for their cruelty, and from what I've heard of the elven kingdom, it's quite beautiful. I'm sure it will all seem like a grand vacation," she said with a watery laugh.

Dareena smiled, more to ease Rona's nerves than anything else. "You're right," she said, taking a dress from her closet and handing it to her maid to fold. "I'll think of it as a great adventure. It isn't every day one gets to travel to a new kingdom," she added with a wink.

"I only wish I could come with you," Rona said ruefully. "I imagine they've assigned you a maid, so I've tucked a list of instructions for her into the bag so she knows how hot to run your bath and what kind of tea you take in the morning."

Dareena laughed. "You are too kind, Rona," she said, kissing her on the cheek. "You have been welcoming since the moment I arrived and have taken such good care of me. I will miss you dearly."

They were nearly finished packing when a knock came at the door.

"Dareena," Drystan said when she opened it. His eyes glimmered with some undefined emotion, his face unreadable. "Could I have a moment alone with you?"

Dareena glanced over her shoulder. "Go on," she said quietly to her maid. "I can finish without you."

Rona nodded. "Please write to us often," she said, hugging Dareena tightly. "I will go mad if I don't hear from you."

Dareena hugged her back, tears pricking at the corners of her eyes. "I will," she promised, and sent Rona on her way.

"All right," Dareena said as she closed the door behind Drystan. "What—"

Drystan didn't give her the chance to finish. He pushed her against the wall and kissed her hard, his hands tearing at her dress. Dareena gasped as the gold and white silk fluttered to the ground, and he slid his tongue into her mouth, deepening the kiss as his hands roamed over her naked flesh. They slid beneath her bottom and gripped her tightly, hauling her up against him so that his hardness pressed directly against her already pulsing core.

"Drystan," she moaned as he blazed a path from her mouth to her ear with his lips.

"This is the last time we'll be alone together," he panted. Dareena whimpered as he sank his teeth into her earlobe, then sucked on it. A bolt of need went through her, and she clawed at the buttons of his deep blue tunic, sending them flying every which way. His skin was hot and smooth beneath her fingers as she pushed the fabric back, his muscles flexing as he carried her to the bed.

"Yes," she hissed as he entered her in one long, firm stroke. Hooking her legs around his hips, she clung tight as he rocked into her, shaking the bedframe with the force of his thrusts. Running her fingers through his thick, dark hair, she kissed his face, his neck, his collarbone, each press of her lips against his skin a benediction, a prayer that the dragon god would keep him safe while she was gone.

Somehow, they would figure this out. And when she returned, she would have all three of them in her bed so they could renew their bond together.

"I love you," Drystan said hoarsely as his thrusts grew harder. Power hummed in the air around him as he drew strength from her, his skin glowing faintly. Dareena arched her hips, pulling him in deeper, urging him to take more, to take it all. This was the last time she would be able to offer this to him, and she gave herself fearlessly, selflessly, digging her nails into his broad back as the orgasm ripped through her. The sound of her name on Drystan's lips shook the walls as he came, his hot seed rushing into her, and afterward, she cradled him, stroking his sweaty back and murmuring sweet nothings as their heart-beats gradually returned to normal.

A knock on the door interrupted the bittersweet moment of bliss. "Dareena?" Alistair called through the door.

"Come in," she called back, tightening her arms around Drystan as he began to move. What did it matter if Alistair saw them together?

Alistair opened the door, and his eyes flew wide. "I wasn't quite expecting to be greeted by the sight of your arse, brother," he said dryly as he nudged the door shut behind him.

"I tried to spare you, but the lady is refusing to let go of me." Smirking, Drystan slid his arms beneath Dareena, then rolled over so that she was on top of him. "Is that better?"

Alistair sucked in a sharp breath, and Dareena hid a smile. She knew exactly how she looked, naked and glistening, her legs open as she straddled Drystan. The space between her thighs warmed, and for a moment, she was tempted to invite Alistair to join them.

"As much as I'm enjoying the view, I'm afraid you'll have to get dressed," Alistair said ruefully. "The duchess is impatient to get back to Elvenhame with her prizes."

"Of course she is," Drystan groused, sitting up. He gently pushed Dareena off, then went to retrieve his clothing.

Dareena gave him a wistful look, then went to clean up and fetch a simple traveling cloak and dress from her wardrobe.

"Here," Alistair said as she began to unbutton the back of the dress. "Let me help you."

Dareena nodded, wordlessly handing him the dress. She could tell by the way Alistair's fingers twitched that he was itching to touch her bare skin, but he merely slipped the dress over her head, then smoothed it over her ample curves. Quickly, he buttoned up the back of her dress, then secured the cloak around her shoulders with a simple gold pin. He was dressed similarly in a brown tunic and cloak, and sturdy boots not unlike the ones he helped her pull onto her feet.

"There," he said, smoothing her hair. "You're ready for an adventure."

Dareena laughed. "That's what I told Rona to console her," she said. "That we should think of this as an exciting adventure."

"Try not to make it too exciting," Drystan said. He slid his arms around Dareena's waist and pulled her in for one last kiss. "You have to come back to us in one piece, after all."

"I will," she said against his mouth, "so long as you and Lucyan can make nice with the elves."

"Lucyan and I will pay whatever ransom they demand," Drystan promised.

"How is Lucyan?" Dareena asked Alistair a bit anxiously. "He looked like he was about to faint when the servants helped him out of that chair."

"Sleeping," Alistair confirmed. "He passed out almost as soon as his head hit the pillow. Do you want to see him before we go?"

Dareena bit her lip, considering. "No," she finally said. "He'll wake up the moment I enter the room, and he needs his rest." Squaring her shoulders, she took Alistair's hand. "Let us go before I lose my courage and bury myself under the covers."

Alistair smiled gently. "I highly doubt that will happen," he said, brushing a kiss against her temple. "You may be small, Dareena, but you have more courage than many of the soldiers I've trained with."

Dareena hoped he was right. She had a feeling she was going to need all the courage she could get to make it through the trials ahead.

FOUR

After they finished their goodbyes, Dareena and Alistair went down to the entrance hall, servants in tow to carry their trunks. The duchess waited for them with a sly smile on her face, flanked by a bevy of elven guards. Two of them took the trunks, while another four closed ranks around Alistair and Dareena.

"This is hardly necessary," Alistair said stiffly, eyeing the wall of shiny armor surrounding them. "We are not planning an escape."

"I never thought otherwise," the duchess said smoothly. "The guards aren't here to restrain you. They're here to protect you."

Protect us? Alistair frowned.

A familiar buzz grew louder—the sound of a large crowd. Alistair tried to peer over Lady Valenhall's graceful shoulder, but the front doors were closed, and from where he stood, he could see nothing through the windows.

"The townsfolk have heard about your unfortunate situation," the duchess explained. "They have come to see for themselves if the royal crown has fallen so low they are forced to give up their Dragon's Gift."

Alistair clenched his jaw.

"You are a horrid woman," Dareena snapped, her green eyes sparkling with anger. Alistair admired her willingness to stand up to the duchess even as part of him wanted to step between them and shield his mate. "Is it not enough that you are getting everything you want? You must humiliate us as well?"

"It isn't about what *I* want," the duchess said, "but what my king wants. And after what Dragomir has done, he wishes to make an example of you."

She waved an elegant, long-fingered hand, and the doors opened. Alistair wound his fingers through Dareena's and held her hand tightly as the guards nudged them into the open. Sure enough, half the town had turned up to see them—every square inch of the courtyard was packed with people, and they all seemed to turn as one to gawk at Alistair and Dareena. Thankfully, there were plenty of guards as well, and they forced the crowd back far enough to make a path to the waiting carriage and horse-drawn cart. The masses clamored as they descended the steps, shouting questions and hurling insults.

"How can you abandon us now?"

"Have the elves really won the war?"

"Who sits on Dragonfell's throne now?"

"Take your brothers with you!" one woman shouted, sounding particularly vehement. She tried to force her way toward Alistair, but a guard held her back. "We've had enough of dragons and their meddling in this country!"

Alistair said nothing, keeping his gaze fixed ahead. He could see from the corner of his eye that Dareena looked stricken, but to her credit she held her tongue, instead focusing on putting one foot in front of the other.

"Almost there," Alistair said to her under his breath, and she gave him the barest of nods.

The driver opened the door of the green and gold carriage and helped the duchess inside. Alistair gently pushed Dareena forward so she could enter behind her, but the footman shut the door, blocking her way.

"I'm sorry, but this carriage is for the Lady Valenhall," he said in the snootiest tone imaginable.

"Excuse me?" Alistair asked, highly affronted. "Where do you expect us to sit, then? Atop the carriage?"

"Don't be ridiculous," the driver said. "Why do you think we brought the cart?"

Alistair scowled. He'd assumed the cart was for the luggage. He glanced at Dareena, who was looking back at the crowd. The shouts were turning into jeers. Blast it. He couldn't waste time out here arguing with the driver—that would only make them look even worse.

"Very well," he said. "The cart it is."

He took Dareena's arm and guided her to the old cart, which looked like it belonged on a farm. There were two wooden benches: a high one for the driver, who was already seated and waiting, and a lower one facing the back of the cart for passengers. He helped Dareena into the cart, then hoisted himself up.

"Your hands," one of the guards said once they were seated. Dareena's eyes widened at the sight of the rope in his hands, but she dutifully held out her wrists, and the guard bound them, and then Alistair's. Alistair knew that the bonds were more ceremonial than anything else—they were fairly loose, and he could escape them with ease. But the crowd watched, and to them they looked like two trussed up prisoners being carted off to Elvenhame rather than "guests."

Once everyone was settled, the elven guards mounted their horses, and they set off. Their caravan rolled slowly through the courtyard and down the drive, giving the crowds ample time to watch them pass and shout more questions and insults.

"Good riddance!" one man cried. He was wearing a black cloak with the hood up, and he hurled a tomato directly at Alistair's head. It smashed into the wall a few centimeters from Alistair's elbow, spattering his cloak with red juice. Alistair gritted his teeth as he plucked the ruined vegetable from the bottom of the cart, tempted to hurl it back at the offender. "At least now we won't have to pay those absurd taxes anymore!"

"It's okay, Alistair," Dareena said, laying a hand on his arm. Her voice soothed him, and he lowered his arm before he did something he would regret. "Don't pay them any mind. We'll be out of here in no time."

"Maybe, but *they* will still be here," Alistair said bitterly. "Do they really hate our kingdom so? I know Father has been heavy-handed of late, but I did not realize there was quite so much discontent."

Dareena sighed. "You wouldn't, cooped up in the castle as you have been," she said. "There are those who resent dragons and dragon born for treating humans like second-class citizens. The Hallowdale family, from my hometown, certainly was that way. They were dragon born, and considered themselves better than anyone else, including the other upper-class families."

Alistair frowned. "Well, that certainly doesn't help our case. And with Father raising taxes…"

Dareena nodded. "There are many who aren't happy with that. Even so, most are content to let the dragons rule, as they want the continued protection of the dragon god over their lands. Someone must be stirring them up."

"The Black Cloak Brotherhood," Alistair said. "That man must be a member." There had been rumors of a growing cult of anti-dragon citizens, but Alistair had never come across one until today. He looked around. Quite a few black-cloaked citizens were in the crowd, shaking their fists at Alistair and Dareena and chanting, "Good riddance!"

"This is not good," Dareena said, huddling closer to Alistair. He let her lean against him, suddenly feeling guilty for letting her console him rather than the other way around. Blast these confounded ropes—he couldn't even put an arm around her with his hands tied like this. "Unless we turn matters around in a dramatic fashion, this civil unrest will only continue to spread. It's going to be very hard for Drystan and Lucyan to bring the people to heel if they believe we are the cause of their problems."

"My brothers are strong and resourceful," Alistair assured her, burying his own worries. "If anyone can figure a way out of this, it's Lucyan. And Drystan will hold the fort down and make sure everything runs smoothly in our absence. We'll be back in Dragonfell before you know it."

"I hope so," Dareena said with a sigh. Silently, they watched as Dragon's Keep gradually dwindled away into the distance and wondered exactly what kind of reception they would get once they arrived in Elvenhame.

FIVE

When Lucyan next woke, it was as if someone had placed anvils over his eyelids and stuffed his mouth with cotton. Groaning, he pushed himself upright in bed and squinted around, hoping someone had the foresight to leave a glass of water. Thankfully, someone had, and as he downed it greedily, some of the lethargy left his limbs.

What in Terragaard had happened to him? The last thing he remembered was the battle in the throne room. His father had smashed him into the wall with his great, spiky tail...

Oh. The rest of the memories rushed in, his heart aching. The elves had come. They'd killed thousands of their soldiers and taken Dareena away in exchange for returning the thousands more they'd taken prisoner. Lucyan's hands fisted in his sheets as he remembered the guilt and horror written all over Dareena's face—she'd felt personally responsible, even though this was in no way her fault.

No, it was Lucyan's fault. And Drystan's, and Alistair's, for not figuring out a way to stop their father sooner. For allowing things to get so bad that their kingdom was only a breath away from annihilation. Dareena was not to blame, and yet she was the one suffering. They'd been too stupid to do anything about it until it was too late.

Frustrated, Lucyan pushed back the covers and rang for his valet to come and dress him. His ribs still smarted some, but a quick glance in the mirror showed no bruises on his face.

"Your Highness," Baromar, his valet said, alarm on his square face as he entered the room. "You really should be abed—"

"I have no time to lay about like an invalid," Lucyan growled. "Not when we are at war. Now fetch my razor."

Baromar did as Lucyan asked. Twenty minutes later, Lucyan walked down the hall, albeit slower than normal, to his brother's office. He might still be in pain, but at least he looked good, clean-shaven and in fresh clothes. He'd pay a visit to the healers later today and take another draught of that foul-tasting but highly effective potion. With any luck, he'd be right as rain tomorrow.

Speaking of the healers, they seemed to be out in full force today, rushing from room to room along with most of the servants, carrying bedding and supplies back and forth. He imagined they were readying all available rooms for the influx of wounded soldiers that would be arriving in the next few days.

"You there." He snagged a servant by the elbow as she was rushing past. "Tell the healers to use my suite."

"Huh?" The servant blinked up at him in confusion.

"My suite," Lucyan said impatiently. "I have a large bed, and several couches and settees. The wounded will have far more use for them than I. Tell the healers they are welcome to them."

"I will. Thank you, Your Highness." The servant bowed, then rushed off to finish her task and do Lucyan's bidding. Some of the tightness eased from Lucyan's chest—it was a small thing, giving up his quarters, but if it could help ease some of the soldiers' suffering, he was glad to do it.

"Lucyan." Drystan shot to his feet as Lucyan entered his office. "You ought to be—"

"In bed, I know," Lucyan groused. He gingerly made his way over to the small cabinet behind Drystan's desk, where his eldest brother kept a stash of liquor.

Sighing, Drystan took the bottle of brandy from him, then fished out two glasses and poured a healthy dose for both of them. He didn't look like he'd slept well. There were circles beneath his eyes, and his skin had a wan look to it.

"I can't believe she's been gone a full day already," Drystan muttered as he lifted his glass. His amber eyes were dull, as if some vital spark had been stolen from them.

In a way, it had.

"I should have been there to see her off," Lucyan said as he flopped into one of the visitors' chairs. Drystan downed his glass in one go, and Lucyan followed suit. The liquid scorched his throat, warming his stomach and taking some of the edge off his pain. "Instead I was passed out in my bed like a useless fool."

"Dareena didn't want to wake you," Drystan said. "She was

worried that if she came to see you it would rile you up again, and you needed your rest."

"Yes, well, as much as I appreciate everyone's concern for my well-being, I don't need you fussing over me anymore. A few cracked ribs are the least of our problems. We need to access the treasury and find out how much gold we have before the elves come demanding their ransom."

"Do you know how to get the door open?" Drystan asked. "I tried to get into the treasury yesterday, but I couldn't find the key."

"Of course," Lucyan said with a wave of his hand. "I figured out where father kept his keys years ago. How do you think I always had enough gold on hand to bribe the guards when we were children?"

Drystan snorted. "I should have known." He pushed himself up from his chair. They made their way to their father's suite, which was located in a tower at the end of the west wing. A strange sense of longing overcame Lucyan as they stepped into their father's rooms—there was a time when he'd sit on his father's knee in the winged armchair by the fireplace, where the king often liked to sit and think in the evenings, or perhaps read a book. Or where he would have barged into the bedchamber in the middle of the night, plagued with nightmares, and his mother would lift up the covers and let him climb into bed with them.

"I miss them too," Drystan said quietly as a fierce longing ripped through Lucyan. They stood together in silence for a long time, letting their childhood memories wash over them—

memories from a time when they had been a happy family instead of the fractured, embittered mess they had become.

"There's a false wall behind this painting," Lucyan said, crossing the room. Drystan gently took down the heavy, framed canvas, which depicted a wild, stormy sea, revealing a large hole in the stacked stone wall. Lucyan reached in and grabbed a cedar box, then opened it and fished out the key to the treasury.

"It's a bit odd, don't you think," Drystan said as he replaced the painting, "that Father chose to move the treasury into his suite."

Lucyan shrugged. "We dragons do like to hoard our treasure, and besides, it isn't like Father was doing anything with these extra rooms." The royal suite had an interesting design—in the center were the main bedchamber and the salon, but surrounding it were four different bedrooms. The dragon kings of old had been fortunate enough to have multiple wives, hence the plethora of rooms, but after their race had been stricken by Shalia's Curse, those rooms had become obsolete. The room on the left had traditionally belonged to the Dragon's Gift, but until their father had taken the throne, the others had sat empty.

"What do you think about refurbishing this place?" Lucyan asked as he crossed the salon to the door on the far right. "We can give Dareena the main bedroom and each take one of these smaller rooms for ourselves. That way we can all be together. We'll need to get rid of these ugly animal heads, though"—he gestured to the stag and bear heads jutting out of the walls— "and I doubt Dareena will care for all the antique weapons strewn about."

Drystan laughed. "I like that idea a lot," he said, the light returning to his eyes as he looked around the space again. "It would be a lovely surprise for Dareena when she returns home. And we could give the weapons to Alistair." As the soldier of their bunch, their youngest brother was fond of weapons of all kinds, and could wield almost anything you could throw at him.

Lucyan smiled, then turned the key in the lock. It had been years since he'd pilfered from the treasury, but he remembered the piles of gold and jewels well—their kingdom was rich. They should have no trouble paying Dareena's ransom, and once they proved to the elves that they had no intention of spilling more blood, he was certain they could negotiate some sort of treaty.

"Lucyan..." Drystan said faintly as the door swung open. "Are you certain this is the right room?"

"I..." Lucyan's jaw sagged. The room was completely empty, save for some cobwebs in the corner. Panic slammed into him as he rushed into the room, looking everywhere, prying at the stones in the walls and floor to see if their father had somehow hidden the treasure from view. But there was nothing. Not so much as a single copper graced the stone floor.

"How could this happen?" Drystan demanded, his face red with anger. "How could Father have spent all our money?"

"He wouldn't have," Lucyan said faintly, leaning against the wall. He looked out the single window toward the Black Mountains. If he stared long enough, would he see his father there, circling the peaks of those chilly mountains, more beast than human now that he'd given in to his madness? "It's more likely that he's moved the treasure somewhere else in his paranoia."

"We'd bloody well better recover it before the elves come knocking again," Drystan growled. "If the other kingdoms find out that we've become paupers, we're done for. Do we have any money at all?"

"Tarius has a petty cash box," Lucyan said absently, his mind racing through various possibilities as he tried to figure out where their father might have hidden the treasure. Most likely, he'd been moving it in small increments over the decades—the treasure was far too large for any one person to carry, even a dragon, and there was the matter of getting it out of the tower unseen. "It will suffice for current expenses until we can recover the treasury."

Drystan nodded. "Lucky for us, taxes are due in the next two weeks," he said. "That will help replenish our coffers. If Father is hiding in the Black Mountains, that is likely where the treasure is, too. We dragons defend our hoards to the death, after all—even in his madness he would not leave all that gold undefended."

"Right. I'll ask Tariana to send some troops into the mountains to scout the caves," Lucyan said.

They found Tariana in the guardroom, in deep conversation with the captain, and took her aside to inform her of the problem.

"Blast it," she growled, her eyes blazing with anger. "I should have known Father would try something like this. He was always going on about how greedy his advisors were, and that everyone was trying to rob from him." She flicked her reddish-gold braid over her shoulder, a calculating look entering her eyes as she considered the problem. "I have a company of soldiers camped out a few leagues from the Black Mountains," she finally said. "I can spare a platoon to scout the mountains. I'll send Xenai with them to make sure they stay on task."

"Excellent," Lucyan said. He wasn't close with Xenai, but knowing that one of his sisters would keep the scouts in line went a long way toward putting him at ease. "Make sure you instruct them not to approach if they find the king's lair, and to only observe and report back with their findings."

"And don't tell them about the treasure either," Drystan warned. "The last thing we need is for some renegade soldier to decide to make off with it himself."

Tariana snorted. "They can try," she said. "Our father would annihilate them all with a single scorched breath if they tried to enter his cave. Still," she added, a troubled look crossing her face, "there is always some idiot who will ignore the dangers and become blinded by greed. I won't tell them what's inside the lair."

Decided, Tariana called for some parchment and a quill, then sent Xenai off to the Black Mountains to mobilize the company. Drystan and Lucyan were just about to leave when someone knocked at the door.

"Lord Shadley!" Drystan cried, letting the visitor in. Lucyan felt a jolt of surprise at the sight of the spymaster, looking travel-worn, the edges of his cloak crusted with dirt, his face and hair dusty from the road. Tariana shot to her feet, and Lucyan stood up more slowly—his ribs had begun to protest from all the walking.

"I'm so glad you made it back safe," Tariana said, throwing her arms around him in an exuberant hug. "Although I confess I am surprised to see you back here so soon."

Shadley smiled as he returned the embrace. "A little birdy told me that there is trouble brewing here in Dragonfell," he said, turning to face Drystan and Lucyan. "I thought you might have need of my services again," he added, bowing.

"Yes, we certainly could," Drystan agreed. "I assume you already know that the elves have taken Dareena and Alistair, and that our father has run off?"

Shadley nodded grimly. "I suppose it is a good thing that the king has abandoned his responsibilities," he said. "I doubt he would be willing to negotiate with the elves if he were still here."

Lucyan let out a disgusted sigh. "No, he would likely just rally our forces and send us all to our deaths," he said. "The envoy who collected Dareena and Alistair hinted that we would have to pay handsomely to get her back, which is proving to be quite a problem, as we have just discovered Father took the treasure with him when he ran off."

Shadley's face paled. "That is a problem indeed," he said. "Is there anything left at all?"

"Only the steward's petty cash fund," Drystan said grimly.

"Do you have any idea where our dear old dad may have hidden the treasure?" Lucyan asked. "We are guessing it is in the Black Mountains somewhere, as that is where he has fled, but it will take weeks to search through all the caves tucked away."

"I'm afraid I can't be of much help in that regard," Shadley said ruefully. "The king never let me access the treasury. I imagine that if I were a dragon, I would have spirited the gold away somewhere that was largely inaccessible to humans, which makes the mountains a perfect choice. If you wish, I can ask around and see if my spies have noticed any suspicious activity."

"Please do," Drystan said. "We need all the help we can get."

As the others continued to discuss their various predicaments, a wave of exhaustion hit Lucyan. Bidding the others a good day, he returned to his suite and climbed back into bed, knowing he still had time before one of the wounded would be needing it. It wasn't like him to be depressed, but between losing Dareena, Alistair, and the treasure, he was finding it difficult to maintain a positive outlook. One of the healers had left another bottle of potion by his bedside, which he downed quickly, then burrowed into the covers and sank into a healing sleep.

He might not have Dareena with him in real life, but perhaps he could enjoy her presence in his dreams.

SIX

The border between Elvenhame and Dragonfell was a two-day journey, and Alistair and Dareena spent that entire time confined to the wagon, save for during the night, when they were given small, separate tents and bedrolls to sleep on. Dareena longed to crawl into Alistair's tent and snuggle with him, to place her head against his chest and listen to his steady, reassuring heartbeat. But as far as everyone knew, she was Drystan's wife, and it would look suspicious if she crawled into her brother-in-law's tent.

Why keep up this charade? she wondered the next day as their cart bumped and jostled over the rough dirt road. They'd taken to wrapping scarves around their faces to protect themselves from the clouds of dust that rose up from beneath the horses' hooves, but even so, Dareena's eyes were constantly watering, and she had to lie low in the cart to avoid the worst of it.

Maybe it's to protect Alistair, she mused, gazing up at him.

He was seated on the floor next to her, his face a mask of stone as he stared out at the endless plains. If they knew that Alistair wasn't merely the king's brother, but a king himself, he would become an infinitely more valuable pawn. She hoped the council wasn't giving Drystan and Lucyan a hard time about this arrangement—as far as she knew, Dragonfell had never had more than one king at any one time. Dareena knew there would be some objections—there always were with any sort of drastic change—but she prayed that the councilmen would see sense and realize there were bigger problems to worry about than how many arses sat on the throne.

As Dareena nearly dozed off in the heat, Alistair hissed.

"Alistair?" Dareena asked, sitting up in alarm. He clutched his chest, his face contorting in pain. "Are you all right?"

"I...I don't know," he gasped, his face pale. "I've never felt anything like this before."

Dareena was about to call for the guards when he relaxed, sagging against the wall.

"That was very odd," he said.

"Did the pain go away?" Dareena touched his forehead—clammy, but no sign of fever. What was happening?

"Not exactly, but it's a dull ache now rather than a sharp pain." Alistair massaged his chest, a troubled look on his face. "I feel as though someone has reached in and yanked away half my strength."

"I wonder if it has anything to do with crossing the border?" Dareena asked, getting to her knees so she could look around. Sure enough, the flatlands had given way to rolling hills. Off in the distance, mountains jutted into the clear, blue sky, and she spotted a vast forest that couldn't be more than five leagues ahead. A sense of peace swept over her as she stared out at the verdant landscape, and as she took in a deep lungful of air, she felt almost invigorated. Guilt swept through her at the thought —what was she doing enjoying the scenery while Alistair was in pain?

"That's absurd," Alistair protested. "Why would the border make any difference?"

But an hour later, Alistair only appeared to be getting worse. By the time they stopped for lunch, he was listless, his normally bright eyes dull, his blond hair limp, his steps dragging as Dareena guided him over to a log so they could sit and eat. The duchess watched them, a smug look in her eyes that raised Dareena's hackles.

"You know what's happening to him, don't you?" Dareena accused.

"But of course. The warlocks crafted an enchantment to make our principal province inhospitable to dragons. Any dragon or dragon born who cross into this territory feel constant pain and are weakened as long as they remain here. Why do you think I allowed you to bring your brother-in-law with you?"

"You're lying," Alistair snapped, glowering at her. "My sister would have reported it if our troops had been struck by such an enchantment."

"Unfortunately, the enchantment doesn't cover all of our lands," the duchess said. "It was quite costly, in terms of both power and money, to set it up, so we have only protected the heartland of our kingdom. The war has mostly taken place in the west, which was no doubt by Ryolas's design. If he had met your sister on the battlefield here, we would have already won the war." The duchess gave them a smirk.

"This isn't right," Dareena protested. "You promised no harm would befall us while we were in your care."

The duchess shrugged. "There is nothing I can do about the enchantment," she said. "But if you insist, I can always send Alistair back."

"You'll do no such thing," Alistair growled before Dareena could answer. "Wherever Dareena goes, I go."

"Suit yourself," the duchess said lightly. Her jade eyes lingered on Dareena for a long moment. "I must say I am disappointed to see that you are not similarly affected. But I suppose the spell does not extend to you, since you do not actually have dragon blood in your veins."

"I suppose not," Dareena said coolly, neglecting to mention the boost of energy coursing through her. She wondered if perhaps she really did have elven blood, and if being in the elven lands was awakening it.

After lunch, they got back in the wagon and continued. On this side of the border, the guards allowed them to discard the bonds around their hands. As Dareena slipped her hand inside Alistair's, some of the tension bled out of his shoulders, and he did not seem quite so miserable. Maybe touching her helped restore some of his vitality, the way having sex boosted his power.

Alistair looked at the sky. "Looks like it's going to rain soon."

Dareena followed his gaze to the storm clouds gathering above them. A few minutes later, she adjusted her cloak as the wind picked up and the air cooled. The trees dotting the landscape swayed, and soon, fat raindrops splashed onto them.

"Find shelter!" one of the guards shouted as the drops quickly grew into a heavy downpour. The caravan headed off the main road, and everyone took shelter beneath a copse of oak trees. The thick canopy spared them from the worst of the storm, but even so, Alistair and Dareena huddled close beneath their cloaks, clinging to each other as thunder and lightning rent the dark sky.

"Dareena," Alistair said in a low voice. "Do you see what I'm seeing?"

Dareena lifted her head to look where Alistair pointed. Her heart jumped at the sight of another caravan, much larger than theirs, headed in the opposite direction. Even through the pouring rain, Dareena recognized their armor—the Dragon Force soldiers who had been taken prisoner. Many of them stumbled through the rain, legs and arms bandaged, while others, too hurt to walk, were carried in carts like the one Alistair and Dareena rode in. The caravan was under guard, but even so, Dareena felt a massive wave of relief.

"They've kept their word," she said, clutching Alistair's hand. "The prisoners are being sent home." Or so she hoped. It was always possible the elves were putting on a charade for her benefit, but Dareena refused to believe that. Besides, there weren't nearly enough elven guards to truly control the prisoners should they try to revolt. This was merely an escort, to ensure the Dragon Force soldiers went straight to the border and did not make any mischief.

Alistair put an arm around her and kissed her brow. "You've

done well," he murmured against her skin. "Even if the commoners hate us right now, the soldiers will remember what you have done for them and will stand by your side when the time comes."

"By *our* side," Dareena corrected. She nuzzled Alistair's cheek, sensing the frustration lurking behind his gentle smile. Dareena knew he wanted to leap out of the wagon and talk to the prisoners—from the way he watched the passing soldiers, he was likely looking to see if his sisters were among them. But she knew the elves would never allow them to get so close—if the soldiers knew their Dragon's Gift and prince were huddled there amongst the trees, there was no telling what might happen. Some of the soldiers might try to fight the guards to get them back, and while they might succeed, such an action would only bring doom upon them. And Alistair knew it, which was why he remained in the cart even though his instincts had to be telling him to go to his people.

"Everything will work out," Dareena said softly, stroking his arm. He leaned into her touch, and she cradled his head against her chest and prayed to the dragon god that they would not be separated once they arrived at the capital. While touching him did seem to alleviate some of his discomfort, she could see that he was still tired and in pain. And though the elves had promised to treat them as guests once they arrived, Dareena knew in her heart that Alistair would need to keep his wits about him for what was coming next.

SEVEN

Three days after Dareena and Alistair left, Dragon's Keep opened its gates to admit the flood of wounded Dragon Force soldiers who poured into the capital. Drystan was relieved that, while there were some terminal cases, most of the wounded were not on death's door. Most would recover once they received proper care.

Drystan, Lucyan, and Tariana had done their best to ensure the Keep was prepared for the influx of soldiers—every available bed had been converted into sick beds, and hundreds more had been set up in the various halls and salons. Even so, the Keep was too small to house them all, and they'd called on the towns-folk to help. There was still plenty of bitterness toward the drag-ons, especially from the Black Cloaks, but the men and women who made up the Dragon Force were still their countrymen, and were welcomed back by and large with open arms.

"More healers are being brought in from the neighboring provinces," Lucyan said. They were all seated around the dining table in the king's suite—the only room in the Keep that had not been given over to the soldiers. "We are still under-staffed, but hopefully these reinforcements shall arrive in the next day or so."

"From what I understand, they may not be needed," Tariana said. "I spoke to Catriona, Ara, and Xenai last night, and they are nearly completely healed. They said their wounds started to mend almost as soon as they crossed the border and that most of the dragon born are healing nicely too. A few days of rest and they should be back on their feet."

"Excellent," Drystan said with a nod. "They can help with the rest of the wounded, then." Despite its name, only a quarter of the Dragon Force's members actually had dragon blood flowing through their veins. Before Shalia's Curse, every soldier had been a dragon—now, with their dwindling numbers, the vast majority were human.

"The soldiers appear to be quite happy with your edict," Lucyan observed. "Exempting them, and their families, from taxes for the next two years was quite smart of you."

"It was the least I could do since we have no money to compensate them," Drystan said. He scrubbed a hand over his beard, the mystery of the missing treasure still weighing heavily on his mind. The scouts had not reported back anything yet—it would take them weeks to thoroughly scour the mountains, and they had to be careful about it or they might well get eaten. "The nobles aren't very happy about it since it's cutting into their profits, but I can hardly explain the reasoning behind my decision."

"Nor should you have to," Lucyan said firmly. "A king does not need to explain every action to his subjects."

"If there is anything important you need me to take care of today, you'd best speak up now," Tariana said, abruptly changing the subject. "I will be leaving Dragon's Keep tonight."

"Tonight?" Drystan echoed. "Where are you off to in such a hurry? We've ordered our troops to back down, so it isn't as if you have a battle to lead."

"Perhaps not, but I am needed all the same." Tariana's face darkened. "I've received word that Ryolas may be executed for his crimes against the crown. It would seem that Arolas, his older brother, has won their father's favor and turned the king against him. I cannot allow Ryolas to die when his actions have saved so many of our people." Her amber eyes glimmered as she got to her feet. "I must find him and free him, if I can."

"Hang on a minute," Lucyan said, snagging Tariana by the wrist before she could leave the room. "You do realize that the moment you cross into elven territory they'll put an arrow through your eye, don't you? You are no mere soldier, Tariana—you're our general, and the princess royal, besides. They'll recognize you on sight."

"I'll disguise myself," she said stubbornly. "I can use hair dye to change my coloring and a cloak to shield my face. It isn't as if I'm going to charge in there wearing my armor."

"Even so, someone may see through your disguise," Drystan pointed out. "I agree we should rescue Ryolas—we owe him a great debt. But there is no reason to rush headlong into danger without doing some reconnaissance first."

"Let Shadley and I find out where Ryolas is being kept first, and the exact nature of his circumstances," Lucyan urged. For once, there was no hint of belligerence in his eyes—he was usually quite standoffish with Tariana, but right now he was only concerned for their sister. "We'll send some spies to Elvenhame. They should be able to get us word on how Dareena and Alistair are faring as well."

"Oh, all right." Tariana sighed and resumed her seat. She still looked troubled, lines of exhaustion plaguing her face, and the fierce, confident aura she usually emanated was nowhere to be found.

Surreptitiously, Drystan scooted a little closer, and draped an arm around Tariana's shoulders. His eldest sister stiffened, not that he blamed her—he couldn't remember the last time either of them had offered the other comfort. But after a few seconds passed, she sighed and leaned into the embrace.

"You really love him, don't you?" Lucyan asked. His eyes narrowed as he studied Tariana.

She smiled. "Not at first. I thought he was far too pretty, and told him so the first time he asked me to dance. I believe my words to him were, 'I would never fuck a man who couldn't hold his own against me outside the bedroom.'"

Lucyan chuckled. "Of course you told him that. How did he worm his way past your icy façade?"

"He challenged me to a sword fight in the garden." Tariana smiled fondly, her eyes shining with the memory. "That fight turned into a tumble in the bushes, and—"

"That's quite enough," Drystan said, holding up a hand. His insides were squirming, and it took everything he had not to cringe. "I've no need to hear about your sexual activities, sister."

Tariana snorted. "So it's perfectly all right for the two of you to discuss *your* sexual experiences together, but not *me*?"

Drystan and Lucyan exchanged uncomfortable glances. "It's one thing to talk about pegging someone," Lucyan finally said, "but quite another to talk about actually *being* pegged—"

"Fine," Tariana said, rolling her eyes. "Anyway, we saw each other every time he came to court, and when I was seventeen, he asked Father for my hand."

Drystan felt like a bucket of ice water had been dumped on him. "He was going to *marry* you?"

Tariana scowled. "I'll have you know that I'm quite the catch."

"No one is calling your sexual prowess into question," Lucyan said with a wave of his hand. "It's just that you're infertile, Tariana, and Ryolas was his father's favored at the time and therefore expected to produce heirs. I'm surprised King Andur allowed it."

"He didn't, and neither did our father," Tariana said with a shrug. "We continued to see each other in secret afterward, knowing nothing would ever come of it. It became much harder once the war started, and now..." Her eyes shone with tears, and she swallowed. "We have to get him back. We *have* to."

Drystan hugged her, his heart aching for his sister. Tariana had a spine of steel—he wasn't used to seeing her so vulnerable. "We will," he promised, kissing the top of her head. "We'll get Ryolas back, and Dareena and Alistair too. And once we're reunited, we'll rain hell down on anyone who tries to split us apart again."

Tariana gave a watery chuckle. "This entire situation is a

catastrophe, but at least it has brought us closer together. It's funny how the catalyst that is strengthening our family bonds is also the same thing that might tear our entire kingdom apart."

Drystan smiled. "It is only in times of adversity that we discover who we really are," he quoted some old saying he'd read in a book somewhere. "It brings me great comfort to know that as siblings, we have each other's backs."

They talked for a few minutes longer, and then Tariana and Lucyan left to consult with Shadley. Drystan was just about to go check on the wounded when someone knocked at his door.

"Lord Renflaw," he said, a little surprised to see the Council Head standing outside. Flanking him were Lords Brimlow and Delvin, both highly influential councilmen. "To what do I owe the pleasure of this visit?"

"We've come to speak with you about some of your recent edicts," Lord Renflaw said. "Might we come in?"

"Certainly," Drystan said, hiding the uneasy feeling forming in the pit of his stomach. He offered the councilmen the chairs his siblings had vacated and poured them each a glass of wine. "How can I help you?" he asked, taking his own seat.

"It has come to our attention that you recently decreed a two-year tax break for all Dragon Force soldiers and their families," Lord Brimlow said. His thick, copper mustache twitched as he spoke, and his elegant eyebrows drew together in a frown. "As you can imagine, this has caused quite a stir amongst your vassals, who rely on this income in order to maintain their lands."

"As I understand it, my vassals have had several good years, and their coffers are quite full despite the war," Drystan said calmly. *Which is more than I can say for myself,* he added silently. "I believe they can withstand two years, and besides, they will still be receiving taxes from the majority of our citizens."

"That may be so," Lord Delvin said in a strident tone, "but you did not clear this decision with the council first. If you had, we would have told you what folly it was."

"You are very close to inciting outright rebellion," Renflaw warned, his eyes glittering dangerously. "The common people, from whom our soldiers are drawn, must not be exempted from taxes. If they get used to such leniency, it could prove fatal for the stability of our country."

"Just as the recent tax hikes have *already* proven fatal for the stability of our country," Drystan snapped. "Or did you not notice the number of Black Cloaks chanting 'good riddance' in the crowd the day my mate and brother were taken away? Our countrymen have long been unhappy with both the war and the taxes needed to fund it. Giving our soldiers a tax break will go a long way toward mollifying them, and might I remind you, the common people vastly outnumber the nobles."

"Is that why you recently submitted a proposal to increase taxes for the ransom fund?" Brimlow asked. "You expect us to take this reduction to our income in silence while approving a tax hike of your own so that you might avoid touching the vast piles of gold in your treasury?" He turned up his nose, and Drystan was tempted to scorch the mustache right off his smarmy face. "I think not, Your Highness."

"Take care how you speak to your king," Drystan growled, clenching his hands beneath the table. The council members exchanged uneasy looks but did not seem inclined to back down. Unfortunately, Drystan could see this from their point of view. Without knowing the treasury was empty, the tax hike he'd proposed made no sense. "If we don't get the Dragon's Gift back, our kingdom is doomed."

"I suppose you'll have to sell off a few plates, then," Delvin said haughtily. "We all know how valuable the Dragon's Gift is —surely she's worth giving up the silverware for."

Drystan swallowed the snarl rising in his throat. "Is there anything else you would like to discuss with me, *my lords?*"

He must not have hidden his anger completely, for the three men before him paled. Drystan realized smoke was pouring out of his nostrils, and he hastily extinguished the fire in his chest. He needed to get a firm hold on his temper, or he was no better than his father.

"You mentioned the Black Cloak Brotherhood earlier," Lord Renflaw said, speaking a bit more gently than before. "Our sources tell us that they have preachers wandering the outlying provinces, spreading anti-dragon propaganda. They claim that dragons are anachronistic, relics of a bygone past, and that it is time for humans to rule Dragonfell."

"Humans?" Drystan sputtered. "That's preposterous. It is called *Dragon*fell for a reason."

"Maybe so," Lord Brimlow said, "but in view of all this unrest, it would be wise of you to court favor with your vassals. As dragon born, we too do not wish to see humans overthrow the current regime, but as you mentioned"—he shrugged a shoulder—"they do make up the majority."

"I see," Drystan said, and really, he did. The councilman

was saying, in not so many words, that Drystan needed them more than they needed him. And until he recovered the treasure and Dareena, the councilman was right. Sighing, he settled into his chair and prepared to listen to the rest of their grievances. He couldn't reverse his edict about the soldiers' tax exemption, not without creating even more civil unrest. But he could promise to consult with them before making any other decisions. As much as he didn't like being questioned, he had to play ball.

He only hoped the council wouldn't back him into a corner as far as his relationship with Dareena was concerned. He knew the idea of all three brothers sharing the throne, and the Dragon's Gift, was unheard of. But Drystan didn't care. His family came first, and the gods help any man who tried to stand in his way.

It took hours for the rain to let up, and even then, Dareena and Alistair were forced to make the rest of the journey in that open cart while a steady drizzle continued. Normally, Alistair would have been able to keep them warm with his dragon fire, but with the enchantment sapping his strength, he was barely able to sit upright. By the time they arrived at Enethar, Elvenhame's capital city and home to Castle Whitestone, Alistair was shivering, his brow hot with fever.

"Help me get him inside," Dareena urged the guards as they pulled up in front of the castle. It was late at night, and far too dark for Dareena to appreciate the castle's splendor even if she had been in any mood to do so.

The guards smirked a little as they beheld Alistair in his sorry state, but the duchess ordered them to do Dareena's bidding. It seemed that she, too, was tired from their long jour-ney, for she swept into the castle without a word, presumably heading to her room for the night. The steward, a tall, reed-thin elf with black hair, showed them to adjoining rooms that were modest for their rank but not uncomfortable. Dareena barely noticed the surroundings at all—the moment they were alone, she opened the adjoining door and hurried into Alistair's room.

"Come now," she said, grabbing his hand. He'd collapsed onto the bed, his big body shaking. "We need to get you out of these clothes."

"S-so c-c-cold," he chattered, his eyes squeezed shut.

It took Dareena a few minutes, but she managed to coax him upright and get him out of his sodden clothes. Once he was naked, she stripped off her own clothing, then burrowed under the covers with him.

"Let's get you warm." She pressed her naked body flush against his. His skin was scalding in some places, ice cold in others, but she let none of that deter her as she wrapped her arms around him and rubbed his back with slow, soothing motions.

Alistair muttered something incomprehensible as he buried his face in her neck, and she nuzzled his cheek.

"There now," she said as his shaking gradually subsided. "You're starting to feel better, aren't you?"

"Much," he mumbled into her neck, and she laughed. Her laugh subsided as he skimmed his hand down her bare back, then gently squeezed her bottom. "You feel good."

Dareena shivered as his hard length pressed into her belly. "You should get some rest," she whispered, even as her nipples began to pebble. He shifted a little, and she bit back a moan as his chest scraped against her breasts.

"I had plenty of rest in that accursed wagon," he said,

nudging her legs apart. Dareena gasped as he slid his fingers between her thighs and cupped her. She was already growing wet, her tender folds aching as he massaged her, and she arched into his touch when he found her clit.

"I guess...a little sex...wouldn't hurt..." she managed as he played with her. A moan tore from her lips when he bent his head and bit down on the sensitive spot where her neck and shoulder met. After all, sex strengthened her dragon princes, didn't it? Perhaps a tumble in the sheets would drive away some of the foul magic plaguing Alistair and replenish his strength.

"That's it," he breathed as she came, clutching at his broad shoulders while she shook from the force of it. Rolling her onto her back, he kissed a scorching path down her chest, then traced slow circles around her nipples until she was gripping fistfuls of his hair, urging him lower. Her hips shot straight off the bed when he took her clit in his mouth, sucking hard, and she clapped a hand over her mouth to muffle her scream as she flew off the deep end again.

"Again," Alistair demanded. He slid two fingers inside her as he continued to lick the sensitive nub, driving her absolutely wild. Unable to control herself, Dareena stuffed part of the sheet in her mouth so she could grab his hair again, urging him on. She was on fire, burning from the inside out with need, and she wouldn't have been surprised if her entire body glowed from the force. Her mind was saturated with need, her heart full to bursting, and she couldn't get enough, she couldn't—

"Mine," he growled, finally slamming into her. She screamed his name as he filled her, stretching her to the fine line between pain and pleasure, and he ripped the impromptu gag from her mouth. He kissed her fiercely, filling her with the taste of him, his tongue deep inside her mouth as he fucked her with single-minded determination. The bed shook so hard beneath them that he gripped the headboard with one hand, and Dareena sank her fingernails into his luscious arse, urging him faster, harder, deeper. The air around them hummed with power as their souls, for a brief moment in time, strained toward each other, determined to become one.

"Yes," she moaned into his mouth as the edge rushed up to meet her. The orgasm hit, a tidal wave of pure pleasure that had her eyes rolling back into her head. Alistair stiffened, and then he came, his entire body vibrating from the force of it. Dareena smiled against his mouth, her walls clenched around his cock as she milked him for all he was worth.

"Mine," he growled again, tucking his face into the crook of her neck. He bit down on her shoulder, a gesture that was somehow possessive and tender all at once.

"Yours," she murmured in his ear as he collapsed on top of her. A soft warmth spread through her as he rolled onto his side, cradling her back against his chest, and she smiled as he nuzzled her neck.

"Yes, I'm definitely feeling much better," he said, and she laughed. "Thank you." He pressed a gentle kiss against her cheek.

"You don't have to thank me." She twisted her neck so she could stick out her tongue at him. "I'm not doing you a favor. This is a mutually beneficial arrangement."

"An arrangement, is it?" He nipped at her earlobe, making her squirm. "I've got some news for you."

"Oh?" She stilled at the serious note in his voice. "What is it?"

He splayed a hand against her belly. "You're pregnant."

Dareena's breath caught in her throat. "Pr...pregnant?" she whispered. Her world seemed to tilt sideways as she looked down at the big hand pressed against her abdomen. Was she really carrying a dragon baby so soon after meeting the princes?

"Yes," Alistair confirmed, a smile in his voice. "I've been around enough pregnant women to recognize the scent. Not to mention," he added, tweaking her nipple, "your breasts are more sensitive than usual."

Dareena squealed, batting his hand away. "Stop that!" she scolded, and he laughed, nibbling her shoulder. The shock of Alistair's impromptu announcement was eclipsed with blinding joy, and she grinned so hard her cheeks began to ache. "I wish Drystan and Lucyan were here with us right now. We must tell them immediately!"

"No." Alistair went still, his voice hard. "We can't risk the elves reading the message first. They can't know about this, Dareena."

The joy vanished as swiftly as it had come. "Damn," she said softly, tears springing to her eyes. For a moment, she'd forgotten all about the elves. "You're right. If the elves find out I'm carrying a child, it will only make me a more valuable hostage."

"I'm sorry," Alistair said softly. "I wish things were different. I wish you were safe at home in your bed, and that we could celebrate together. Instead, you're in enemy territory, and you're saddled with a useless lug who can't even shift."

"Oh, hush." Dareena turned in his arms so she could cup his face. "It's not your fault that you're not up to your usual strength," she said. "The same thing would have happened to Lucyan or Drystan. I'm glad to have you with me, Alistair." She kissed him gently. "I don't know what I would do if you weren't by my side."

"Neither would I," he said, tucking a strand of hair behind her ear. "Your eyes are more luminous than usual," he observed, a curious note in his voice. "I noticed it after we crossed the border—you seemed to glow with new vitality."

Dareena nodded. "I've long suspected I have an elven ancestor in my family tree," she explained as she traced the lines on Alistair's face. "I think being in the elven lands might be awakening something inside me."

Alistair's eyes lit with hope. "Perhaps you're capable of elven magic, then. I might be useless, but if you are able to harness your power in any way—"

"We'll be able to better protect ourselves from whatever Prince Arolas has planned," Dareena finished. From what Tariana had briefly told her, she knew he was the real enemy, not the king. "I'll see if the king will let me access the library. Perhaps I'll find something that can get us out of here, or at least alleviate your symptoms."

"My little bookworm." Alistair smiled fondly, then tucked her head beneath his chin. "If anyone can find the answers to our problems between the pages of a manuscript, it's you."

As Dareena pressed her cheek against his chest, she listened to the steady thrum of his heartbeat and let it rock her to sleep. Tomorrow, they would visit with the High King and find out if there was anything they could do to convince the elves to let them go.

And maybe, just maybe, Dareena would discover more about her elven heritage, too.

NINE

The next morning, Dareena and Alistair were woken by a bloodcurdling scream.

"What is it?" Alistair jumped out of bed, ready for battle. Unfortunately, he was also stark naked, and the maid who'd opened the door only screamed louder at the sight of him, her eyes popping so wide Dareena wondered if she would have to reach out and catch them before they landed on the floor.

Certainly, it was possible the woman had never laid eyes on a specimen as fine as Alistair. But did she have to act as if she'd never seen a naked man before?

"By the gods!" She pointed a shaking finger at them. "You… with your brother's wife…!"

Oh.

"It's not what it looks like!" Dareena clutched the sheet to her chest as she sat up, trying to find the words to explain. But really, what was there to say? It *was* what it looked like. She was in bed with Alistair, and as far as the elves knew, she was *Drystan's* wife.

An assumption she would have to correct immediately, she decided.

Dareena and Alistair exchanged helpless glances as the maid whirled about and left the room. "I wonder if I should call her back?" Dareena muttered as the door slammed shut behind her. She was going to need some help dressing this morning, after all.

Alistair sighed. "I suppose I should have sent you back to your own room last night," he said, perching on the edge of the bed. The muscles in his broad back flexed as he ran a hand through his shoulder-length blond hair.

"Nonsense." Dareena wrapped her arms around him from behind, pressing her bare breasts against his back. His warm body felt so good against hers—she was tempted to pull him back under the covers with her and make love with him again. "You need me, Alistair. For whatever reason, touching me makes you feel better."

"You're damn right it does," Alistair growled playfully, twisting around to catch Dareena's mouth in a steamy kiss. She clung to him for a long moment, their tongues tangling, as heat gradually built in her veins. If she reached forward right now, Dareena knew she would find his cock, hard and ready for her already. Her pussy clenched with need at the thought of lowering herself onto him, of riding him until they both saw stars.

"You should go back to your rooms," Alistair said, reluctantly pulling away. "I imagine the reason that maid came to wake us is because the king wishes to see us today, and the last thing we need is for her to come back and see us *in flagrante delicto*."

Dareena laughed and slid off the bed. "No, I imagine she would have a conniption." Giving Alistair one last, longing look, she opened the adjoining door and returned to her own room.

After donning a robe, Dareena spent the next twenty minutes unpacking her trunk. She'd picked out the dress she was going to wear to see the king—a gown of deep red velvet that went beautifully with her complexion—and was laying it out on the bed when a different maid returned with a breakfast tray. Dareena ignored the speculative look in the elven woman's eyes, merely thanking her for the food and asking her to draw water for the bath. She imagined the prudish maid from before had already told the other servants about her "adulterous" activities, and word was spreading like wildfire throughout the castle.

Dareena finished her food just as the maid returned with a bucket of steaming hot water and a wash cloth. Shrugging off her robe, Dareena let the maid bathe and dress her in the gown and matching slippers, then style her hair. The woman did an excellent job, her deft fingers weaving it into braids and piling them atop her head in an elaborate crown.

"You look lovely, Miss," she said when she was done.

"Lady," Dareena corrected automatically. "Miss" Dareena Sellis had died the day she'd drunk from the dragon goblet, though she hadn't known it at the time. She was the Dragon's Gift now, carrying a dragon baby in her womb. She was far more than a mere "Miss."

"Lady," the maid repeated with a nod. A faint smile curved

her lips, and Dareena wondered if the news about her and Alistair didn't bother this new maid. Perhaps not all elves were prudes after all. "I am Mari. I've been assigned to serve you for the remainder of your stay."

A knock came at the door before Dareena could respond, and the maid opened it to a guard on the other side. "The king commands your presence in the throne room," he said stiffly. Alistair stood behind him, flanked by a second guard. He already looked pale again, Dareena noted with some concern. How long would the boost she'd given him last under such duress?

"Of course." Dareena rose gracefully from her chair. The guard stood aside to let her pass, and she went to Alistair immediately. The moment she slipped her hand in his, she felt the air in the hall shift, and the guards gave them both stern glances. But Alistair's cold hand began to warm in hers, and she only held it tighter, refusing to let go. The elves could look down on them all they wanted—if skin-to-skin contact helped Alistair fight the effects of the spell, she would cling to him with her dying breath if necessary.

Thankfully, the guards made no attempt to separate them. As they were herded through the halls toward the audience chamber, they got more than a few strange looks from various nobles and residents living in the castle. Dareena ignored them and looked around curiously. The castle was fashioned entirely from white stone, but there were various stained-glass windows set high in the walls that made the stone bloom with wonderful colors and shapes. Tapestries depicting various scenes in history added further color, and statues of important elven figures flanked entrances and stairwells.

The castle steward waited for them outside the throne room, dressed in a deep green and gold tunic—the royal colors, Dareena had gathered. His face was inscrutable as he opened the doors to the throne room, and Dareena's breath caught as she beheld the splendor within.

Like the rest of the palace, the room was built of stone, but here, the pillars were carved into trees so lifelike Dareena would have thought them real if not for the color. The trunks stretched up and up and up, until the branches curved over the arched ceiling, twigs and leaves tangling on either side as they crossed midway. Between the pillars, steps led to a second landing where members of the court could come and watch the proceedings, and below, on either side of the aisle, were azure pools with shimmering orange fish swimming beneath the clear water. There were a number of elven nobles gathered on the landing, watching with expressions ranging from curiosity to boredom to outright disdain. Amongst them was Lady Valenhall, and flanking her were two men Dareena judged to be her son and husband, though age was hard to tell with elves.

The room quieted as Dareena and Alistair arrived, the silence broken only by their footsteps rasping against the stone floors as they approached the dais. Like the gallery, the throne itself was on the second landing, and behind it, carved into the wall, was a tree even more gigantic and stunning than the pillars. Unlike the stone forest lining the room, this one was in full color. The greens and browns seemed so alive, Dareena wondered if the tree was real.

"My king." The steward bowed once they'd reached the steps leading to the dais. "Presenting Dareena Sellis, the Dragon's Gift, and Prince Alistair, of Dragonfell."

Dareena looked up at the king, and it took great effort to fight against her instinctive need to bow before him. She had never seen a likeness of Andur, High King of the Elves, but he was nearly identical to the picture she'd conjured of him. Long, pale blond hair, a handsome, ageless face with fine-boned features, and eyes of pure silver that gave nothing away. He wore a tunic woven of some otherworldly material that seemed to shift and shimmer before her eyes—impossible to pin down exactly what color it was —and his head was wreathed with a crown of antlers. She met that silver gaze squarely, trying to gauge his measure, and though there was that aura of wisdom and mystery she expected from such a powerful gaze, there was also a brittleness there, as if something had recently broken and was desperately trying to mend.

His son, she thought, feeling unexpected sympathy for him. What must it be like to realize that your favorite child had been going behind your back and consorting with the enemy?

Her eyes flicked to the left, away from Andur. There stood an elven woman with chestnut hair and lovely green eyes, dressed in a pale green gown, every inch embroidered in gold. The shape of her mouth and chin told Dareena the obvious— she was the princess. And to the king's right, the raven-haired man in shining armor and a green and gold cape much too fine for the average soldier must be Prince Arolas. His cold blue eyes bore into hers, and a smirk curved his lips as he looked her up and down.

"Prince Alistair, Lady Dareena, this is Andur, High King of the Elves, and his children, Arolas, Crown Prince of Elvenhame and General of the Elven Host, and Princess Basilla."

"Enough with the formalities," Arolas said in a bored voice. "We know very well who they are, and vice versa. What I would like to know," he said, his smirk turning into a disgusted sneer, "is why the servants are whispering about finding you in bed together."

Dareena's cheeks burned. "I don't see how that is any of your business," Alistair growled.

"Considering that you are our guests, I find the matter quite pertinent," the High King said. "Does King Drystan know that you are bedding his wife? How can we assure her safety if we allow you to steal into her rooms every night? Are you attempting to supplant your brother by planting your own seed in her before he gets the chance?"

"Please, Your Highness," Dareena said, taking a step forward. "It isn't like that at all. Drystan is—"

Arolas made a slicing motion with his hand, and Dareena choked as her mouth filled with air. Try as she might, she couldn't speak, and she was forced to breathe in through her nose lest she pass out. From the pained noise Alistair made, she guessed the same had been done to him.

"There is no need to make excuses," the prince said, his eyes glittering. "I suppose you can't be faulted for bedding the prince. After all, it was what you were created for, was it not?" His cold gaze slid over Dareena like a physical caress, and she burned with anger and humiliation. She wanted to slap the smug, condescending look right off his face, but she could do nothing from her position so far below him.

That will change, she vowed fiercely as she glared up at him. One way or another, she would find a way to turn the tables so that *she* was on top.

In an act of pure defiance, she moved closer to Alistair and took his hand in hers. Murmurs swept through the gallery, and the High King's eyes narrowed.

"Perhaps we *should* let them explain themselves, Father," Basilla said, looking curiously at their joined hands. "They have to know word of this will spread back to Dragonfell. Could it be that we've made the wrong assumption about which of them is king?"

"Nonsense," Andur scoffed. "Dragonfell would never have turned over both its king *and* its Dragon's Gift as hostages. No one is that foolish. Still," he said after a beat of silence, "it would be best if we did not send word back to the new king about his wife's infidelity. We do not wish to devalue them."

"I've seen the reparations you and Father have written out," Basilla said to Arolas. "The sum is quite high. What will you do if they do not pay?"

"Oh, they will," Arolas said, smiling wide. "The Dragon's Gift is far too valuable for them to refuse. If they do not, she will be executed. Which does not bother me in the slightest," he added with a shrug. "As far as I'm concerned, putting an end to the dragon line once and for all can only be a good thing for us."

TEN

Late at night, four days after Dareena had left Dragon's Keep, Lucyan stared into the bottom of his whiskey glass and wondered how the hell he'd managed to sink so low.

Just a month ago, he would have never imagined growing depressed over a woman. They were a dime a dozen in his life, easily accessible. Married, single, virginal, whorish, it hadn't mattered—he'd had them all. And while he'd delighted in the time spent between pair after pair of legs, the moment they were out the door, they were also out of his head and heart.

He'd never become attached to one before. Not until Dareena. And the woman who held his heart in her precious hands was hundreds of miles away, far beyond his ability to protect or cherish her.

Alistair is one lucky bastard, he groused to himself as he put his feet up on the coffee table. If his father had been here to see it, he would have had a fit, but since Dear Old Dad had run off into the mountains with their treasure, he had no right to complain about how Lucyan treated his furniture. He and Drystan had moved into the king's suite, since all the other available rooms were being used to treat the soldiers. The servants had already taken down the animal heads and would busy themselves replacing the linens and furniture once the soldiers were back on their feet. He couldn't wait for Dareena and Alistair to come back so they could enjoy the space together.

Speaking of Alistair, he wondered how his brother was faring. As much as he envied him for being able to stay by Dareena's side, he also knew that his brother was likely in pain, or at least discomfort, right now. His spies had reported to him that the elves had paid the warlocks to help them cast a strong anti-dragon spell over the heartland of their kingdom, which would weaken any dragon who crossed the border and prevent them from either shifting or breathing fire. It was the equivalent of cutting Alistair's balls off, and Lucyan was all too glad he didn't have to endure that.

Lucyan considered switching to port instead of whiskey, then a knock came at the door. Groaning, he heaved out of his chair and opened the door to find Shadley. The grave look on his face sobered Lucyan right up, and he opened the door wide to let the spymaster in.

"What is it?" he asked, closing the door behind them.

"I've been investigating the Black Cloak Brotherhood, and something interesting has come to light," Shadley said, taking a seat in one of the chairs by the fire. Lucyan retook his chair and poured a glass for both him and Shadley. "I have reason to suspect that the oracle is behind their sudden rise to prominence."

Lucyan choked on his mouthful of whiskey. "The oracle?" he sputtered, once he could draw enough breath to speak. "But he is the dragon god's mouthpiece. What reason would he have to support a cult that is the antithesis of whom he serves?"

"I don't know, and these are only suspicions as of yet," Shadley warned. "But rumor has it that behind closed doors, the oracle is telling people that he worries that perhaps Dareena used some kind of warlock trick to fool everyone into believing the dragon god had given her his blessing. He says that it would explain why such tragedy has befallen the royal family—Dragomir running off without formally abdicating or choosing an heir, you and Alistair not stepping aside for Drystan, and, of course, the Dragon's Gift stringing along all three of you instead of choosing one."

Lucyan gritted his teeth. "She's not 'stringing along' any of us," he said. "Ours is a mutually agreed upon relationship, and we have reason to believe the dragon god himself has blessed it." Dareena had told Drystan about the prophecy she'd found before she and Alistair had left. Of course, soothsayers spouted gibberish all the time, but they also spoke true prophecies from time to time, and that one had been quite specific.

Shadley shrugged. "Be that as it may, all of this coupled with the recent military defeat is lending credence to the idea that Dareena may not be legitimate."

"That's ridiculous." Lucyan slammed his glass on the table. "I won't stand for this," he said, shooting to his feet. "I'm going to visit the oracle immediately and demand he recant these vicious rumors."

"Your Highness." Shadley got to his feet and gently grabbed Lucyan by the elbow before he could storm off. "It's the middle of the night. The oracle is hardly in any position to be receiving visitors."

"Oh. Right." Lucyan blinked, shaking his head in an attempt to clear it. He'd imbibed far too much tonight. "Well, what do we know about the oracle, Shadley?" he asked, resuming his seat. "I confess I've never been much interested in religion and have not spoken to him much. I've only ever seen him the times Mother and Father dragged us to the temple for some ceremony or other, but I remember him being a nice enough man. Why would he turn on us after all these years?"

"It's odd," Shadley said, leaning back in his seat. The firelight reflected in his dark eyes as his gaze grew contemplative. "Before your mother's death, the oracle spent most of his time at the temple and rarely came to Dragon's Keep unless he was called. But after she passed, he and your father became quite close. I daresay he was a trusted confidante."

"That *is* odd," Lucyan said, tapping his forefinger against his chin. "The oracle is supposed to be above politics. Why the sudden change in behavior?"

Shadley shrugged. "I asked him about it once, and he merely said that the dragon god urged him to take a more active role in the goings-on of the kingdom," he said. "I couldn't very well argue with him since he is the only person who ever talks to the dragon god."

"And why is that?" Lucyan demanded. "If we dragons are

supposed to be descended directly from the gods, why does he talk to some human instead of us? Why don't we have a direct line?"

Shadley blinked in surprise. "But you do," he said. "Every dragon has the ability to commune directly with our god."

Lucyan stared. "Why do I not know about this?"

"I'm surprised your father never told you. Luckily, I read about it myself a few years ago while doing research in the library. We can go down there right now, if you like, and see if I can unearth that passage."

"Please, lead the way," Lucyan said, hope stirring in his chest for the first time. The library held some fond memories, as he and his brothers had spent so much time down there with Dareena. It seemed only fitting that he'd find an answer to their problems between the dusty pages of an old tome, as Dareena had done for them before she'd been taken away.

ELEVEN

The next morning, Lucyan rose bright and early and called for his horse to be saddled. By the time he'd returned from the library, Drystan had been fast asleep in bed, and he saw no reason to wake his brother. Neither of them had gotten much sleep recently, so Lucyan merely left him a note informing him of his whereabouts before riding off to give the oracle a surprise visit.

Targon Temple was a two-and-a-half-hour ride from Dragon's Keep, and Lucyan used the time to think. Shadley had indeed come through with the secret ritual for how to commune with the dragon god, and he wondered if the oracle used the same method, or if the dragon god spoke to him through different means. Had his father ever spoken to the god? If he had, Lucyan couldn't imagine it had been recently. Why had the dragon god allowed their father to descend into madness? If they truly were his descendants, should he not have done something to intervene?

What if the oracle is right? an unbidden voice whispered in his head. *What if Dareena really isn't the Dragon's Gift, and all their suffering is the dragon god's way of punishing us for choosing wrong?*

"Don't be ridiculous," he muttered to himself. Of course Dareena was the Dragon's Gift. How else was it she could strengthen them every time they made love? He'd seen Drystan shift just before he'd lost consciousness during that fateful battle and had felt the hot flashes and intermittent weakness himself. Dareena had changed them, and was bringing them closer together with every kiss and caress.

Gods, how he missed her. If he closed his eyes, he could imagine the feel of her lips on his flesh, the way her luscious curves molded perfectly into his hands as he ran them down her bare body. His cock began to harden at the mere thought of her standing before him, those perfect breasts jutting proudly from her chest, her thighs parted just wide enough for him to catch that flash of pink petals beneath her thatch of dark curls.

Wrong time, wrong place, he scolded himself, shifting uncomfortably in his saddle. He forced himself to think about the oracle's wrinkled face instead, and exactly what he would say to the old bastard when he saw him.

Eventually, the woods surrounding him grew quiet, a familiar, hushed reverence permeating the chilly air. Up ahead, the trees gave way to a wide clearing, and Lucyan could clearly see Targon Temple, the most sacred place in all of Dragonfell. Despite the feelings of anger and bitterness the oracle had inspired in him, a sense of peace and contentment swept over Lucyan as he drew closer.

The oracle himself might not have the purest intentions, but there was no doubt in Lucyan's mind that this was a holy place.

Lucyan dismounted his horse a few paces away from the dragon fountain, then handed the reins off to an attendant before bending over to wash his hands and mouth before entering the building. The temple loomed a few yards away, a massive, two-story structure built from wooden beams painted vermillion, their sacred color. Golden runes shimmered along the edges of the roof, the pillars, and the entrance—protective symbols that would repel anyone who approached with ill will.

Lucyan drew in a deep breath and expelled what little anger lingered in his heart. He didn't *actually* mean the temple ill will, but he wasn't sure the runes distinguished the difference. Steadier now, he climbed the steps, then handed his shoes to another attendant.

"Do you know where I can find the oracle at this time of day?" Lucyan asked the attendant. He'd timed his visit to ensure he missed the morning prayers, having no intention to kneel on the floor for an hour and a half and chant rhythmically with the priests and acolytes. That time was much better spent getting what shut-eye he could.

The attendant smiled. "He is in his office upstairs."

Lucyan thanked the woman, then gave her a coin as a donation and stepped over the threshold. Woven rugs cushioned his bare feet, sparing him from the worst of the frigid cold that had seeped into the floorboards overnight. Ahead, on the other side of the wide, open space, was a shrine with a statue of the Fiorlax, the dragon god, and various offerings gathered around him. Lucyan bypassed the shrine, and those praying in front of it, in favor of the staircase that hugged the left side of the building. He lightly traversed the rickety steps, then turned down a hall lined with several rooms.

Lucyan had met the oracle enough times to know him by scent, so he easily picked out his office. "Enter," the oracle commanded when he knocked, and Lucyan raised his eyebrows. He sounded far too imperious for a man of the cloth, though perhaps he had a right to be, as the "only" man who could speak to the gods.

"My prince!" The oracle's eyes widened as Lucyan pushed the door open, and he got to his feet. He'd been sitting behind his desk, which, while neat, was covered in stacks of paper. The office itself was spacious and nicely appointed, with a large glass window overlooking the gardens on one side and a fireplace and chairs on the other. Bookshelves lined the wall behind his desk, and over the mantle was a gorgeous depiction of the dragon god soaring over Terragaard, his scales shining gold as he spewed flame into the night.

"This is a most unexpected surprise," he said, smiling broadly as he approached Lucyan. Lucyan noted the smile did not reach his eyes, and he detected the change in his scent—the man was nervous, and not at all pleased to see him. But he shook the oracle's hand anyway and accepted his invitation to sit down. "Have you and your brother come seeking guidance?"

"Just me, I'm afraid," Lucyan said as the oracle poured tea for them both. Lucyan surreptitiously sniffed at it to make sure the man hadn't slipped anything untoward in his cup, but it simply smelled like berries and hibiscus, so he took a sip.

"Understandable," the oracle said after taking a drink

himself. "I'm sure that neither of you can afford to leave for very long now that the king has left the responsibility of the entire kingdom on your shoulders."

"Indeed," Lucyan said, with more than a hint of bitterness in his tone. "We have many problems to deal with, and I was hoping you might be able to assist me with one of them."

"Of course," the oracle said eagerly. "Anything I can do, you need only ask."

"What I'd like you to do right now," Lucyan drawled, leaning back in his seat, "is tell me why you've been spreading nasty rumors about our mate."

"O-our mate?" the oracle repeated, his eyes widening in confusion. The fear in his scent grew sharper, and Lucyan bit back a wolfish smile.

"By 'our' I am referring to me and my brothers," he said. "Surely you know about the prophecy, the one that states the three of us can break Shalia's Curse if we join with the Dragon's Gift all together?"

The oracle's cheeks colored. "I told Lady Dareena to disregard that nonsense," he said stiffly. "That prophecy was told by a soothsayer with a well-known propensity for madness."

"Aren't all soothsayers known for flirting with madness?" Lucyan asked pointedly. "I hear it's a requirement for regular communal with the gods."

The oracle's eyes narrowed. "I don't like what you're insinuating."

"And I don't like that you're trying to change the subject," Lucyan said. "Do you take me for a fool? My spies have informed me that you are telling others that Dareena is not the true Dragon's Gift, and that she cheated the ritual. Why are you taking such great pains to malign her, especially when she is not here to defend herself?" His voice deepened into a growl.

The oracle held up his hands. "I said nothing of the sort!" he protested. Lucyan bared his teeth, letting out a plume of smoke, and the oracle's bald head grew shiny with sweat. "My prince, why would I do such a thing? I myself was right there when Dareena was blessed by the god—I would be calling my integrity as the oracle into question by suggesting that I could be hoodwinked. Of *course* she is the Dragon's Gift."

Lucyan frowned. The man had a point, and yet... "I see no reason why my spies would lie."

The oracle shrugged. "Sometimes rumors are only that—rumors. There is no question that Dareena was chosen by the dragon god to bear his next descendants. However, this business about the three of you being her mates must come to an end," he said firmly.

"Like hell it will," Lucyan said. "We've already decided."

"Well, un-decide it," the oracle demanded. "Dareena was charged with the task of choosing one of you as a mate, and choose she must. In order to save the dragon dynasty, she must mate with the strongest of you, which means you and your brothers will need to fight to the death to win her hand."

"And how the bloody hell do you know that?" Lucyan asked, horrified at the prospect. Fratricide? The very idea made him sick inside.

"The dragon god told me," the oracle said, as if that were obvious. "He spoke into my ear just as I was drifting off to sleep last night."

"Oh, so it's that easy?" Lucyan's voice was rife with sarcasm. "The dragon god sidles up to you in bed and whispers sweet prophecies in your ear?" He couldn't believe the audacity of the man. Lucyan had half a mind to rip his throat out, if only to stop him from speaking more lies.

"Just what are you insinuating?" the oracle asked, outraged. "You may be a prince, but I won't have you sitting here in my office, drinking my tea while you insult me!"

"Of course not," Lucyan said silkily, rising from his chair. He set his cup of half-finished tea on the table and gave the oracle an exaggerated bow. "Thank you for your time and your counsel, Oracle. I will discuss this with my brother henceforth. In the meantime, I would appreciate your discretion on this matter, at least until the Dragon's Gift has returned from Elvenhame."

He turned and strode out the door, leaving the oracle sputtering behind him. Keeping an unhurried pace, he headed down the steps, then left another coin with the attendant at the door as he collected his shoes. There was no need to give the temple staff any reason to suspect that the meeting had gone badly. With any luck, the oracle would keep his mask on and pretend that he was a do-gooder instead of the lying sack of horse dung he really was.

But as soon as Lucyan mounted his horse, he gave rein to some of his anger, urging the beast into a gallop. Heart pounding, he leaned forward in the saddle and gave the horse free rein to run. The wind sang in his ears, ruffling his short, red hair as they raced along the path and cooling the rage that stung his cheeks and ears.

Finally, when the mountain trail grew steeper and more treacherous, Lucyan pulled his horse back to a trot. Even if the dragon god *had* commanded him to fight his brothers to the death, he would never do it. He'd lived in the womb with them —he couldn't contemplate the idea of driving a sword through their hearts. And Dareena would never condone such barbaric behavior. She loved them equally—Lucyan was certain of that.

Mind made up, Lucyan stopped in Paxhall to send a quick message off to Drystan, then turned his horse around and made his way to the remote cave Shadley had told him about. *Fuck the oracle,* he thought with a grim smile. It was high time he spoke to the dragon god himself.

TWELVE

Four hours. It had only been four hours since Drystan had risen from his bed, and he already craved a stiff drink.

He sat at his desk, a ledger open in front of him, as he tried to make sense of their finances. The king had fired their treasurer years ago, insisting on taking over the accounting himself—an unusual practice for a king. Now that he'd made off with the treasure, Drystan knew why. The petty cash fund would cover their expenses until the taxes came in, but as Drystan pored through last year's tax collections, he realized they would not have enough to cover the coming year's bills if they also had to pay a hefty ransom.

Damn the elves. Those bastards had them by the balls, and they knew it. Drystan sincerely hoped those scouts had found his father's lair—they had to get that treasure back or they were doomed.

The financial logistics weren't the only thing making Drystan's head pound. He'd woken up to find Lucyan and Tariana both gone. *Bloody hell, can't I sleep in for a few hours without the world going to shit?* Lucyan had told him he was off to visit the oracle, and Tariana had decided to run off and rescue Ryolas after all despite his insistence that she stay at the Keep and make herself useful. He'd expected Lucyan back by now, but instead he'd received *another* note, this one saying that his brother wouldn't be back until nightfall, and in the meantime, not to trust anything the oracle said.

Maybe I need to get out of this stuffy castle for a bit, he told himself. When was the last time he'd gotten some fresh air? *Not since he'd battled with his father*, he thought ruefully. He really ought to get some flying practice in, now that he knew how to shift. Under normal circumstances he would be doing it every day, but with the stress of the past week, he could barely think about shifting, let alone flying.

The idea was quite appealing just now, so he closed the ledger, then made his way back to his rooms to change into a robe. His father had usually worn one when he went flying, as it was easy enough to shuck off—normal clothing was torn to smithereens during the change. But Drystan was only halfway to the royal suite when the steward waylaid him.

"My prince," he said, sounding slightly out of breath as he bowed. Drystan had half a mind to instruct the servants to call him and his brothers "king," but he'd held off as he wasn't certain that was accurate. They were a triumvirate now, were they not? Or would Dareena rule alongside them as well? What did you call a group of four rulers, anyway? Drystan didn't see why she shouldn't have a say in the goings-on of the kingdom—

she might not have been brought up as royalty or bred to rule, but she had a far better understanding of the common people's needs than either he or his brothers did.

"What is it?" Drystan said irritably. Surely not *every* damn thing in the castle needed his attention, did it?

"The delegation from Elvenhame has arrived," the steward said. "I've shown them to a suite of rooms and told them I would send word as to when you are available to meet with them."

Fuck. They were here already? Part of Drystan was relieved, but the rest of him felt sick at the thought of negotiating with the elves when he had barely two coppers to rub together.

"Tell them I will dine with them tonight," he said wearily. "And send Taldren and Catriona to my chambers, please."

The steward bowed and hurried off to do his bidding. Drystan dragged his heels as he continued toward the royal suite, his dream of taking a few hours for himself evaporating. As he closed the door to the suite behind him, he was overcome with the urge to burrow beneath the bed covers and shut out the world.

Really, how had he ever thought he was ready to take on the responsibility of ruling the kingdom? A surge of white hot anger rushed through him, and in that moment, he hated his father more than ever for giving into madness. He should have spent more time grooming them instead of trying to keep them away from the throne, and he damn well shouldn't have run off with every blasted coin to their name.

But instead of hiding beneath the covers, Drystan grabbed a bottle of cognac and three glasses, then settled in to wait.

"By the gods, Drystan," Catriona said as she and Taldren entered the room fifteen minutes after Drystan had called for them. "You look like hell."

"Hello to you too," Drystan said dryly, lifting his glass to her. Catriona was his fifth-born sister, and she looked much better than she had when she'd been brought back to the castle, her blonde curls shining and lustrous instead of matted and dirty, her creamy skin healed of all bruises and cuts and glowing with health. She wore the same tunic dresses all his sisters wore when they were at home, elegant enough to befit their stature but economical enough to throw on armor and rush into battle if necessary.

"Is there anything we can do to help?" Taldren asked as he and Catriona joined Drystan by the fireplace. He still wore the guard uniform—Alistair had reassigned him to the Keep after they'd rescued him from the elves. "It can't be easy, picking up the pieces after your father."

"I heard that the elves have arrived," Catriona said, swishing the contents of her glass. "Is that why you've summoned us here?"

"Yes. With Tariana and Lucyan both gone, you are the closest family I have." His other sisters had already flown back to rejoin the troops—Catriona was still here only because her wounds had taken the longest to heal. He paused for a moment, trying to gather his thoughts. "You both have spent time in Elvenhame recently. Do you have any reason to believe the elves are planning to backstab us?"

Taldren shook his head. "Ryolas treated me well enough for

a prisoner," he said. "He was no crueler than he had to be, and he did release me."

"What of Arolas?" Drystan asked Catriona. "Have you ever had the occasion to meet him?" He'd run across the elven prince once or twice in his younger years, before the war—he was a smarmy bastard, used to getting his way, with a tendency to look down on others.

"Arolas is a manipulative cunt," Catriona spat, her eyes glowing with anger. "It's a shame I never got to meet him in open battle. I would have made it my personal mission to run my sword through him." Her hand clenched so hard around her glass it started to crack, and she quickly put it down before it exploded, to Drystan's great relief. "He used to yank at my pigtails when I was a child, and once he forced me to sit on his lap for nearly an hour at a party. The pig was nearly a man by then—he had no right putting his hands on me at that age, or any other for that matter. Mother gave him a right scolding when she found him, and she never let him near me again, but..." She trailed off, shuddering a little. "I don't know what he's capable of, to be honest."

Drystan's stomach roiled at the picture Catriona painted. "And I've sent Dareena into the clutches of that monster?" He groaned, putting his face in his hands.

"Dareena has Alistair to protect her," Taldren reminded him. "She will be fine."

"Not if Alistair is being incapacitated by that foul spell," Catriona pointed out. "I don't really expect Arolas to try anything with her—she is a valuable hostage, after all, and unless he cuts out her tongue he knows she will tell you all about it at the first opportunity. But as far as the treaty…it's hard to say. King Andur will keep his word, but Arolas is manipulative, and he has the king's ear now. He will have done his best to ensure that the king fucks us as hard as he can with this deal."

"Bloody fantastic," Drystan growled. He had half a mind to seek out the elf delegation and send them back to the elven king as a jar of ashes, but that wouldn't get Dareena back. He talked with Taldren and Catriona for a little longer, but since Drystan couldn't tell them the full extent of the situation, they weren't much help. Tired of going around in circles, Drystan sent them away, then gave in to his urge to hide under the covers and took a long nap, ordering his valet to wake him an hour before his supper meeting.

By the time he went down to meet the elves for supper, he was feeling somewhat better, his raging headache reduced to mere tension in his neck and shoulders. To his great annoyance, Lucyan had still not returned—he knew his brother had said nightfall, but Drystan had hoped he would be back sooner so he wouldn't have to endure these negotiations alone. Lucyan was far better at this sort of thing.

The elves were already waiting in the dining room when he arrived—two men and two women. They rose as he entered, and he greeted them individually, shaking their hands and noting their cold stares and smug smiles. *Perhaps they'd been taking lessons from Arolas,* Drystan thought as he seated himself at the head of the table. He wouldn't be surprised to learn the prince had picked the delegates himself, or at least nudged his father into selecting the ones of his choosing. Rumor had it that the High King had not been himself since he'd jailed Ryolas—it was very likely that, in his grief, it was far easier for Arolas to manipulate him than it had been in the past.

The five of them made small talk as they were served a full seven-course meal, starting with a clear, spicy soup and working their way to the main entrée, a tender roast duck that melted in the mouth, served with new potatoes and a side of cabbage sprouts. The tension in the room was so thick, Drystan could have sliced it with a serving spoon, and it only seemed to grow the closer they got to the end of the meal.

Finally, when the table had been cleared and dessert was brought out, the conversation turned to business. "Thank you for this splendid meal," Lord Parkas, a raven-haired elf with a long, hooked nose, said. "Your hospitality is much appreciated."

"It's the least I can do after you've traveled all this way," Drystan said graciously. "I hope you've found your rooms comfortable."

"We have," Lady Maliwood, a gray-eyed elf with fire-red hair cropped close to the nape of her neck, said. "It's a shame we'll only be enjoying them for a single evening, but we must be on our way in the morning."

"Of course." Drystan inclined his head. "I assume you have a list of terms drawn up."

The delegates nodded. "Pre-signed by the king," Lord Thranar said, pulling a scroll from his sleeve. He passed it up the table to Drystan. "Sign it now, and you'll have your brother and your Dragon's Gift safe and sound in the Keep walls by tomorrow night."

The thought sent a pang of longing through Drystan, but he hid it behind a mask of indifference as he opened the scroll.

Sure enough, King Andur's seal was affixed to the bottom, and there was a line for Drystan to sign as well. Andur had assumed that he was king after what Drystan had said to Lady Valenhall, so no other signatures were required, though he would have to speak to the council before he signed off on anything.

He wondered how things would work once the four of them were reunited. Would all of them have to sign off on everything? Or would they each be delegated to handle certain types of matters, and only ones of the utmost importance would require a vote between them? They would have to hash all that out when Dareena and Alistair returned.

One thing at a time, Drystan, he told himself, and pushed the thought out of his mind. He carefully read the demands, and his eyes grew wider with every line. The salient points were:

- That Dragonfell give its unconditional surrender.
- That the Dragon Force be reduced to a quarter of its current number and only used to defend Dragonfell's borders.
- That during this time, Dragonfell will allow itself to be occupied by the Elven Host, who would provide "protection" from outside kingdoms.
- That a permanent envoy from Elvenhame be installed in Dragonfell's court.
- That Dragonfell will pay the sum of a hundred thousand gold crowns for the safe return of Alistair and Dareena, plus a ten percent tax for the next five hundred years in war reparations.

"This is absurd!" Drystan exclaimed. He snapped the scroll shut and handed it back to the delegates, resisting the urge to tear it into tiny scraps and shove it down their throats. "A hundred thousand gold crowns, *plus* ten percent? Your king is out of his mind."

"I believe it is *your* king who has recently lost his mind, not ours," Lady Eanor, the delegate sitting on his left, said with a smirk. "Our king is quite well, and he understands how valuable your Dragon's Gift is. He said to tell you that if the terms for their release are unpalatable to you, that he will accept fifty thousand crowns instead, and that Alistair would be released in ten years after working off the remainder of the debt."

"And if I refuse?" Drystan asked, sounding far calmer than he felt.

"Then you will never see them again," Lord Parkas said simply.

Dead silence descended upon the room as Drystan frantically scrambled for a solution. Even if he did recover the treasure, did they really have enough to cover such an outlandish sum? He would do anything to get Dareena back, but the thought of beggaring the kingdom...and not to mention the ridiculous request about quartering their army...

"What if I paid the ransom in land instead of gold?" Drystan finally said.

The delegates exchanged surprised glances. "What land do you have to give?" Lord Thranar asked. "Are you prepared to relinquish part of Dragonfell itself?"

"No," Drystan said. "But there is a province in the west called Dawnfall that we conquered some centuries ago. Though it belongs to us, we do not technically consider it a part of Dragonfell."

"Dawnfall is not a very large province," Lady Eanor said with some disdain. "Surely you could offer us something better?"

"I would also be willing to throw in Kalakas Island," Drystan said.

The elves leaned in, their eyes gleaming with interest. Kalakas Island had belonged to them some two thousand years ago before the inhabitants had declared their independence and managed to free themselves from elven rule. Not fifty years later, Dragonfell had swooped in and taken it for their own, and the elves had wanted it back ever since.

"I must say, I am quite surprised by your counteroffer," Lady Maliwood finally said. "It is well-known that dragons hoard their gold jealously, but they are even more possessive of their land. Why is it that you would rather not pay us?"

Drystan shrugged. "As I said, those two pieces of land are not truly part of Dragonfell, and Kalakas Island was originally an elven territory. My father was a warmonger, no doubt about it, but I assure you, my lords and ladies, that my brothers and I do not share his bloodthirsty tendencies. I throw in Kalakas Island in the hopes that you will consider it a gesture of good-will. I will, of course, insist upon certain trade agreements, but overall I think it is quite a good deal."

There was another beat of silence as the elves considered this. "We are not authorized to negotiate territory or trade concessions," Lord Parkas finally said. "We will need to send a missive to our king and wait for instructions."

Drystan gave them a wide smile. "I guess you will be staying more than one night after all then," he said, getting to his feet and signaling the end of the meal. He had no intention of handing over any lands—he simply needed to offer them something to chew on to prevent them from hurting Dareena or Alistair. Hopefully Lucyan would have something useful to offer once he returned from wherever the hell he'd gone off to, preferably something that they could use to free their mate and sibling. Drystan was coming up empty. Unless his brother put that brilliant mind of his to use, they were well and truly fucked.

THIRTEEN

By the time Lucyan arrived at the cave, the sun had long set, and his stomach cramped with hunger. It was a damn good thing he hadn't eaten breakfast before he'd left—the ritual for summoning the dragon god included fasting for an entire day. He'd drunk deep and often from his canteen during the journey, refilling it several times to keep the hunger pangs at bay, but with his extraordinarily high metabolism, fasting was particularly hard on him.

"This had better be worth it," he muttered as he dismounted from his horse.

It had taken Lucyan quite a while to locate the cave in question—it was hidden halfway up the cliffside overlooking a vast lake thirty miles south of Paxhall. Since the pathway to the cave was narrow and treacherous, he left his horse at the top of the cliff rather than forcing him to wait directly outside. While the animal grazed, Lucyan stripped off his clothes and dunked himself into the cold, clear spring nearby, then changed into a fresh pair of clothes.

He had to look his best for the dragon god, after all.

Once he was presentable, Lucyan climbed back down to the small opening leading into the cave itself. He had to duck to enter, and even so, the moss hanging from the entrance slid over his hair like ghostly fingers, making him shudder. But the same sense of peace and contentment he'd felt at Targon Temple swept over him, and he let out the breath he'd been holding as the apprehension prickling at his scalp vanished.

"All right," Lucyan said, pulling the torch he'd picked up back in Paxhall from his belt. He blew a gentle stream of fire atop it, igniting the beeswax. He had to hold the torch low to keep from accidentally lighting the moss on fire—it seemed to hang everywhere, so thick it was almost as if Lucyan was staring at a forest while hanging upside down in the air. His keen ears picked up the sound of critters skittering about, but as he did not see or smell anything dangerous, he disregarded the noises and continued walking.

About ten feet inside, Lucyan came upon a simple stone slab no higher than his waist. The sigil of the dragon god was carved into the flat surface. Lucyan frowned, wondering why there were no signs of previous offerings. Surely there would be something if his ancestors had visited this place, and yet the slab was as smooth and pristine as it had likely been the day it was carved. The hairs on the back of Lucyan's neck rose as he placed a gold ring on the stone, then kneeled before the tiny altar and clasped his hands together.

Please, Fiorlax, he prayed, invoking the dragon god's name.

Accept my offering, and speak to me as you have done with my ancestors.

Lucyan didn't know what to expect. The only reason he believed in the gods was because of Shalia's Curse, but even so, he wasn't much for prayer. Why hadn't he sent Drystan to do this instead? He wasn't as devout as Alistair, but since his younger brother wasn't here, Drystan would have done just fine.

He half-wondered if maybe he would feel a gentle gust of wind, a stirring in the air, maybe a whispered word. But there was no sign that the dragon god had heard him at all. The minutes passed in utter silence, the only sound in the cave that of his breathing and the movements of the critters who dwelled there.

"This is ridiculous," he finally said, when his knees started to ache in earnest. As he pushed himself to his feet, the air around him grew hazy. He gripped the wall, feeling woozy...

I must admit, I had thought you would hold out longer than this, a deep voice echoed in his head. His vision blurred, and then everything around him changed. He was at the top of a mountain, his knees buried in several inches of snow, and he was so high up that there was only fog, the clouds obscuring the world below. And above, hanging in the sky, was a giant golden dragon with eyes of pure flame.

"By the gods," Lucyan croaked, his mouth dry. The dragon was at least a hundred feet tall, twice the size of his father, with a wingspan that seemed to stretch endlessly. Warmth radiated from the enormous beast, melting the snow around him into puddles and turning the frozen ground to mud.

Did you think I was not real? The dragon cocked his giant

head. There was no censure in his booming voice, only curiosity. *That I would not come?*

"I...there was a moment..." Lucyan trailed off, not wanting to offend the god. Really, what was there to say? "Thank you for answering my prayers, Your Eminence," he said, bowing his head.

The god snorted, emitting a stream of fire from his nostrils that scorched the air. *I cannot remember the last time anyone called me Your Eminence,* he said. *I quite like the sound of it.*

Lucyan's lips twitched. "When was the last time you were called upon?"

Three centuries ago, by your great-grandfather, Barimius. He wished to know my opinion on what to get his wife for their twentieth anniversary.

"You can't be serious." Lucyan gaped up at the dragon, certain that the god was pulling his leg. Had his ancestors really dared to bother the dragon god for something so trivial?

The dragon god laughed. *No, I am not,* he admitted. *Your grandfather and father have come to see me since then, though sporadically, and the last visit was some thirty years ago. But the conversation I had with Barimius was the last one I truly enjoyed. Once, I had a much closer relationship with my descendants than I do now.*

The dragon god's voice carried genuine sadness, and pity stirred in Lucyan's heart. "What did my father ask you the last time you spoke to him?" Had madness started to take root in him already?

The dragon god was silent for a long moment. *He came to beg me for a cure to the curse,* he finally said. *One of his daugh-*

ters was in tears—she had fallen in love with a male and wanted to marry him, but she could not due to her inability to bear children.

Lucyan went still, remembering Tariana's story. She hadn't seemed very distraught when she'd told them about Ryolas's offer of marriage being shot down in flames, but if it had really been so many decades ago, she would have buried those feelings deep. Could his father have come here seeking answers on his eldest daughter's behalf?

Unfortunately, I was unable to give your father the answer he sought, as the time was not right. But it would seem that your Dragon's Gift has found what he could not. The dragon god smiled, baring rows of sharp teeth that sparkled like diamonds.

Lucyan's heart leapt. "So, you really did intend for all three of us to wed Dareena, then?" That the dragon god had given him a real answer was more than he could have hoped for.

Yes, and don't let that imposter fool you into thinking other-wise, the dragon god said. *It is a good thing you came to me right away—if one of you dies before Dareena gives birth to her child, you will ruin all chances of lifting Shalia's Curse.*

Lucyan felt as if someone had yanked the rug out from beneath him. "Dareena...what? Are you saying she's pregnant already?"

Indeed. She is a few weeks along. Alistair has already informed her.

The heavy weight that had been sitting on Lucyan's shoulders dissipated, and he wanted to dance. "A child!" he cried, his heart filling with elation. "Do you know which of us is the father?"

Does it matter? the dragon god asked. *All three of you will care for that babe as though he were your own. I brought the four of you together because this situation is far too complicated for a single ruler to handle. Working together, you may just have a chance.*

A son. Lucyan stared up at the god, stunned. They were to have a son, on the very first try. It was unheard of. "I...thank you," he said fervently, bowing his head again. He had never felt so humbled in his life, but as he knelt before the dragon god, gratitude overcame him.

"You said the oracle was an imposter?" Lucyan asked, his brain finally catching up. "Has he always been one?"

No, the dragon god growled. *His real name is Mathias Black, and he is a warlock. You should kill him sooner rather than later, as he murdered the real oracle some six years ago and took his face and name for himself. He has been subtly manipulating the population, turning the masses against us, as part of a larger plan to take over both Dragonfell and Elvenhame.*

"I knew it," Lucyan spat. "The warlocks killed my mother, didn't they?"

Yes, the dragon god confirmed. *They are the true enemy, though after all that has transpired between Elvenhame and Dragonfell, the elves are not your friends either. Dareena and Alistair are not safe at Castle Whitestone—you must get them back before it is too late.*

"We'll need to recover the treasure first," Lucyan said, his mind racing. "The ransom—"

Never mind the ransom, the dragon god said. *Arolas is a petty bastard—he has not said as much to his father, but he would sooner see the dragon line end than accept any sum, no matter how high. If you play your cards right, you can get them back without paying, but much depends upon the elves. They must do something treacherous or dishonorable so that their goddess will be forced to concede a boon.*

"And how am I supposed to make that happen?" Lucyan demanded. "I cannot very well manipulate the elves into doing such a thing from all the way over here."

All in good time, the dragon god said, sounding amused. He waved a hand, and the world turned hazy again. Lucyan tried to speak, but his mouth felt as if it had been stuffed with cotton. The world turned black around him as he sank to the ground, and the last thing he heard was the dragon god's chuckle before he lost consciousness.

By the time Alistair and Dareena were escorted back to their rooms, his sickly pallor had returned, and he was beginning to sweat with fever again. A healer was sent to look at him, but once determining that it was dragon sickness resulting from the spell, she merely gave him a potion to cool his temperature, then left him to suffer.

"You have to let me in to care for him," Dareena snapped, flinging her door open so she could scold the guard posted outside their chambers. She could hear Alistair moaning in pain, and it was driving her mad with anger and fear for his health. "Someone needs to mop his brow and make sure he's comfortable."

"We've been given orders not to leave you two alone together," the guard said sternly. "Prince Arolas doesn't want you tupping each other again."

Dareena's cheeks burned with anger. "Does that sound like a man in the mood for 'tupping?'" she demanded, stabbing a finger toward Alistair's door. Some protective instinct surged inside her, eroding her common sense, and she marched right up to the guard, close enough to grab his sword. The guard merely looked down his nose at her—he dwarfed her by a good head and a half, and obviously did not consider her a threat. "He's sick, and if he dies on your watch, there will be grave consequences."

The guard's eyes flicked toward the door, then back at her. "Very well," he said grudgingly. "But no funny business. I'll be right outside."

"Of course," Dareena said sweetly, stepping aside. The guard opened Alistair's door for her, then waved her in. He was tangled up in the sheets, tendrils of hair clinging to his sweaty brow, and Dareena felt a wave of pity as she looked upon his pain-contorted face.

"There now," Dareena said soothingly as she untangled him from the bedding. She was tempted to undress him again so she could give him skin-to-skin contact, but she was acutely aware that the guard could come back in to check on them at any moment, so she merely climbed under the covers with him and snuggled up against his big, trembling body.

"I-I'm supposed to take c-care of you," Alistair chattered as he wrapped his arms around her. He tucked his face into her hair and breathed deeply, likely soothing himself with her scent. "Not t-the other way around."

Dareena kissed the top of his head. "We are partners, Alistair," she said as she rubbed his back. "We take care of each other."

He only sighed deeply, relaxing into her embrace. Gradually, the shivers subsided, and the next thing Dareena knew, he was snoring lightly into her hair. Smiling a little, she played with the ends of his hair, twisting the silky blond locks around her fingers as she used her presence to keep the warlock spell at bay. She knew another bout of sex would rejuvenate Alistair again, but with that guard listening in the hall?

A knock came at the door, followed by the sound of a familiar voice. "Hello?" Princess Basilla called. "May I come in?"

Dareena blinked in surprise. She tried to get up to answer it, but Alistair mumbled something unintelligible and tightened his grip around her. "Yes," she called back, even as an apprehensive shiver came over her. What would the princess say when she saw them together?

The princess entered the room, still dressed in the same pale green and gold gown from before. She looked a bit startled to see Dareena and Alistair in bed together, but the surprise morphed into a small smile as she pulled the chair out from beneath the small writing desk and sat down next to the bed.

"The two of you look cozy together," she said, sounding almost wistful. Her green eyes, a shade lighter than Dareena's, trailed over Alistair's sleeping face, and she kept her voice low. "Almost as if you belong together."

"We *do* belong together," Dareena said possessively, pulling Alistair tighter against her.

"Then why is it that you are married to Drystan instead?"

"I'm not married," she said, exasperation creeping into her voice. "There has been no time for a wedding. But when we do marry, I will be wedding all three of the brothers, not just one. I am already bound to all of them—I can feel the connection in my heart, just as clear as they do."

"That's right," Alistair said, finally opening his eyes. He pinned Basilla with a fierce stare that said there would be hell to pay if she tried to separate them, anti-dragon spell or no. "We belong to Dareena, and she belongs to us."

Basilla stared at them for a long moment, her eyes round with shock. "I have never heard of such a thing," she finally said, "but I suppose I myself would not mind having three lovers, so long as they do not boss me around too much. Unfortunately, my father has other plans." Her voice colored with displeasure as she flicked a skein of hair over her shoulder. "He plans on marrying me off to Mordan, the crown prince of Shadowhaven. There is no formal engagement yet, but Father has been strongly hinting at the possibility—I imagine I am to be some form of payment in exchange for the help the warlocks have given us recently."

"I met Mordan once," Alistair said, sitting up with a frown. Dareena propped some pillows beneath him and slid her hand in his own, afraid of breaking contact with him. "Long ago, when he was still a youth. He was a pale, sly boy, and liked to slink around and eavesdrop on his betters. He always looked like he was up to something. Animals tended to go missing when he came to visit—cats and dogs and the like. One time, my sister Ara scolded him when she noticed him sneaking pastries out of the kitchens without the cook's leave. The next morning, she found her beloved calico out on the terrace, the body wrapped up in its own entrails."

Basilla recoiled, and Dareena clapped a hand over her

mouth as her stomach pitched. "That is beyond awful," Dareena said, her lip curling in disgust. "How could a young boy be capable of such cruelty?"

Alistair shrugged. "Some people are born bad," he said. "Others are made that way by their fathers. I don't know the warlock king very well, but my impression of him as a young man was that he was not a man to cross, and he had a dark aura around him."

Basilla sighed heavily. "At least I will be able to insist upon separate apartments if I am forced to wed him," she said. "What of Shadowhaven itself? Do you know what the capital is like?"

"My brother Lucyan told me it was a large, sprawling city full of magic and metal. There are as many metallurgists and factories as there are potion and spell shops."

"Metallurgists?" Basilla echoed, sounding horrified. "That sounds terrible! Elves cannot abide such things—they hamper our magic, and too much exposure can shorten our lives. Our own armor and weapons are crafted of mithril—the only metal we can stand to be around."

"Well, never mind separate apartments then," Dareena said, alarmed at the thought of Basilla wasting away in a similar manner to Alistair. "If you marry him, you'll have to insist on a separate residence entirely."

"Too true," Basilla said firmly. "Outside the capital, and far away from all those nasty metals."

"You mentioned that your magic is earth-based," Dareena said casually. "Can you tell me a little more about how that works?"

"Oh, it's the most wonderful thing," Basilla said, her eyes

lighting up. "We gather energy from our surroundings—some elves find it easiest to pull from the air, some from the trees or the oceans, and others from the ground itself. We can use that energy to perform certain spells, though nothing quite so advanced as the warlocks. We excel at healing, and can manipulate the elements—as I tend to pull my magic from the air, I wield air best, though another elf might be better able to control water."

"That's fascinating," Dareena said, leaning forward. "Would you be able to heal Alistair, then? Touching me seems to help him some, but the moment I pull away he begins to deteriorate again."

Basilla bit her lip. "There is nothing I can do to permanently undo the effects of the warlock spell," she said. "However"—she leaned forward and pressed her hand against Alistair's forehead—"I can help reduce the impact a bit."

The air in the room shifted, and Basilla's hand on Alistair began to glow. Dareena watched as the tension bled out of his face and shoulders and healthy color seeped back into his cheeks.

"Wow," Alistair said as Basilla pulled away. He sounded deeply relieved. "I feel much better."

"See?" Basilla beamed. "It should last you for a few hours." Her smile faded a little as she looked at Dareena again. "It is a pity that only elves can do it...and yet, you said that touching him keeps the sickness at bay. How does that work?"

"I think it has something to do with being the Dragon's Gift," Dareena said. "The guard let me in to care for him, but I fear that he will separate us again and Alistair will fall ill over the night."

"Well, that won't do at all," Basilla declared, getting to her feet. "You are our guests, and we promised to keep you safe and healthy. I must be off now, before my lady-in-waiting comes looking for me, but I will tell the guard to keep the two of you together."

"Thank you," Dareena said fervently. "You are too kind."

Basilla gave her a sad smile. "It is the least I can do after all you have been through."

"She seems quite sympathetic to our plight," Alistair said after she'd closed the door behind her. "Not what I expected at all from Arolas's sister."

"She is also Ryolas's sister," Dareena reminded him. "Perhaps the siblings get their temperaments from different relatives."

They listened as Basilla ordered the guard to leave Dareena and Alistair in peace and allow them to stay together. The guard sounded skeptical and told her that he would need to clear it with Arolas, much to Dareena's consternation. She heard his armor clank as he strode off down the hall, followed by the soft pitter-patter of slippered feet.

"Sounds like we are alone," Alistair said, slipping his arms around her waist. He pressed a kiss into the back of her neck, sending a pleasant shiver down her spine. "Shall we take advantage?"

Dareena giggled, turning to face him. "We've got to keep up your strength, don't we?" she asked, twining her arms around his neck. She kissed him deeply as he pushed up her skirts, his big hands making quick work of her underwear. He squeezed her bare bottom as she rubbed herself against his growing erection, and she moaned into his mouth as her pussy ached with need for him.

"Already wet," he murmured against her mouth, sliding his fingers against her folds. He undid the buttons on his trousers, then lowered her onto his waiting shaft. The two lovers moaned in unison as Alistair's cock filled Dareena, and she gripped his shoulders hard, riding him.

They made love three times—once for themselves, and twice more for Drystan and Lucyan, whom they both missed terribly. The third time, as Alistair pounded into Dareena while her legs were locked around his waist, he splintered the wooden headboard by gripping it too hard.

"Blast it," he cursed, wrenching his hand back. "That bloody hurts." Wincing, he carefully picked the splinters out of his bleeding hand.

"Let me see that," Dareena said, sitting up. She gently took his hand in her own, and after fishing out the last few splinters, decided to try the trick that Basilla had told her about. Closing her eyes, she focused in on the air around them. At first, she felt nothing, but as the seconds passed, her chest stirred. She could sense a low hum in the air around her—an undercurrent of power, she realized with some excitement. She tried to grab hold of it, but it slipped out of her mental grip.

"What are you doing?" Alistair asked.

"Hush!" Eyes still shut, Dareena tried again. She was unsuccessful the second time, but the third, she managed to snag a small tendril of power. Holding tight, she envisioned it going into Alistair's hand, merging with his flesh and encouraging his skin to knit back together.

"By the gods," Alistair said, and her eyes flew open. He stared down at their joined hands, an astonished look in his eyes. "You...you healed my hand!"

"It works!" Dareena squealed. "It was quite hard, which makes me think that air may not be my element...though it could just be that having only a tiny bit of elven blood makes it more difficult to use the magic. Still," she said, marveling at his newly healed hand, "this is very encouraging." What else could she do with this newfound power? Would she be able to draw more from the air with practice?

"Indeed, it is," Alistair said. He pulled Dareena back under him, his eyes gleaming with renewed vigor, and she gasped as he cupped her between her legs. "Now," he said, leaning in to nibble on her earlobe, "where were we?"

FIFTEEN

Drystan sat at the dining table in the royal suite, scowling at the array of jewelry spread before him. Several rings, heavy gold cuffs, a silver torque, a variety of gems...it wasn't even close to the ransom the elves had demanded, but perhaps he could use the profits to pay the wages of the castle staff. He had a set of jeweled daggers that might also fetch a nice price, though he was loath to give those up—they had been a coming-of-age present from his mother and had great sentimental value.

What does it matter? Drystan thought gloomily, running a hand over his beard. He'd neglected to trim it the past few weeks, and it had grown longer, to the point that he could catch the thick strands and twirl them around his finger. If they didn't find a way to get the elves to back off, there would be no staff left to pay. Even with their recovered numbers, the Elven Host could still annihilate them. Losing three of Drystan's sisters had dealt a heavy blow—their bodies had been ruined beyond recognition, so the elves had burned them to ashes and returned them in urns. They would have a proper ceremony to mourn that loss once all of this was behind them.

If such a day ever came when they had the luxury of time to mourn.

The door banged open, and Lucyan stormed in. Drystan sat up in alarm—his brother's shirt was torn, his hair was disheveled, and his face and clothing were smudged with soot.

"What the hell happened to you?" Drystan demanded.

"Fucking Black Cloaks," he fumed, his teeth bared and eyes blazing. "A group of them ambushed me on the way back here, and I was forced to char them all." His fists clenched and unclenched as he made his way to the liquor cabinet. "We're out of whiskey," he snapped, pulling out a bottle of port.

"That's because you keep drinking it all," Drystan said as Lucyan brought the bottle over with two glasses. "Not that I have any room to talk, but with finances so tight, we should probably lay off the spirits."

Lucyan snorted, eyeing the jewelry on the table as he poured a glass for each of them. "Is that why you have all your valuables out?" he asked. "You're trying to replenish the alcohol fund?"

"More like I'm trying to figure out how to pay the staff wages," Drystan said. They had spent a great deal of the petty cash fund on medical supplies to treat the wounded, and they needed to stretch their remaining funds until the taxes were brought in.

"You're not going to do it by selling off your belongings," Lucyan said. He knocked back his drink in one go, then swiftly poured another. "That will ruin the notion that we are not destitute and scrambling for cash. I have an emergency fund stored away—I'll fetch it for you so you can pay the staff wages."

"Thank you." Drystan sighed in relief, then took a sip of port. "Now would you mind telling me where the bloody hell you've been all day? And why I should steer clear of the oracle?"

"Shadley has informed me that the oracle has been spreading rumors that Dareena's status as the Dragon's Gift is not legitimate." Lucyan's eyes flashed. "I decided to pay him a visit and see if there was any truth to that."

"That's absurd," Drystan protested. "The oracle proclaimed her himself. Why would he go back on that now and risk damaging his own reputation?"

"That is exactly what he said to me," Lucyan said, taking the seat to Alistair's right. "He said that of course Dareena is the Dragon's Gift, but that the prophecy she found is bollocks. According to him, the dragon god has decreed that Dareena must mate with the strongest of us, and that the three of us must fight each other to the death to win her hand."

"To the death?" Drystan recoiled, his blood turning to ice. He couldn't imagine trying to kill his brothers over anything, even Dareena. "That's impossible. The dragon god could not have decreed such a thing."

"He didn't," Lucyan said archly. "I went and spoke to him myself."

"You *what*?"

"Apparently," Lucyan went on, as if he hadn't just dropped an anvil on Drystan's head, "there is a sacred cave a half day's journey from here that our ancestors used to commune with the dragon god. Our father knew about the cave, as did his father before him, but he never got around to telling us about it. Shadley discovered the information in an old tome in the library, and I followed the instructions and summoned the god."

Drystan stared at Lucyan. "That's...how was it?" he asked faintly. He tried to wrap his mind around actually speaking to the dragon god face to face. He had no idea such a thing was even possible! "Did you actually gaze upon him? Or was his brilliance too great to behold?"

"His brilliance was manageable," Lucyan said dryly. "He seemed quite cross that nobody had come to visit him in so long. He also confirmed what I suspected—the oracle is an imposter. He said the man is really a warlock named Mathias Black, and that he killed the original oracle six years ago and took his position. He is a plant, and has been working to topple our kingdom from within."

"Unbelievable." Drystan scrubbed a hand over his face. "And he is sitting comfortably in the temple right now, free as a bird?"

"Yes," Lucyan said darkly. "And that is not all. The dragon god said that Dareena is pregnant, and that we need to get her and Alistair out of Elvenhame before great danger befalls them. They are not safe there."

"Pregnant?" Drystan cried. For a moment, he was giddy with happiness, but his mood plummeted as the rest of what Lucyan said caught up with him. "It seems that just when I think things can't get any worse, they do." Guilt swamped him at the thought of Dareena in harm's way, and pregnant with their child... "Did the dragon god say anything about the babe?"

"He confirmed that the child, as well as the four of us, are the keys to breaking the curse," Lucyan said, "which makes it even more important for us to get Dareena and Alistair back. The dragon god said we should focus on coming up with a plan to get them to safety rather than scramble to come up with funds for the ransom. He seemed to insinuate that if we play our cards right, everything would turn in our favor...though of course he didn't say exactly which cards to play."

Drystan sighed. "Of course not. That would be far too easy." He drummed his fingers on the table. "It seems that we have two main tasks to focus on—eliminating the oracle, and rescuing our mate and brother."

Lucyan nodded. "The oracle is a tricky one," he said, his gaze turning pensive. "He is a favorite of the people, so if we kill or imprison him, that may make our political position even worse than it already is."

"We cannot allow him to run amok and continue to make mischief," Drystan protested. "He has murdered at least one man that we know of, and possibly more. And who knows how many state secrets he has fed the warlocks?"

"He's probably managed to worm a great deal of information out of Father, in the guise of being his confidante," Lucyan said darkly. "We will have to kidnap him under the cover of darkness, without alerting anyone that we have him or that he is in our dungeons."

"Right. We'll have to ensure only the most trusted guards watch him," Drystan said. "We don't have anyone else in the dungeons right now—that will make it easier. As far as the public is concerned, he will simply have disappeared in the middle of the night."

"I'll assign the task to Taldren and Catriona," Lucyan decided. "Those two are well-trained and stealthy enough to make it happen. As for Dareena..." He trailed off, mulling over what few options they had. "I'll go and break them out myself."

"Are you mad?" Drystan said with a scowl. "You can't go to Elvenhame. That anti-dragon spell the warlocks gave them will weaken you as soon as you go over the border."

"Ahh, warlocks." Lucyan gave him a crafty smile. "The nice thing about them is they often have the cure as well as the poison. I purchased a protective amulet from a warlock a few years ago that wards against hostile magic—it should work to shield me from the spell."

Drystan chuckled. "Of course you did." His brother was ever resourceful—Drystan often wondered just how many tricks he had in that proverbial bag of his, and if they would ever run out. "I suppose you ought to go—after all, Tariana likely doesn't have any such protection herself, and she went running off to rescue Ryolas this morning."

Lucyan rolled his eyes. "Naturally," he said. "Love makes fools of us all, doesn't it? I imagine that if you weren't anchored down by your sense of duty and honor, you might be the one rushing off to Elvenhame instead of me."

Drystan smiled. "Very likely," he said, "but you are the better man for that job, Lucyan."

Lucyan got to his feet. "I'll go make the preparations now," he said. "Shadley has a cache of charms that his agents use to disguise their looks—I'll go borrow one and then pack for the journey."

"Good." Drystan stood and clasped his brother in a hard hug. "Bring them back safely, Lucyan," he said roughly, a rare swell of emotion tightening his throat. He'd already sent one brother to the enemy. He couldn't bear it if he lost both.

Alistair and Dareena were sound asleep when footsteps marching up the hall woke him. The hairs on his arms stood on end, and he quickly sat up, buttoning his tunic shirt and pulling his trousers on again.

"What is it?" Dareena asked sleepily, curling her fingers around his arm. "Where are you going?"

"It's Arolas," Alistair growled, getting to his feet. He could smell the bastard a mile away. "He's coming for me."

The door banged open, and Arolas marched into the room with a pair of guards. "As I thought," the elven prince sneered, raking his cold blue stare over Dareena's barely covered form. "The moment my guards turn their back, the two of you are at it like rabbits again."

"Don't touch me," Alistair snarled as the guards marched forward. He tried to fight them off, but they were in close quarters, and he was worried about accidentally hurting Dareena. Gritting his teeth, he struggled against them as they bound his arms behind his back, clamping shackles around his wrists tight enough to make them smart.

"Since you don't know how to keep your cock in your pants," Arolas said with a cruel smirk, "I'm carting it, and you, off to the dungeons to help preserve what's left of the lady's honor. Take him away," he said to the guards with a snap of his fingers.

"You can't do this!" Dareena cried as Alistair was dragged away. He met her frantic gaze, and his heart clenched with guilt and anger as he continued to struggle. He could already feel his strength waning. In a few hours, he would not have enough energy to lift a finger, never mind brawl with a bunch of elves.

"You promised not to mistreat us," Dareena said fiercely to Arolas. "If you take him away from me, he will grow sick again."

"Perhaps you should have thought of that when you allowed him to spread your legs like a common whore," Arolas said.

Alistair saw red, and he lunged for the prince despite his hands being tied. The guards yanked him back and dragged him through the door, but not before he saw the prince's gaze drift over Dareena's body, lingering on the outline of her bosom through the sheets. "But then again, perhaps King Drystan already knows of your proclivities and has made his peace with them. I wonder if he would mind if I took a turn with you?"

"You insolent pig!" Dareena's hand cracked against Arolas's cheek as the guards shoved Alistair down the hall

Pride surged through him, along with a healthy dose of fear at the thought of her alone with Arolas. Would the elven prince really take advantage of her? From what Alistair knew, dragons disgusted the man, but Dareena wasn't a dragon. And if she truly had elven blood...

Grief and rage burned at Alistair's throat as the guards hauled him off to the dungeon—an oubliette, he discovered as they lifted a trapdoor and threw him into the darkness below. He hit the ground hard, his shoulder smarting, and the scents of piss and sweat and dung immediately assailed his nose. The waiting jailer hauled him to his feet, and Alistair stumbled through the dimly lit hall, his eyes adjusting. The hall was lined with small, cramped cells, and from the moans and whimpers he heard, several were occupied.

"Enjoy your stay," the jailer sneered. He untied Alistair's hands, then shoved him into a cell at the end of the hall. The door clanged shut behind him, and Alistair sank onto the hard, wooden bench, his stomach sinking with dread. A fever was already coming over him—far too quickly, considering he'd only been separated from Dareena mere moments ago.

Was it from the Change, or was the anti-dragon spell stronger down here? he wondered, passing a hand over his burning forehead. Gods, he was so tired of feeling sick and helpless, like a weak dragonling instead of the strong, magnificent prince he was born and bred to be.

Either way, Alistair felt like death was seeping into his bones, filling him with pain and weakness, robbing him of his will to live. He drifted into a dark, shadowy dream where he followed the sound of Dareena's voice crying out to him to help her. In the dream, he could hear Arolas laughing, and the sounds of her screams, and he ran faster, trying to get to his mate before the elven prince could rape her, or worse.

But as far as he ran, he couldn't catch up, and the screams went on and on. He was stuck down here, Alistair realized dimly, and he sank to the ground in his dream, tears running down his face as he tore at his hair in agony and despair. Stuck, with no way to help his beloved no matter how hard he tried.

SEVENTEEN

Get your kitchen wares here! Pots and pans! Ladles and cutlery! Sharpen your knives!" Lucyan called as he trudged through the small town of Idlewood at a pace that was slowly driving him mad. "The tinkerer is back in town, and his prices can't be beat!"

"Louder," the tinkerer ordered, a stern look on his wizened face. He sat beside Lucyan on the bench, his big, rough hands gripping the reins as he steered the mule. "How am I going to make any coin if you keep whispering like that?"

"I'm yelling as loud as I can," Lucyan said crossly. "I'm not used to being a herald." Or *an apprentice, for that matter,* he thought to himself, but there was nothing he could do about that. The tinkerer was a good friend of Shadley's, and sneaking into the elven kingdom under the guise of being his apprentice was an excellent disguise, since the tinkerer was one of the few humans allowed to travel freely between the kingdoms. The elves could not work normal metals due to their inability to tolerate it, and yet mithril was too costly to spare on pots and pans and the like, so they allowed humans like the tinkerer to come in and peddle their wares. The tinkerer was especially popular amongst the human population—elven households could only tolerate a limited number of the tinkerer's wares, but the humans had no such issue.

"Mr. Haveshamer," a little girl cried, scampering out of a nearby house. She wore a pale pink dress, and her dirty blonde hair was pulled back from her adorable round face into pigtails. "Do you have any lollies today?"

"For you? Always." The tinkerer gave her a jovial smile and plucked one of the candies from a tin. "That'll be a haycopper," he said.

The little girl gave him the money, and as she scampered away, more children came out of their homes, along with their parents. Before Lucyan knew it, they were doing a brisk business, housewares practically flying off the cart. By the time they made it through the rest of the town, they'd offloaded a good tenth of their wares.

"Not bad," the tinkerer said approvingly as he counted the coins in the till. "We'll eat well tonight, Ramsey," he said, using Lucyan's assumed name.

They stopped at the local inn—a two-story establishment with eight rooms and a small, cozy pub. While the tinkerer sharpened his knives, Lucyan unhitched the mule from the cart. As the animal drank from the trough next to the small stable behind the inn, Lucyan idly listened to the two inn staff members smoking pipes out back. He had no fear of anyone recognizing him—the charm Shadley had given him had turned his red hair dull brown, his amber eyes slate gray, and his features bland and unassuming. No one would guess that he was a dragon prince, especially not in the rough, patched-up tunic he wore.

"We're going to have to turn her out, you know," one of the men said ruefully. "She has no coin left for her meals, never mind the room."

"Aye," the second man said, "but I feel bad, turning her out when she's so ill. She was limping when she came in, but at least then she still looked as though she could crack a few skulls, if need be. Now she can barely walk out the door. We'd have to drag her."

"Which would be no mean feat," the first man said. "I've never seen a woman so tall and muscular. I thought she was a man before she lowered her cloak."

Lucyan froze. A tall, muscular woman, sick as a dog...could it be? It had been several days since he'd left Dragon's Keep, and though under normal circumstances Tariana would have reached Castle Sunstone by now, she would be hampered by the anti-dragon spell. Quickly, he stabled the mule, then went through the back door of the inn. Now that he was paying attention, he picked out Tariana's scent easily—it was faint, down here on the lower level, but as he crept up the stairs, it grew stronger, along with the scent of blood and rot.

"Blast it," Lucyan growled. He fished a set of lock picks from his pocket and opened the door. Inside, Tariana lay on the narrow bed in nothing but her underthings, her skin flushed and coated with sweat, her face contorted in agony. She'd dyed her hair brown, and had likely used the cloak hanging over her chair and the makeup smudged on her face to hide her features, but Lucyan would recognize her anywhere. Her left thigh, wrapped in a bloody bandage, emitted a terrible odor. The wound had not been treated properly, and with the anti-dragon spell hampering her ability to heal, rot was setting in.

Lucyan approached slowly, doing his best not to startle his sister, but even so, her eyes flew open, and she shot upright, a dagger clenched in her fist. "S-stay back," she stammered, her eyes wide and her body trembling.

"Shhh." Lucyan pulled the charm ring off his finger, revealing his natural form. "It's me, Tari."

"L-Lucyan?" Tariana dropped the knife and went limp. Cursing, Lucyan yanked the amulet, which he wore on a leather cord around his neck, over his head and placed it over Tariana's. Unscrewing the cap on his canteen, he brought it to her lips and gently coaxed her to drink.

"There now," he said as her temperature began to cool. "You're all right."

"Thank you," she gasped, wiping her mouth with her hand as she leaned back against the pillows. "How did you find me?"

"The staff were talking about a sick woman," Lucyan said, sitting down on the edge of the rickety bed, "and I figured out it was you from their description." Sighing, he smoothed a sweaty strand of hair from his sister's face. "What did you do to yourself, Tari? You look like shit."

Tariana cracked a smile. "You haven't called me that since you barely came up to my knee," she said. The fond look in her eyes made Lucyan vaguely uncomfortable.

"Yes, well, seeing one's sister on her deathbed can do strange things to a man," Lucyan said. "What in blue blazes happened to your leg?" he asked, twisting around to take off the bandage. Now that Tariana's powers weren't being hampered anymore, the wound would heal better if it was exposed to the air rather than suffocated by these nasty strips of linen.

"I was trying to rescue Ryolas," she said bitterly. "I flew as fast as I could to reach him—Shadley's spies reported he was held in Fort Arrowhill. I made sure to stay high above the clouds so the elves would not notice me, but as I approached the fort, the same magic Arolas used to defeat our sisters took hold of me, and I was forcibly changed back into a human. I landed hard on the roof and impaled my leg on one of the spikes. It was one of the most excruciatingly painful moments I have ever endured, and as I lay there, waiting for an opportunity to escape, I overheard the soldiers mention that Ryolas had been bundled off into a cart several hours before I arrived. They're taking him to the capital," she said in a choked voice, her eyes gleaming with tears. "He'll be executed there."

Lucyan winced. "I'm so sorry, Tari." He tossed aside the ruined bandages so he could take her frail hand in his. "How did you escape?"

"A combination of luck and sheer grit." Tariana covered her pain with a grim smile. "The fort was hosting a party to celebrate their great 'victory' over Dragonfell, and many of them were drunk. A guard heard me land on the roof, and when he came up to investigate, I killed him and took his clothes. Once I was certain no one was around, I snuck down to the stables and stole a horse. He's in the stable."

"Amazing." Lucyan shook his head in wonder. He wasn't

sure if he had the fortitude to endure what she had—he was no weakling, but neither was he a soldier. "I am on my way to Castle Whitestone now to break Dareena and Alistair out. I will do what I can to free Ryolas as well."

"Castle Whitestone?" Tariana gasped. "Lucyan, it is even more dangerous for our kind there than it is at Fort Arrowhill. You will be slaughtered if they catch you!"

"I'm well aware, but I do have the advantage of the amulet," Lucyan said. "Besides, the dragon god is watching over me. I know it will turn out all right."

Tariana gave him a skeptical look. "You've never been one to place your faith in the gods."

Lucyan chuckled. "That was before I talked to the dragon god myself."

Tariana's eyes went wide as he told her about his visits with the false oracle and the dragon god. "I would be inclined to outright dismiss your story if you weren't the one telling it," she said when he finished. "But as you are the most cynical of us all, I believe you. If the oracle is an imposter, and if Dareena and her babe are in mortal danger, then of course you must go."

"Yes, but while I'm here," Lucyan said, sliding his arms underneath Tariana, "why don't we get you outside so you can heal and shift before I go?"

Tariana nodded. Quickly, Lucyan put his disguise charm back on, then swaddled Tariana in her cloak and carried her down the stairs with her clothes in hand. He received a strange look from one of the guests on his way down, but thankfully no one else saw them. Fast as he could manage, he brought Tariana to a copse of trees just outside the town, then deposited her on the ground so she could change. The air shimmered around Tariana, heating up with dragon fire as her form blurred, stretching and elongating into a magnificent beast with red-gold scales and long spikes jutting from the top of her head and all along her spine.

Lucyan couldn't help but feel a pang of envy as his sister stretched her long, sinuous form—he wished he could shift, and wondered how long it would take for that instinct to kick in. It had happened for Drystan...had his brother attempted it since that day? With all that had been going on, likely not.

Tariana let out a low rumble, then nuzzled her snout against Lucyan's chest in farewell. "Safe flight, sister," he said, stroking her warm, smooth hide, and a surge of affection swelled his heart. "Tell Drystan I said hello."

Tariana nodded, then backed away to give herself room. With a single flex of her powerful haunches, she launched herself high into the air, then pumped hard with her wings to propel herself above the clouds.

Lucyan bent down to pick up the amulet she'd left on the ground as he watched her go. The headache that squeezed at his temples disappeared the moment he put it back on.

Alistair must feel a hundred times worse, Lucyan thought grimly as he headed back to the inn. He needed to convince the tinkerer to pick up the pace, for he had a feeling that if they delayed much longer, he would be too late to save his brother and their mate.

EIGHTEEN

On the fourth day of Dareena's "stay" in Castle Whitestone, the guards finally gave her leave to walk about the castle and grounds. Since they considered her helpless and weak, they did not require her to have an escort, though they did forbid her from going anywhere near the dungeons to visit Alistair.

This last bit infuriated Dareena, as she was certain that a visit would do him some good. Even holding his hand for an hour a day would alleviate some of his sickness, but the guards refused to hear of it, and Arolas had left the castle, so she could not appeal to him. She tried the king as well, but he would not see her—apparently, he was too busy taking care of state matters to entertain her for even a few moments.

Frustrated, Dareena went to the one place that might offer answers—the library. Much of the tomes were inscribed with elven runes, impossible for her to read, but after careful searching, she managed to unearth a slim tome written in the common alphabet that turned out to be a primer on elven runes. She spent the next day teaching herself to decipher the symbols, and slowly, painstakingly went through other tomes, hoping to find another primer that could teach her the basics of elven magic.

Eventually, she came across a manuscript titled *Magic for Beginners*, which turned out to be exactly what she was looking for. She learned that elven magic best functioned in Elvenhame itself but worked reasonably well outside the country, though it took longer to gather the amount of life force needed to cast spells. As Basilla had explained, there were many sources from which to draw energy, and each elf tended to draw from some sources better than others. The author warned against the dangers of taking too much from any one plant or animal unless the circumstances were dire, as doing so could kill it.

"Hmm," Dareena said aloud, pondering this concept. Was it possible to use this aspect of elven magic as a weapon? Could she kill someone if she was able to drain their energy? Of course, she would have to do it quickly, or they would fight back, and Dareena wasn't sure she was capable of it since her elven blood was so diluted. But surely elves had done this sort of thing in the past. She couldn't imagine at least one of them hadn't tried.

"Lady Dareena?" a familiar voice asked, startling Dareena. She looked up from the manuscript to see Princess Basilla standing a few feet away, a puzzled look on her lovely face. "What are you doing down here?"

"Oh, just a bit of light reading." Dareena closed the book and laid it face down. "I've no one to talk to, and things have gotten awfully boring."

"You could have come to seek me out," Basilla said, taking a seat next to Dareena. "The guards told me they saw you come down this way, but I confess I didn't believe them at first. I had no idea you could read—Arolas said you were a commoner."

"I am, but I had to learn to read as part of my job," Dareena said. "I was the assistant to an innkeeper and helped him with his books and such."

"Really?" Basilla seemed fascinated by that. "Did you ever imagine your life would take such a drastic turn?"

Dareena laughed. "Certainly not," she said, looking around. "The last thing I expected was to become the Dragon's Gift, never mind being carted off to the elven kingdom and held as ransom."

Basilla flinched guiltily. "I wish things didn't have to be this way," she lamented. "You and your mates are not responsible for what King Dragomir has done. And yet, I understand my father's position as well. This war has cost us precious time and resources, and our people never laid a finger on your predecessor. We deserve reparations for what we have suffered."

"I agree with you," Dareena said, "but I do not agree that Alistair should be forced to waste away in the dungeons, sick and in pain because of this awful anti-dragon spell. Please, Basilla," she said, grabbing the princess's hand, "you *must* help me get him out of there. If Alistair should die, there will be no peace between our peoples."

A troubled look crossed Basilla's face. "Do you really think he will die down there?" she asked.

"I don't know." Dareena's stomach knotted at the very thought. She was sick at the idea of Alistair down there, all alone, likely living off moldy bread and water while he wasted away. "But he was in very bad shape when we arrived, shaking and with fever. I know he's a dragon, but even he cannot withstand such sickness forever."

"I will speak to my father, but I'm afraid I cannot promise anything. He has shut me out completely—Ryolas was brought back yesterday, and he refused to listen to my pleas to visit him. The only person he will listen to is Arolas, which troubles me greatly. It is not like Father to sit back and let others make decisions for him."

"Grief does strange things to people," Dareena said, though she wondered if there wasn't something more sinister afoot. The warlocks had sunk their claws deep into Elvenhame. Could it be they had done something to the king? Perhaps Arolas had struck some bargain with them? It was obvious the elven prince cared for no one other than himself. She would not put it above him to force his father off the throne so he could take the crown for himself.

"Do you know anything about Shalia's Curse?" Dareena asked. "I've always been curious to know if the elves have a different version of events to what I learned as a child."

"I'm sure the bedtime stories differ between countries," Basilla said with a small smile. "I believe there is a book lying around here somewhere about the origins of the legend. Let me see if I can find it."

Basilla came back a few moments later carrying a slim tome in her elegant hand. "I've read this more times than I can count." She handed it to Dareena. "I'm one of the priestesses who tend Shalia's temple here in the capital, though it is mostly an empty title—I only go for special ceremonies. This book is part of the reading list we are required to get through as part of our training."

"A priestess?" Dareena cocked her head as she studied Basilla. "What does the elven goddess think about one of her priestesses spending time with the Dragon's Gift?"

Basilla laughed. "She has not said, but I imagine she would not be thrilled to hear of it. I can't bring myself to care, though—all this old enmity between our people is quite silly. As far as I'm concerned, the curse should have been lifted a long time ago. Perhaps if it had, we wouldn't be stuck in this dreadful war."

Dareena smiled. "I agree. Lifting the curse would go a long way toward mending this old wound, I think." She was tempted to tell Basilla about the prophecy she'd discovered, but she wasn't certain it would be wise to trust her with something like that when they barely knew each other.

Basilla's gaze turned thoughtful. "You know, I could search the old temple records and see if I can find any more information on the curse," she said, rising. "I have to go there this afternoon—the head priestess requires me to visit monthly." She screwed up her face in distaste.

Dareena laughed. "Well, you wouldn't want to keep her waiting." She looped her arm through Basilla's. She walked the princess out, then returned to her room, the two books hidden in the voluminous folds of her skirt. She would study up on the curse's history, then see if she could find a good spell from that magic primer to practice. She didn't expect miracles, not overnight, but she needed to find a way to free herself and Alistair before Arolas returned. She had a feeling the prince was looking for any excuse to visit misery upon them, and she wanted to be long gone before he decided to execute them, or worse.

NINETEEN

By the time Drystan finally turned in for the night, he was exhausted. With Lucyan, Taldren, and Catriona all gone off to perform various missions, he was the only one left to hold down the fort, and it took everything he had to keep a brave face and not let the courtiers know how much this was all getting to him.

Drystan collapsed onto his bed, instantly falling into a deep sleep. He wasn't certain how long he lay floating in the blissful darkness, but gradually, the shadows morphed into a hazy picture, and the next thing he knew, he was looking up at his mate.

"Dareena?" he whispered, reaching up to cup her cheek. She smiled, turning her face into his palm so she could press her lips against his skin, then moved lower down his body. Drystan reached for her, wanting to hold her in his arms, but she pushed his hands away and pulled down his trousers, freeing his rapidly swelling member. Drystan hissed as she took his cock in her small, dainty hands and began to pleasure him.

"Yes," he groaned, arching his hips into her as she slid her hand up and down his shaft. Gods, that felt so good. "Please, don't stop."

"Mmm," Dareena purred, lowering her mouth onto his cock. Her hot tongue swirled around the head of his shaft, making him see stars, but something about her voice seemed off. He reached for her, and though his hand should have met dark, silken tresses, he instead felt tightly coiled curls.

"What the hell?" Drystan barked, sitting up in bed. He blinked hard, adjusting to the darkness, and in the moonlight, Lady Dalmouth knelt between his legs—one of the noblewomen who had come to see him with her father earlier today. She was stark naked, the silvery light highlighting her milk-white skin, and her heavy breasts bounced as she recoiled, no doubt repelled by the anger in his gaze.

"I'm sorry to startle you, Your Highness," she said, her eyes wide. "It's just...you looked so tense earlier when my father and I spoke with you in the throne room. I thought perhaps you were missing Lady Dareena and needed someone to take your mind off her."

"You thought wrong." Drystan grabbed her dress from the chair and yanked the garment over her head, then ushered her out of his suite. "Don't *ever* do something like that," he snarled, shoving her into the hallway. "If I catch you in my quarters again, I will banish you from the Keep permanently."

He slammed the door in her shocked face and stormed back to his room, shaking with anger. Unfortunately, his cock was still hard and aching—he missed Dareena so fiercely that Lady Dalmouth's touch had stirred up the longings he'd buried so deep. Sinking onto the mattress, he wrapped his hand around his cock and slowly moved his hand up and down, just as he'd dreamed Dareena doing. If he closed his eyes, he could see her again in his mind's eye, that combination of innocence and lust on her gorgeous face as she knelt between his legs and worked his cock. He watched as she rose onto her knees, long-lashed eyes closing as she touched herself with her free hand, her fingers growing slick with cream...

"Oh gods," Drystan groaned as he came, shooting his seed all over his belly. The release was both satisfying and somehow hollow—beating himself off wasn't the same as coming in Dareena's tight pussy and planting a babe deep inside her. He hoped the dragonling growing in her belly was safe and not being adversely affected by the anti-dragon spell. The pregnancy was in the early stages yet—if Lucyan could get Dareena and Alistair out of there, they might be able to avoid any lasting damage to the babe.

That child was the key to lifting the curse. Drystan knew it in his heart as surely as he knew that all four of them were meant to be together. He couldn't allow any harm to come to that baby, no matter who or what he had to sacrifice to ensure its safety.

Drystan mopped up the mess on his stomach with a rag, then lay back down to sleep. He was just drifting off again when a knock came at his door, and he quickly yanked the sheet up to cover himself.

"Who is it?" he snapped, thoroughly irritated. It had better not be another trollop, or he would lose what little remaining patience he had.

"Catriona." His sister pushed open the door, a triumphant smile on her face. "We got him."

"You did?" Drystan sat upright, excitement pumping in his veins. "The oracle is in custody right now? Where is he?"

"In the deepest, darkest cell we have," Catriona said with a cruel smirk. "Capturing him was all too easy—a simple sleeping potion slipped into his drink allowed us to carry him out of the temple without raising the alarm or dealing with any of his foul magic tricks. He won't wake for some hours, but he'll be ready for you to interrogate in the morning."

"Excellent. We'll do so after breakfast."

Catriona bid him a good night, and Drystan went back to sleep, a great weight sliding off his shoulders. For once, something was finally going right around here. He drifted off with a smile on his face, clinging to the hope that he would get something useful out of the warlock spy, and that, in the meantime, Lucyan was making headway on his efforts to rescue Dareena and Alistair.

Alistair groaned back to consciousness and scrubbed away the crud encrusting his eyelids to find himself in the same dark cell he'd passed out in. He still burned with fever, but not quite as bad as before. As his stomach rumbled, aching for sustenance, he wondered just how long he'd been out, and how often the jailers brought food.

Gritting his teeth against the pain and weakness in his limbs, he pushed himself upright and looked around the small space. Aside from the bench, there was a chamber pot for him to do his business in and a small jug of water on the filthy floor. Alistair fell upon it like a rabid animal, drinking down half the pitcher in one go. Panting, he sat and wiped his mouth with the back of his hand, wondering if he should dump the rest of the water over his head. As a dragon, heat didn't usually bother him, but this sickness was downright miserable.

"Bloody hell," someone growled. Alistair started—the voice sounded as if it was coming from right above him, but that was impossible. "I'm going to strangle that bastard if I ever get out of here!"

Alistair spotted an air vent a few feet above his head. Curious, he stood on the bench, ignoring the wave of dizziness that passed over him, and pressed his hands to the wall to steady himself. "Hello?" he called through the vent. "Who are you planning on strangling?"

Silence. Then, "My backstabbing whore of a brother," the voice said. "Who are you?"

"Alistair of Dragonfell." He leaned his forehead against the wall and gave a near-silent sigh of relief as the cool stone eased his fever a bit. "I'm guessing you are Prince Ryolas?" He vaguely recognized the voice from when the prince had met him and his brothers in the forest.

"Indeed," Ryolas said, a bitter note in his voice. "Not that the title seems to be worth much these days. They've clapped me in iron chains—bad business for an elf, as you probably know."

"Damn." Alistair felt a pang of sympathy for the elven prince. "And your father has no issue with this?"

Ryolas snorted. "He won't even allow me to explain myself," he said sadly. "I don't know if you know the particulars—"

"Tariana explained it to me," Alistair said. "The two of you were staging the battles to avoid casualties."

There was silence for a long moment. "I'm not sure I'll ever see her again," Ryolas said in a hollow voice. "I would have liked to tell her I love her one last time."

"As would I," Alistair said morosely. He would have liked to kiss Dareena one more time too, but at least he'd held her in his arms and made love to her before he'd been dragged off. And she would have his brothers to comfort her if he didn't make it out of here. But Tariana—he'd seen the fierce love in her eyes when she'd talked of Ryolas. She would be devastated if she lost him.

"You're certain you'll be executed?" Alistair asked. "Without even a trial?"

"I would have one if my father were in his right mind," Ryolas said.

"What do you mean?"

Ryolas hesitated. "My father isn't mad the way yours is," he said, "but he isn't himself as of late. The High King of Elvenhame has never been one to sit back and let others take charge, and yet he has let Arolas take the reins. It is almost as if my dear brother has already become the new king. He's got me in the dungeons awaiting the gallows, he's marrying Basilla off to that nasty warlock prince.... Soon, there will be no family left to challenge his decisions."

"Yes, the king seemed remarkably passive," Alistair said. "Do you think the warlocks could be involved somehow?"

"If they are, there is nothing we can do about it from here," Ryolas said grimly. "I knew it was a bad idea for us to ally with the warlocks, but Father insisted—he was a child during the War of the Three Kingdoms and remembers the dragons' treachery all too well. Back then, the dragons really were the enemy. But now, I am not certain our sights are fixed on the right enemy."

"Neither am I," Alistair said. He wondered if Lucyan was tugging on this particular thread, which Dareena had uncovered the day she'd found that dragon scroll in the library. Their middle brother knew more about the warlocks than anyone else; if anybody could find the true culprit behind this mess, it was him.

Whether or not Alistair lived to see such a day remained to be seen.

After Lucyan and Tariana went their separate ways, he managed to convince the tinkerer to hasten their pace toward the capital. They arrived at Enethar just as the sun was setting over the beautiful city, setting the elegant, spiraling buildings aflame with gold and red. Relief washed over Lucyan as they entered the town—tonight, he would finally be able to do some reconnaissance, and find out how his mate and brother fared behind the walls of Castle Whitestone.

Lucyan and the tinkerer made their way to an inn a few blocks from the castle. The city hummed with life and activity, an air of peace and harmony that Paxhall lacked. Lucyan spied no pickpockets or thugs skulking in dark alleys, no homeless people panhandling in the streets—everything was clean and shiny, everyone was courteous, smiling and nodding as they passed, many of them coming up to the wagon and buying items.

If Lucyan didn't know better, he wouldn't have thought this was a country at war.

"Ahh, here we are," the tinkerer said as they stopped in front of a green and white two-story building. Warm, inviting light spilled out of the windows, and the heavenly smell of freshly baked meat pies lured them closer. "The Whistling Willow. My favorite place to stay in Enethar."

They booked two rooms and ate some of those delicious meat pies, washed down with honey mead. The tinkerer retired to his room afterward, and while Lucyan, full and sleepy, was tempted to do the same, he instead pulled his cloak around his shoulders and walked out into the rapidly darkening night.

Castle Whitestone was perched atop a hill overlooking the entire city. It towered above Lucyan as he traversed the winding streets, approaching the castle from the west, studying the exterior with his keen eyes for any weaknesses. He counted twenty guards manning the battlements, and that was only what he could see from his angle. The walls were thick and high, and as he drew closer, he saw an additional four men stationed at the front gate.

"Excuse me," he said, flagging down a passing woman. "I grew up in Idlegrove, and this is my first trip to the capital. Are tourists allowed inside the castle?"

"Sometimes, if you can get an official to vouch for you," the woman said. Her gaze darted to the castle towers, and Lucyan wondered at the troubled look on her lined face. "But these days it is nigh impossible. No one who is not an elf is allowed past the gates. Even the human servants who work in the castle are no longer allowed to come and go freely—they are forced to stay in the servants' quarters and are only permitted to visit with their families at the gate."

"That's too bad." Lucyan frowned up at the castle. He should have thought to ask Shadley for an elven disguise—as a human, there was no way for him to sneak through the gate, and in his natural form, the elves would put an arrow through his heart the second they spotted him.

If only I could shift, Lucyan thought morosely. But then again, would that really do any good? He remembered how Tariana had been gravely injured when she'd tried to rescue Ryolas from that fort—the magic that had forced her back into human form was very likely in effect at the castle, too.

Still, being able to shift might be handy when they made their escape. Alistair would likely be very weak from being exposed to all that anti-dragon magic. Lucyan would have to carry him and Dareena too. The fevers preceding the change had already come and gone. Did Lucyan have the power to change into a dragon as Drystan had done back in the throne room?

Turning away from the castle, which he could do nothing about, he gazed out at the rolling hills, which were almost completely invisible to his eye now that the sun had set. *They would be a good place to practice,* Lucyan thought as he trotted down the hillside. He hailed a small wooden carriage, big enough to fit no more than two, and paid the young elf driver to take him to the outskirts of the capital. From there, he hiked a good two miles away, until he was well into the hills, certain no one could see or hear him.

"All right, Lucyan," he muttered to himself as he sat atop

the hill. He took a deep breath and rubbed his hands together, mentally preparing himself. "You can do this. Change into a dragon."

Closing his eyes, Lucyan did what he had often done as a child—he clenched his hands tight at his sides and *willed* himself to change as hard as he could. Every muscle in his body strained as he mentally grasped for whatever that *something* was that would help him morph from his puny—if handsome and well-muscled—human form into the glorious, fire-breathing, winged beast that his people worshipped and feared.

Unfortunately, all Lucyan got for his valiant efforts was a tension headache. "Blast it," he growled, opening his eyes. He yanked a fistful of grass from the hill and tossed it, only for the wind to blow it straight back at him. "It would have been nice to get some instructions!" he yelled to the dragon god as he wiped dirt and grass from his face.

Does a baby bird receive instructions the first time it tries to fly?

Lucyan frowned. That had *sounded* like his voice...and yet, the words weren't his. Had the dragon god spoken to him? Or had that bit of snark come from his subconscious?

In any case, he didn't see how that was relevant—birds relied on instinct, which was why they needed little instruction to get airborne. And yet...was that what Lucyan was missing? Was he not listening to his instincts? Or was the problem that there was nothing for his instincts to respond to?

How was Drystan able to change in the first place? Lucyan thought back to that time. Their father had slammed him into the wall with his tail. Lucyan's ribs twinged with phantom pain at the memory. Just before he'd lost consciousness, he'd seen Drystan's eyes flare red with shock and anger, and then...

He hadn't actually seen his brother change. The darkness had taken him before it had happened. But Drystan had been angry, filled with hate and fear because Lucyan had been injured. Necessity had spurred him to change, to face their father in battle before he destroyed them all.

Closing his eyes, Lucyan focused his attention not inward, not on his desire to change, but on his desire to have Dareena back, safe and sound in his arms. He pictured her sweet, smiling face in his mind, then imagined it morphing, changing to grief and fear. She screamed his name as a pair of elven hands wrapped around her upper arms, dragging her away—

Lucyan snarled as fire flared in his chest, burning hot and bright as rage consumed him. He channeled that energy into his all-consuming need to save Dareena, to rescue her from the cruel bastards who had taken her away and burn their enemies to cinders. Something inside him snapped, and pain rippled through flesh and bone as his body stretched and changed, becoming something far bigger and stronger. Wings sprouted from his shoulder blades, scales popped up from beneath his skin, and his jaw elongated and filled with far more teeth than he could ever remember having.

By the gods. He opened his eyes, and suddenly he could *see*. He zoomed in on a coyote chasing after a rodent, both animals clear as day despite only a sliver of moon hanging in the sky to illuminate his surroundings. He could count the individual blades of grass through the night sky, *see* the currents drifting in the air around him—his wings flexed instinctively, wanting to catch the updraft, and without further thought he launched himself into the darkness.

He managed to jump about thirty feet in the air with a powerful bound and snapped his wings out. The wind buffered them, and he coasted for a bit, relying on his instincts to read the current. His heart pounded as he pushed himself higher, his blood singing with exhilaration as cloud mist brushed over his scales. He was really doing this! He was flying!

After only a few minutes, his wings burned from the strain. He coasted to the ground, landing only a few hundred yards from where he began. Panting, he tucked his wings against his sides, then craned his neck to get a good look at himself. The moonlight shimmered over his scales, a brilliant red-orange, as if each scale held a flame within itself. Stretching, he preened a bit —he'd look magnificent to anyone who could see him.

Magnificently useless, so long as you're in Elvenhame.

Lucyan huffed. True, he couldn't use his wings or dragon fire to break into Castle Whitestone. But he would eventually figure out a way to worm past the castle's defenses. And in the meantime, there was no reason he shouldn't hone his flying skills. With that thought, Lucyan flexed his wings and launched himself into the air again.

Drystan might have been the first to shift, but Lucyan intended to be the first one to master the sky so he could carry their beloved mate home.

TWENTY-TWO

Dareena spent the next few days studying the elven books she'd taken from the library and practicing magic every second she had. Which turned out to be quite a lot, as she had nowhere special to be. Princess Basilla liked to stop in at lunch to check in on her, the servants brought Dareena her meals, and Mari, the maid, came every morning and night to dress and undress her, but aside from that, she saw no one. She half-expected Arolas to come back to her room and accost her, but the prince was nowhere to be found.

Likely bossing around his soldiers, she thought, and not without bitterness. Oh, if only Ryolas were still in charge! Dareena had never met the younger prince, but if Tariana was smitten with him he had to be a noble man. He never would have separated her from Alistair.

"My lady?" Mari knocked on the door, startling Dareena. The clock on the wall told her it was barely four, far too early for the maid to come. Hastily, she shoved the books beneath her pillows, then smoothed the bedspread.

"Come in!" she called, and Mari opened the door. "What are you doing here?"

Mari bustled in. "The royal family wishes you to dine with them tonight."

Dareena's eyes latched onto the shimmering teal dress hung over her maid's arm—it wasn't one of hers. Who had sent it?

"I'm to get you ready."

Dareena's palms grew sweaty at the idea of sitting down to a meal with her captors. "Is Prince Arolas back?" she asked, rising from the bed so Mari could help her out of her day dress.

"He is." Mari hesitated. "You should try not to provoke him this time if you can help it, my lady. He was quite furious after your last...encounter."

Dareena bit her lip. She remembered quite well how angry Arolas was after she'd slapped him and called him an insolent pig—he looked ready to strike her himself, and might have done so if Princess Basilla hadn't come storming into the room, in a towering rage herself. The royal siblings had argued fiercely about Arolas's decision to jail Alistair, and had taken the conversation out of Dareena's room, to her mingled disappointment and relief. Basilla had come to her the next day and apologized for not being able to stop it—she had no power to challenge Arolas's decisions, and he would not listen to her no matter how insistent her arguments.

Gods, would she be able to sit across the table from him and keep a pleasant smile on her face while he leered at her? She knew he wanted to bed her—apparently his hatred of dragons did not extend to her body, or perhaps it was a gesture of dominance. After all, if he could successfully bed the dragon king's mate, that meant he was more powerful, didn't it?

Please, a voice in her head sneered. *Any one of my mates could crush him like the cockroach he is if not for this awful spell.*

Dareena allowed her mind to drift as Mari dressed and coiffed her, curling her mass of dark hair and fixing it atop her head with sparkling pins. The dress fit her like a glove, and as Dareena finally looked at herself in the mirror, a shiver crawled down her spine. Had Arolas ordered it for her? Had he imagined peeling her out of it afterward? The very thought made her nearly lose her appetite, and she swallowed hard against the bile rising in her throat.

"There." Mari smoothed out a non-existent wrinkle in her gown. "You look ready to eat."

"Do you mean I look like I am ready to go eat, or that I look like I am ready to be eaten?" Dareena asked wryly.

Mari laughed. "Can it be both?"

Shaking her head, Dareena pushed all thoughts of Arolas out of her mind, and as the guards escorted her to the dining room, she imagined she was going to have dinner with her mates instead of the elves. The brothers would love seeing her in this dress—it flattered her figure perfectly, the bodice lifting her ample bosom and highlighting her small waist before it flared out into voluminous skirts. Her heart warmed as she imagined the hungry looks in their eyes as they debated between devouring the food on their plates or devouring her. But then, was there really a reason they couldn't do both? A smile curved her lips at the thought.

"My lady." The guard's voice snapped her out of her reverie. "We're here."

The warm tingles that had spread through Dareena's blood vanished as the door to the dining room opened and she laid eyes on the royal family. King Andur sat at the head of the table, with Arolas and Basilla at his elbows. Relief flooded through her as she noticed the empty seat to Basilla's left—Lady Valenhall was seated next to Arolas, and at the foot of the table sat a dark-haired man Dareena had never seen before.

"Lady Dareena," the king said as they all rose from their seats. Dareena inclined her head, trying to be gracious even though all she wanted to do was rush out of the room. "It's a pleasure for you to join us."

"Indeed," the duchess said as Dareena opened her mouth to respond. "You're just in time—another few minutes and surely I would have fainted from hunger."

"Perhaps if I had been given advance notice, you wouldn't be made to suffer so, Lady Valenhall," Dareena said coolly as she took her seat. The duchess's eyes sparkled with annoyance, and the man at the other end of the table raised his eyebrows. But Dareena didn't care—let them think what they would. They already believed her to be a harlot. What more damage could she do?

"I don't believe we've been introduced," she said to the man as servants set plates of salad in front of them.

"How rude of us," Arolas drawled. Dareena forced herself to meet his gaze even though he made her skin crawl. "Lady Dareena, this is Count Silus Kianor, envoy from Shadowhaven's court and a trusted friend. Count Kianor, this is Lady Dareena

Sellis, the Dragon's Gift. Or should it be All Dragons' Gift?" His lips curled into a cruel smirk.

"Arolas!" Basilla snapped.

"No, that's all right," Dareena said coolly, picking up her utensil. She forked up a bite of salad and looked straight into Arolas's eyes. "I do have quite an appetite," she said before putting the fork in her mouth.

The atmosphere in the room turned awkward, even as Arolas's smirk turned downright smug. "Whatever arrangement you have with the dragon brothers is none of our concern," the duchess said in a clear attempt to wrangle the conversation back within the borders of propriety. "So long as your country agrees to our demands."

Dareena swallowed a retort. "I have no reason to believe that my mates won't cooperate," she said, "unless they hear of how terribly you've treated Alistair. Do you know he rots in the dungeons below even now, like a common prisoner?" Dareena leaned forward, pinning the duchess with a fierce look. "You promised we would be treated like guests. Does the word of an elf mean so little?"

The duchess stiffened. "I had not heard of this mistreatment," she said defensively, turning to Arolas. "Is this true?"

"It is," Arolas said, "and I see no reason not to leave him there. Spending a few days in the dungeon is the least any of the dragons deserve after all they've put our country through. I care not what you promised them."

"Father!" Princess Basilla said, sounding scandalized. She turned to the king, who had an almost detached look on his face, as a spectator to a sport rather than a participant. "Are you really just going to sit by and do nothing while Arolas soils our good name?"

"Don't talk about me as if I weren't in the room, sister," Arolas snapped. "I am not the one behaving dishonorably. The dragons have yet to come through on their end—if they had paid the ransom by now, your little dragon friends would be free. It seems the negotiations will be protracted, though of course I could be persuaded to speed them up." His gaze lingered on Dareena's bosom, making her stomach twist.

"It is very likely the dragons are stalling in a bid for time," the count said, his deep voice smooth as the surface of a dark lake. He stroked his beard as he considered Dareena. "Rumor has it that the entire fortune of the dragon kingdom was stolen away by Dragomir, and that his sons are searching for it as we speak. But it is unlikely they will recover it—the former king may be mad, but he is still the stronger dragon. I doubt they will be able to pay even a fraction of the ransom."

"I don't know anything about that—"

Arolas pounded his fist on the table before she could finish her sentence, sloshing their wine glasses.

"How dare these pathetic beasts toy with us, as if we are not to be taken seriously!" His face turned red as he bared his teeth, and Dareena flinched as his angry gaze clashed with hers. "If your 'mates' insist on playing games," he hissed, "then perhaps I need to give them an incentive to take us more seriously. Guards!" He snapped his fingers. "Bring the dragon prince here."

"Arolas," the king said, stirring from his stupor for what seemed like the first time. "Is this really the right time?"

"Yes, really?" Basilla interjected, her face pinched with anger. "Can we not enjoy a meal every once in a while without you making a spectacle of some sort?" She locked like she wanted to rake her nails across Arolas's face, and Dareena couldn't blame her. Similar thoughts were going through her head, even as part of her was excited to see Alistair's face again. She hoped he hadn't fared too badly in the oubliette.

The servants brought out the next course—poached salmon—as if nothing were amiss. Dareena couldn't even bring herself to pick at the food—she watched the door anxiously, waiting for the guards to come back. To be fair, she wasn't the only one not in the mood to eat. Basilla looked downright mutinous, and the duchess looked a bit uncomfortable, taking small bites of her food as she observed everyone at the table.

"So," Count Kianor said, breaking the tension-filled silence, "Princess Basilla, have you considered Prince Mordan's marriage proposal?"

Basilla, incredulous, opened her mouth, no doubt intending to deliver a scathing retort. But before she could, the door opened. Dareena and the princess gasped as Alistair was dragged in—his wrists and ankles were shackled, his clothes torn and dirty, and his matted hair hung over his face as he was hauled inside, barely able to stand upright.

"What have you done!" Dareena cried, shooting to her feet. She tried to rush over to Alistair, but Arolas waved a hand, and a gust of air pushed her back against the wall.

"I'd advise you to stay back," Arolas said as he rose from his seat. Alistair finally lifted his head, and Dareena let out a breath of relief as she saw his eyes blazing—they were filled with hatred, but at least they had life in them. "You wouldn't want to get blood all over your skirt."

"Wha—" Dareena began as Arolas yanked a sword from one of the guard's sheaths. The sword gleamed in the candle-light as he swung it high, and Dareena's heart leapt into her throat.

"No!" she screamed in horror as he chopped off Alistair's right arm at the elbow with a single swing. Dareena followed the arc of spraying blood with mingled shock and disbelief, and the duchess shrieked as some of it spattered her face. Alistair roared with pain as he dropped to his knees, his other arm still firmly in the second guard's grip—the first guard was holding the severed arm, a stunned look on his face.

This can't be real, she thought numbly as she stared at Alistair's bloody stump. *I'll wake up in just a moment, and all of this will be gone.*

"Box that up and send it off to his brothers, would you?" Arolas asked with a lazy wave of his hand. He smirked at Dareena as he spoke. "Make sure it is delivered promptly, and with my compliments. I wouldn't want it to be a rotted mess when it arrives."

Dareena doubled over and heaved the contents of her stomach all over the carpet. Bile stung at her throat as she wretched on her hands and knees, her body shaking with grief and rage. How could Arolas do such a horrid thing? And how could she have stood by and watched it happen, without lifting a finger to stop it?

As Dareena vomited, she was vaguely aware of the activity in the room around her. Princess Basilla rushed over to Alistair to heal the wound, the duchess was calling for aid, and the king, it seemed, had been roused from his stupor.

"What has gotten into your head, boy?" he demanded, sounding appalled. "Have you lost your mind?"

"I'm the only one who still has my mind," Arolas retorted. "I'm doing what's best for the kingdom, Father."

"You have gone too far!" the king shouted. "Our office made a promise that neither of these prisoners would be harmed, and you have broken it!"

A servant helped Dareena to her feet. She took the glass of water he offered and drained it, then clutched it in her hand, wondering if she could use it as a weapon against Arolas. If she broke it, perhaps she could stab the shards into his neck.

Shaking, Dareena forced herself to look at Alistair. He lay on the floor in a pool of his own blood, unconscious, but thankfully Basilla seemed to have healed the wound itself. Shame flooded over Dareena—she should have been the one helping him, and instead she'd let Basilla take care of it while she fell apart. What kind of mate was she?

"Thank you," Dareena croaked as Basilla rose, the skirt of her off-white dress covered in blood. Dareena moved toward her, then stopped, a warning tingle running down her spine. The princess's eyes had turned milky white, and there was a slack look on her face as she turned to Arolas.

"Prince Arolas of Erethar, son of the House of Aelosham," Basilla boomed in a voice that was most definitely *not* her own, "you have brought great shame and dishonor upon your family, and upon the office whose power you wield."

"G-goddess," Arolas stammered, sinking to his knees.

Everyone else in the room followed suit, even Dareena and the count—Shalia might not have been *their* god, but it was never wise to be anything less than deferential to a deity. "It was not my intention to commit any harm against our people."

"And yet you have," the goddess said coldly. "By breaking your word, you have forsworn yourselves—I cannot protect you from the dragon god's retaliation. King Andur," she said, and the king jerked as she pinned him with her white gaze, "your eldest son is not fit to be your successor. I suggest you name either Ryolas or Basilla as your heir and remove your youngest son from the dungeons. It is clear you have put the wrong one there."

Basilla's eyes flickered back to green as the goddess left her. She stared down at Arolas in shock. "By the gods," she said, her voice faint with shock. "That was the last thing I suspected."

"You bitch!" Arolas shot to his feet. "Playing horrid tricks like that! I'll have you beaten for daring to speak such blasphemy!"

He lunged for her, but the guards grabbed him, wrestling him away from Basilla. "That's quite enough," King Andur said firmly. "Guards, take him away."

"What?" Arolas's eyes bugged out of his head as the guards clapped restraints on him. "You can't do this to me, Father! I am your son!"

"Bring back Ryolas while you're at it," Basilla ordered, ignoring her brother. "After all, our goddess commanded it, did she not?"

The guards nodded, wide-eyed. They dragged the protesting Arolas away, careful not to step on Alistair, who was still passed out on the floor. Dareena rushed over to him and sank to the ground beside him, taking his left hand in hers. Oh gods...his poor arm...

"Don't worry." Basilla put a soothing hand on Dareena's shoulder. "We'll get him back to your rooms and resting up nicely in no time." She turned to face the king. "Father, in light of the goddess's commands about choosing either Ryolas or me as a successor, I refuse the match with the warlock prince. I do not believe such a union would be pleasing to our goddess."

"You can't do that," Count Kianor protested, looking alarmed for the first time. *He barely batted an eye when Alistair's arm was severed, which speaks volumes about him,* Dareena thought as she fumed. "This alliance was already promised!"

"I'm afraid this matter must be reviewed," the king said firmly, quashing further protest. "Count Kianor, I think it would be best if you returned to your own house for some time. It is clear that we have much to sort out before we can make any kind of decision about furthering our alliance."

"Very well," the count said stiffly. He rose from his chair and left, his robes swirling about him as he stalked out the door. Dareena was glad to see the back of him—after all that had happened, she knew a warlock could be nothing but trouble, and besides, she was happy that Basilla had finally found a reason to escape that horrible betrothal. Even so, Dareena had a feeling they were not done with the warlocks yet. Even if they'd bought themselves a little reprieve, it was more imperative than ever that she find a way to get them out of here once and for all.

That will be three silvers," Lucyan said as he placed an entire set of cooking pans on the makeshift counter at the rear of the wagon. He held out a hand for the coins, all the while burying a sigh. Part of him wanted to be out in the hills, practicing his flying, but to do so during the day, when anyone could see him, was folly. Besides, he needed to keep an ear to the ground so he could catch any bit of news about the goings-on of the castle; there was always a chance that an opportunity to sneak in would present itself, and Lucyan damn well wasn't going to miss it.

Lucyan completed the transaction with the woman, then did a quick count of the till. "There's a good lad," the tinkerer said, ambling around the cart. He patted Lucyan heartily on the back. "My sales have doubled since I started traveling with you —you are quite a good salesman. Perhaps I shall keep you around permanently!"

Lucyan chuckled. "I'm afraid the gods have different plans

for me," he said. The tinkerer was a good fellow—he'd even offered Lucyan a commission on his sales, which Lucyan had politely refused—but Lucyan far preferred the company of his brothers, not to mention their mate.

"Mr. Haveshamer!" an elven girl called, running toward them. She looked about thirteen—though as an elf, she was probably twice that age—with long, braided black hair and a pretty face with skin the color of fresh milk. "Mother told me you were back in town!"

"Naleena," the tinkerer cried jovially, wrapping her in a quick embrace. "You've grown a bit since the last time I've seen you." He held her out at arm's length.

"A whole inch," she said proudly. "Last year I only grew half as much. It's very exciting, though not nearly as exciting as the news this morning!"

"News?" Lucyan interjected, his instincts humming. "What news?" It was still early in the morning, and they hadn't heard much.

"Oh, it's just beginning to make the rounds—the castle folk have been trying to keep it quiet, but of course they can't keep such a secret locked away forever." The girl lowered her voice conspiratorially. "The word is that Prince Arolas lost his mind last night. He heard that Dragonfell has been stalling on the negotiations, and in a fury, he took a sword to the dragon prince they have as a hostage."

"A sword?" Lucyan demanded. "What are you saying? That the prince stabbed him?" Fire began to build in his chest, and he had to dampen his anger—the last thing he needed was for smoke to start billowing out of his nose. That would blow his cover for certain.

"Well, it's not clear what happened," the girl said, a troubled look on her face. "Some say he was stabbed in the chest, others say his legs were chopped off, and one person even said that Prince Arolas used a knife to peel the skin off the dragon prince's face." She shuddered. "I know the dragons are the enemy, but I can't help feeling pity for him. No one knows if he even survived the assault."

"Excuse me," Lucyan said, barely able to choke out the words. He briskly strode away, ignoring the tinkerer as he called after him. The fire was burning hot and bright in his chest now; if Lucyan stayed to hear the rest of what the girl had to say, he would lose it completely.

How is this possible? he fumed, storming up the hill toward the castle without being consciously aware of where his feet were taking him. The other pedestrians took one good look at his face and crossed to the opposite side of the street. The elves had promised that his brother and mate were to be treated like guests and that no harm would come to them. Rage boiled his blood, and his tendons stretched with the beginnings of the change. He wanted to shift right now and launch himself at the castle so he could burn those treacherous elves to a crisp with the fire blazing inside him.

But he could not do that, for the same reason that he could not practice flying in broad daylight. If there was a chance the guards were wielding the stupid warlock magic that had brought down so many of his sisters, he couldn't risk an assault on the castle. So Lucyan forced himself to take deep breaths until his heart slowed to a manageable level, his mind no longer quite so clouded by anger and grief.

What if Alistair wasn't dead? After all, these were just rumors, and dragons were notoriously difficult to kill. If Arolas had indeed stabbed him with a sword, Alistair was no doubt in bad shape—the anti-dragon spell would prevent him from healing. But he could still be alive, and if he was hanging on, even by a thread, Lucyan needed to help him.

Mind made up, Lucyan asked for directions to the nearest apothecary and tailor. Armed with a handful of coins, he bought a dark coat, tinted spectacles, a hat, a large leather bag, and a number of potions, poultices, and bandages. On its own, the disguise would hardly be sufficient, but coupled with the illusion charm, Lucyan managed to pass it off.

"Excuse me," he said, approaching the castle gate. The guards turned to look at him, their gazes wary—Lucyan imagined the entire staff was a bit shook up after hearing their general had lost his marbles. He hoped Arolas had at least been taken to task by the High King, though with Lucyan's luck lately, he wasn't holding his breath.

"I'm sorry, but no humans are allowed through the gates, by order of the king," the guard said.

"What about a dragon doctor?" Lucyan asked, straightening to his full height and doing his best to look self-important. "I'm Doctor Otho Harrigan. I've heard that you have an injured dragon within these walls, and I've come to offer my services. Unless your king doesn't mind if a political hostage dies on his watch?"

The guards exchanged glances. "What do you mean, you're

a dragon doctor?" the second guard asked suspiciously. "I've never heard of such a thing."

"I spent a good five years of my life serving at the pleasure of Dragonfell's royal family before I packed up and moved here," Lucyan said proudly. "You wouldn't believe how many cases of scale rot I've had to treat, amongst other issues. If the prince is truly ailing, I may be able to help him."

"How do we know you're not a Dragonfell spy sent here to break the dragons out?"

Lucyan snorted. "Do I look like I'm capable of such antics?" he asked, holding his bag open for the guards to inspect. "There are no weapons in here—only healing potions and supplies. Check my pockets if you wish—I have nothing to hide."

The guards did, patting him down thoroughly, but all they found was the amulet and the charm, which looked like simple jewelry. "Wait here," the first guard said, leading Lucyan into the guardhouse just inside the gate. "We'll speak to the steward and see if your services are needed."

Lucyan settled into a chair to wait. He did his best to look bored, though inside, he was filled with nervous excitement. The plan was working thus far—he hadn't been turned away yet! With any luck, the elves would agree to let him see Alistair. If Lucyan could get the amulet around his neck, Alistair might just be able to heal himself if he was given enough time.

Then again, Lucyan thought darkly, *the elves might not want to help my brother.* If they suspected that Dragonfell would not be able to pay the ransom, there was no reason to keep Alistair alive, or Dareena, for that matter. Fear coursed through him, turning his skin cold despite the warm weather.

Gods, he hoped that scouting party would find his father's lair soon so they could recover the treasure. Alistair would be a devastating loss, but Lucyan didn't think he would be able to stand it if anything happened to Dareena. He and his brothers had a responsibility to protect the kingdom and clean up after their father, but Dareena was blameless in all of this. She did not deserve to be cooped up in a foreign castle and treated like a prisoner, and if she died, Lucyan didn't think he would be able to live with himself.

The door to the guardhouse opened, and Lucyan sat up straighter as the guard from earlier came in. "Come, Doctor Harrigan," he said briskly. "The Princess Basilla would like to meet you."

"Of course." Lucyan got to his feet and hid the triumphant smile threatening to curve his mouth. He followed the guard through a side entrance into the castle, up two flights of stairs, and into an elegant office appointed in shades of pale pink and gold.

"Princess Basilla," the guard said. "This is Doctor Otho Harrigan, the man I told you about."

"Princess." Lucyan bowed deeply. "At your service."

"Thank you," Princess Basilla said. She was seated behind a white desk—a stunning woman, Lucyan observed with some detachment, with long, shining chestnut hair, a beautiful face, and green eyes disturbingly similar to Dareena's. "Please, Doctor, have a seat."

Lucyan did. "So, it is true that there is an ill dragon here?" he asked. "The rumors seemed outlandish, but when I heard, I knew I had to come and offer my services."

Princess Basilla nodded. "My fool of a brother lost his temper last night and decided to take it out on one of our hostages," she said, the skin around her mouth tightening with displeasure. "He has lost an arm, and is doing very poorly right now."

Rage flared up in Lucyan again, and he squashed it quickly before it could show on his face. "Is the arm the only injury the prince suffers?" he asked.

"Injury, yes," Princess Basilla said. "But the anti-dragon spell has also affected his health. I believe he would recover on his own if not for the magic, but there is nothing I can do about that save for sending him back to his own country. And that, the king will not allow."

"Of course," Lucyan murmured, noting the pity in Basilla's eyes. So she was more like her younger brother, Ryolas, he mused, though that did not necessarily mean she was sympathetic to all dragons. "The spell will hamper my work, but I mixed up some potions specially formulated for dragons. They should help boost his healing."

"Excellent." Princess Basilla rose from her chair. "Let's get you to him, then. I fear the prince may be dying, so there is no time to waste."

TWENTY-FOUR

"Oh, Alistair." Dareena sighed as she mopped his sweaty brow with a cool cloth. "I wish there was something I could do to ease your suffering."

"You *are* doing something," Alistair said, his voice rough with pain. "Every time you touch me, you're helping."

Dareena bit her lip. She'd been healing Alistair with her magic every few hours, but it wasn't having much effect—he'd been exposed to the anti-dragon spell for too long. All the healing did was keep him from getting worse, but his time spent in the dungeons, away from her, combined with the trauma of having his arm severed, had brought him close to death's door. His forehead was scalding, his face was lined with exhaustion, and his body shook with racking coughs that sounded like death rattles.

"It should have been me who lost that arm," she said dully, dipping the cloth in the bucket of water. She squeezed the cloth to wring the water out, her knuckles going white as she imagined her hands around Arolas's throat. He'd taken Alistair's sword arm, and for a soldier, that was almost worse than death. Even if he trained himself to fight left-handed, he might never be as good as he once was.

Alistair gripped her wrist and turned her around to face him. "Don't say such foolish things," he said fiercely. "I can handle losing an arm. I could handle losing my life if it meant keeping you safe. But I couldn't abide anything happening to you."

"Nor could I abide anything happening to you," Dareena cried. "The reason Arolas went after you is because of his jealousy. If I had not provoked him—"

"You did *nothing* wrong," Alistair growled. He pulled her flush against his body and kissed her quick and hard. "Being beautiful and opinionated does not give any man the right to your body, or to be angry that someone else is sharing it instead. It is not your fault that Arolas is such a vile maggot."

Dareena opened her mouth to respond, but Alistair's eyes rolled back into his head. "Alistair!" she cried as he passed out, his head thudding against the pillow. "Please, please don't get any worse," she begged, pressing her hand to his forehead. She tried to pull more magic from the air and feed it to him, but her mental muscles were already overtaxed from doing so multiple times throughout the night. Tears of exhaustion and grief seeped from her eyes, and she swiped at them in frustration. Why was she so useless?

"Dareena?" The door behind her opened, and she turned to see Princess Basilla hurry inside, a strange, bespectacled man wearing a long coat and carrying a satchel following her. "This is Doctor Otho Harrigan. He has worked with dragon patients before and says that he can help Alistair."

"A dragon doctor?" Dareena rose, looking the doctor up and down with skepticism. She wished Alistair were awake—if the man was a charlatan he would be able to sniff him out immediately. "I've never heard of such a thing."

"I assure you, I have spent a great deal of time amongst dragons." The man brushed past Basilla and approached the bed. "Please move aside, Lady Dareena, so I can look at him."

Dareena frowned—there was something familiar about the man's voice. "Very well," she said warily, giving him some space. It couldn't hurt to have the man look at Alistair—perhaps there was a potion in that bag that could help ease his pain. "But I'll be watching."

"As you should." Something very much like affection glimmered in the doctor's eyes for a split second as their gazes met. But before Dareena could think about it much more, he bent over Alistair, checking his pulse and feeling his forehead. He rolled up Alistair's sleeve to expose the newly-healed arm, which had been severed at the elbow.

"Whoever healed this terrible injury did excellent work," the doctor said. Dareena was surprised to hear the note of anger in his voice, but perhaps any doctor would be outraged on behalf of their patient.

"I did what I could for him," Basilla said, "but I'm afraid I am of no help with his illness. Perhaps being a dragon makes him resistant to my elven magic."

The doctor nodded grimly. "I should be able to help him,

but I need some time and space. I'll call for you when I have news."

"Very well." Basilla squeezed Dareena's hand gently, a gesture of comfort and solidarity that made Dareena's throat swell with tears. She was so grateful to have the princess as an ally—without Basilla, she would have likely given in to despair already. "I'm only a shout away if you need me," she said before she left.

Dareena turned back to the bed just in time to see the doctor pull a necklace over his head. "What are you doing?" she demanded as she watched him fasten the chain around Alistair's neck. "Is that some kind of warlock magic?"

"As a matter of fact, it is," the doctor said in a voice she would recognize anywhere. Shock reverberated through her as she tried to reconcile what she was hearing with what she was seeing. "Look, Dareena," he said, his tone hushed. "It's working already."

Dareena stared at Alistair. Sure enough, his entire body had relaxed, and the shaking started to subside. "By the gods," she whispered, drawing closer to the doctor. "Lucyan...is it really you?"

"It is," he whispered back, turning to face her. "I'm sorry it took me so long to come after you."

"Oh, thank the gods," she sobbed, throwing herself into his arms. She finally let the grief and terror from the past week free, tears flowing freely down her cheeks as she shook from the force of it. Lucyan kissed the top of her head and held her tight, murmuring sweet nothings. She clung tightly to him, basking in the warmth and comfort of his embrace.

"There, there, miss," he said aloud, likely for the benefit of the guards, who could hear her crying from the hallway. "It'll be all right."

Dareena pulled back so she could look up at Lucyan's face. "What is all this?" she whispered, cupping his cheek. He was nearly unrecognizable, though enough of him remained in his new features that she could see it now that she was really looking. "How did you get here? What does that necklace do?"

"The necklace has an amulet with a shielding spell that wards against hostile magic," Lucyan explained. "Shadley gave me a ring that changes my features, and he also put me in touch with a tinkerer who travels freely between Dragonfell and Elvenhame. I've been posing as his apprentice."

"I'm so glad you're here," she said, hugging him fiercely. "We have to get out of here. Arolas has been sent to the dungeons, but his father is not quite right. If we truly haven't the funds to pay the ransom, our lives are in danger every moment we remain."

"I agree," Lucyan said. They both looked down at Alistair, who was sleeping peacefully now. "But we'll need my dear brother at full strength first."

ucyan and Dareena stayed by Alistair's side for the next hour, talking quietly amongst themselves as they monitored him. Basilla had come by earlier, and after seeing that Alistair was improving, gave Lucyan permission to tend to him for the rest of the night.

While Alistair rested much easier wearing the amulet, the anti-dragon spell affected Lucyan. His chest had constricted, making it hard to draw breath, and weakness had settled into his muscles.

"I don't know how he's lasted this long," Lucyan said, shaking his head. He clasped Dareena's hand loosely in his own —touching her seemed to help a bit. "It seems I got here just in time."

"You really did," Dareena said. She squeezed his hand tight, though her emerald gaze did not stray from Alistair's face. "I've been trying to heal him, but I'm still new to this magic, and I've taxed my abilities to their limit. I don't know what I would have done if you hadn't arrived."

"Heal him?" Lucyan turned in his chair to look at her fully. "What do you mean?"

She turned to meet Alistair's eyes. "Do you remember that day you took me out for a picnic? When I told you that I suspected I had an elven ancestor in my family tree?"

"Yes." Lucyan looked down at the ring on her finger. "You were telling me that's where you thought your green eyes came from."

She nodded. "It turns out green eyes aren't the only thing I've inherited," she said. "I can also use elven magic, to a limited degree. I found a primer in the library and have been practicing daily. "

"Really?" Lucyan asked, astonished. Shock and delight filled him as he looked her up and down—his little minx continued to surprise him. "Have you learned many spells? What abilities do you have?"

"I can heal and do a few other things," Dareena said, "but I'm afraid I couldn't do a demonstration right now even if I wanted to. I've depleted all my energy." She passed a hand over her face, which looked drawn and exhausted.

"Go get some rest." He took her hands and pulled her up from the chair. "You're no good to us if you're tired."

Dareena hesitated. "I don't want to leave him," she said, glancing at Alistair's prone form.

Lucyan gently gripped her shoulders, drawing her attention back to him. "I'll let you know as soon as he's awake." He leaned in and pressed a soft kiss to her lips. Despite his lethargy, his loins stirred at the sensation of her lush lips on his, and he had to pull back before he took more from her than she could give. "Go now," he said.

Dareena left, and Lucyan sank back into the chair, resuming his vigil. He had no idea how long it would take for Alistair to heal—it could be hours or days. There was no precedent for this —dragons were rudely healthy creatures and not prone to illness or injuries that required lengthy recovery. But Alistair had been exposed to the anti-dragon spell for more than a week, and for that matter, so had the baby growing in Dareena's belly. Could they really afford to wait days for Alistair to heal? He hated the idea of leaving his brother behind, but their babe's safety was paramount. Was it better to try to spirit Dareena out now, while the babe was still in its early stages of growth?

No, a voice in his head said. *The dragon god made it clear that all four of you must survive for the curse to break.*

Right. Leaving Alistair behind was not an option. Lucyan closed his eyes, praying to the dragon god to speed his brother's recovery. The longer Alistair took, the weaker Lucyan himself would grow.

As the hours dragged on, Lucyan found it harder and harder to stay awake. Natural exhaustion coupled with the anti-dragon spell made him drowsy, and eventually he began to nod off.

"Lucyan?" Alistair croaked, startling him. His eyes flew open, and he grinned at the sight of Alistair staring back at him through heavy-lidded eyes.

"Ah, so you recognize me?" Lucyan asked, keeping his voice down as he perched on the edge of the bed. Before she'd left, Princess Basilla had ordered the guards to move to the end of the hall to give them some privacy, but even so, he didn't want to risk them overhearing.

Alistair gave him a weak smile. "You can't fool me with that getup," he said. "I'd recognize your foul stench anywhere."

Lucyan chuckled. "Wonderful to see you too," he said, clapping Alistair on the shoulder. "How are you feeling?"

"Like someone has placed two tons of bricks on me," he admitted. "I'm weaker than a kitten, but at least I'm alive." He glanced down at his severed arm and grimaced. "Though I must admit, I was hoping that part was a dream."

Lucyan winced. "I'm afraid not," he said. "With any luck, you'll be able to heal that once you've made your first shift."

"That's not going to happen so long as I'm within these walls," Alistair said. His brow furrowed. "How is it that I'm on the mend? I feel like hell, but that's a lot better than I was feeling before."

Lucyan tapped the amulet resting against Alistair's bare chest. "Warding amulet," he explained. "It protects against hostile magic. I wouldn't have made it here without it."

Alistair smiled. "Trust you to have something like this in your arsenal," he said. He lifted his head a little, glancing around the room. "Where is Dareena?"

"Sleeping," Lucyan said. He glanced toward the door, a wave of longing washing over him. As much as he was glad to be by his brother's side, he yearned to be with his mate. Part of him had been terrified that he would never see her again when the elves had taken her away, and the thought of being separated from her again, even by a mere wall, tore at him.

"Go to her," Alistair urged, reading him perfectly.

Lucyan frowned. "Are you certain?" he asked. "You're hardly recovered."

Alistair waved a hand. "I just need to sleep the rest of it off, and as much as I appreciate your concern, the idea of you watching me while I sleep is a bit disconcerting. Besides, I know you're beginning to feel the effects of the anti-dragon spell. Touching Dareena helps ward off the symptoms, especially if you're not wearing any clothing."

"Really?" Lucyan's eyebrows rose at the suggestive tone in Alistair's voice. "You don't mind?"

Alistair snorted. "Give me thirty seconds and I'll be unconscious again," he said. Indeed, his eyelids fluttered. "She's missed you fiercely, Lucyan," he mumbled. "Go to her."

"Thank you, brother." Lucyan leaned over and kissed his brother's forehead as he slipped back into sleep. He tucked the covers around Alistair, then opened the adjoining door connecting their rooms. Hopefully the guards wouldn't come in to look for him, but if they did, he would just tell them he went to check on Dareena.

"Lucyan?" Dareena asked sleepily as he lifted the covers. Her eyes widened as she noticed he was stark naked—he'd stripped off his clothes before approaching the bed. "I thought you were watching Alistair?"

"He woke up briefly, then told me to go snuggle with you to conserve my strength before he passed out again," Lucyan said, pulling her against him. "At the rate he's healing, I suspect he shall be right as rain in the morning."

"Thank the gods," Dareena said fervently, hugging Lucyan tight. They stayed there for a long moment, simply savoring their embrace. Lucyan breathed in Dareena's scent, and his chest loosened. Even with her nightshift in the way, her touch was making him feel better.

"Alistair said that skin-to-skin contact was best to combat the effects of the anti-dragon spell," Lucyan said, toying with the hem of Dareena's nightshift. Slowly, he pushed the thin cloth up her leg, his hand skimming the silky-smooth skin of her thigh.

"Did he?" she purred, leaning into him. Lucyan's blood thrummed in his veins as he felt her nipples harden beneath the fabric, and he hissed when she nipped at his chin. "How much skin?"

"He didn't specify," Lucyan said, his hands sliding up her ribcage. Dareena gasped as he cupped her breast, and he smiled wolfishly at her. "But I'm thinking we should try for as much skin as possible. We wouldn't want me getting weaker, would we?"

"No, of course not," Dareena said breathlessly. She lifted her arms above her head so Lucyan could pull the nightshift over her head, then wrapped them around him and kissed him deeply. Lucyan growled at the taste of her as he slid his tongue into her mouth, his cock hardening even more as it pressed against her hip. She felt so fucking good in his arms, even better than he last remembered. And his last memories of them in bed together were pretty damn good.

"If we were back home," Lucyan said, rolling Dareena onto her back, "I would make you scream loud enough to wake the stable boy." He cupped her breast, and she moaned softly when he slid his thumb over her taut nipple. "But since we're in enemy territory, we'll have to be a little more discreet."

Dareena's eyes blazed as she reached for the pillow next to her head. "Do whatever you want to me, Lucyan," she panted, stripping off the pillow case. "The guards won't be able to hear a thing."

Lucyan chuckled as she balled the pillowcase up and stuffed it into her mouth. "I remember how shy you were when you first came to the castle," he said, gently massaging her nipples. She arched into his hands, the cloth muffling her moan. "And now look at you. You're wanton now," he said, leaning in to bite down on her left nipple.

Dareena moaned again, her sounds of pleasure loud enough only for Lucyan to hear. She rubbed herself shamelessly against him as he licked and sucked her nipples, and Lucyan sucked in a sharp breath at the feel of her wet pussy sliding against his thigh. He reached between them to slide his thumb along her slippery folds, and her hips came off the bed, seeking out more. Part of Lucyan wanted to draw this out, but a larger part of him wanted to feel her come beneath him, watch her fall apart as she screamed her pleasure into that self-imposed gag, so he stroked her faster, finding her sweet spot with ease. In no time her eyes glazed over, color spilling across her cheeks as she strained against him, seeking that release.

"There you go," he said as she went over the edge. He thrust his cock into her as she shook from the force of it, then bit back a curse as her inner walls clamped down on him. He bit down on the inside of his cheek to keep from coming, but it was so bloody hard with Dareena bucking against him, frantically milking him for every bit of pleasure she could get. Bracing his hands on the bed, he quickened his pace, refusing to let her catch her breath even as she started coming down from the high.

"You are so bloody perfect," he panted, ripping the gag out of her mouth. He kissed her deeply, swallowing her breathy moans as he fucked her, wanting to make her come again. She clawed at his back, nails sinking into his skin, and the pain spurred him on, driving him even deeper into her.

Finally, Dareena's body went rigid beneath his, and her pussy clenched tight around him again. Lucyan groaned into her mouth as her orgasm pushed him over the edge, and his vision went white for a moment as he became overwhelmed by the wave of utter bliss. Winded, he collapsed onto his elbows and buried his head in the crook of Dareena's neck, breathing in their combined scents as he fought to catch his breath.

"You truly are the Dragon's Gift," he said when he could speak again. His exhaustion evaporated as renewed energy that only Dareena could give surged through him.

"Was there ever any doubt?" Dareena asked teasingly. She reached up to cup his face, her green eyes filled with satisfaction and tenderness.

"No," Lucyan said. He slid down Dareena's body to press a kiss to her abdomen. "Not anymore. Our son is growing in your womb." He had no idea if the child was from his seed, but it didn't matter—as far as he was concerned, it was as much his as it was Drystan's or Alistair's. "I can't wait until your belly begins to round," he said, nuzzling her damp skin.

Dareena smiled. "We'll be back home then,' she said, a dreamy look in her eyes. "All four of us together again."

"Yes, but we need to get out of here first." Lucyan rolled onto his side and propped up his head to face Dareena. "You said you learned to manipulate your elven magic. It turns out I too have a new trick up my sleeve—I can shift."

"You can?" Dareena sat up, her face lighting up with joy. "Oh, Lucyan, that's wonderful!" She threw her arms around him and hugged him tight. "You must be thrilled. Can you fly?"

"A bit," he said, "though that will not help us much until we can get beyond the castle walls. I cannot risk any of the guards taking me down with that horrible warlock magic."

"No, you certainly cannot," Dareena said. "Although, do you think it's possible your amulet might protect you? It has worked against the anti-dragon spell so far."

"The warlock warned me that the amulet might fail if it tries to combat more than one spell at a time," Lucyan said ruefully. "As much as I would like to try, we would find ourselves in even more dire straits if we accidentally destroyed the amulet in the process. Tariana flew over the border to try to rescue Ryolas before he was brought to the castle, and she nearly died thanks to that blasted warlock magic," he growled. "Luckily, I came upon her and helped her heal with the amulet, and managed to convince her to go home by promising I would rescue Ryolas if I could."

"I'm glad you did, because a rescue is no longer necessary," Dareena said. "Arolas was thrown into the dungeons after what he did to Alistair, and Ryolas was released. He is confined to his quarters, and resting comfortably, from what Princess Basilla has told me."

"Thank the gods," Lucyan said, relief sweeping through

him. That was one less burden for him to worry about. "It will be far easier to escape if it's only the three of us. If we can successfully sneak out of here, I can carry you two on my back and fly to Dragonfell. Do you think you might be able to use your magic to make us invisible?" he asked, remembering how Ryolas and his men had done so in the forest.

Dareena shook her head. "Invisibility is beyond the purview of nature-based magic," she said. "If we had your invisibility cloak I might be able to strengthen it a bit, but I could not fashion such a spell myself."

"That is unfortunate," Lucyan said. "And no, I no longer possess the cloak—Shadley managed to lose it while he was fleeing Paxhall. What about offensive spells? Can you use your magic as a weapon?"

"Oh yes," Dareena said. She sat up and reached for the drawer in the bedside table, and the sheet slid down, exposing her round, lovely breasts. Lucyan's cock twitched, and he gripped the bedspread to keep from reaching for her again—the conversation at hand was far more important than his sexual desires. "Here is the primer I was telling you about." She turned back to show him the slim volume in her hand.

"This is written with elven runes," Lucyan said, flipping through the pages. "You've already taught yourself to read this?" He shook his head, amazed at her aptitude, though perhaps he shouldn't be. She'd learned those dragon runes awfully fast when he'd taught her.

"Well, I sometimes still refer to the alphabet book Basilla gave me," she admitted, "but yes, I've come a long way." She took the book from him and flipped it open to a passage. "This is a technique that produces a humming noise that is very harsh on the ears. It can be used to stun dogs and wolves, or other creatures with sharp hearing."

"Like elves," Lucyan said, nodding. "Or even dragons."

Dareena smiled, turning to another page. "This one here talks of taking the life energy and forming it into a weapon," she said. "Some people fashion it into spears, others shoot it from their hands like arrows."

Lucyan's eyebrows rose. "That sounds handy," he said. "Have you tried any of these?"

Dareena shook her head. "I couldn't risk the guards overhearing," she said, glancing toward the door. "But now that they're no longer right outside..."

"You could try it now," Lucyan finished. "At least the weapon thing. I'd advise against the humming noise—they would definitely hear that."

Dareena nodded. She rose from the bed and covered her body in a dressing gown, much to Lucyan's disappointment. Lucyan quickly dressed, then joined her, not wanting to be on the receiving end of whatever she summoned.

"This may not work," she warned, raising her hand. "I've gotten a little better at gathering energy from the air, but this could require more than I can manage."

"Just do your best," Lucyan said. He stood back and watched as Dareena focused on her hand, pursing her lips. The air in the room shifted, and sure enough, he could feel the hum of power as it gathered around her. By the gods, he hadn't doubted her when she told him she could use elven magic, but hearing it was quite different from watching it at work.

"It's working," Lucyan said, his voice hushed but excited. Her hand was glowing, sparks crackling in the air around it. "Come on, Dareena, you can do this!"

Dareena sucked in a breath. The light grew brighter, and suddenly, a glowing whip unfurled from her hand. It crackled as it hit the floor, throwing off sparks, and Lucyan's eyes widened. A few of the sparks left scorch marks on the floor and walls.

"I—I did it!" Dareena exclaimed. As soon as she said the words, the whip flickered out of existence. "Or at least, I did for a moment," she said, a little put out.

"Damn right you did." Lucyan gathered her into his arms and kissed her soundly. "Don't look so disappointed—this is excellent news! With a bit of practice, you'll be wielding that whip in no time."

The two of them returned to bed to snuggle for a little while, and they slept until sunrise. Rays of pink and gold peeked through the curtains when Lucyan opened his eyes, and he nuzzled the back of Dareena's neck. This was the best night of sleep he'd gotten in a long time.

"Time for me to get up," he said, kissing her neck. "I've got to be in Alistair's room before a servant shows up."

"Mmm." Dareena turned in his arms, her eyes half-lidded. "I'll join you."

Lucyan dressed quickly, reluctantly putting his disguise back in place while Dareena donned the dressing gown again. They returned to Alistair's room to find him sleeping peacefully and looking significantly improved from last night.

"Morning," his brother rumbled, pushing himself upright.

His sleepy gaze moved between the two of them, and he smiled knowingly. "The two of you look well-rested."

"As do you," Dareena said, smiling. She sat down on the bed next to Alistair and felt his forehead. "No fever," she said, "and your color looks good. I believe you're back to normal." She ran her fingers through his messy blond hair as she kissed him.

"And here I thought I was the doctor," Lucyan teased as Dareena cuddled Alistair. A pang of jealousy hit him, but it was less about Alistair holding Dareena's attention and more about the fact that he couldn't rejoin her in bed. But he was Dr. Harrigan again, and it would raise some very awkward questions if he was found in bed with her by one of the elves.

"You are," Alistair said, grinning, "and your treatment was quite effective. Though I suppose you'll be wanting your medicine back," he added, unfastening the amulet from around his neck.

"You should wear that for as long as possible—" Lucyan began, but just then someone knocked on the door. "Who is it?" he called as Dareena jumped up from the bed, an alarmed look on her face. Lucyan remembered that Drystan had given the elven duchess the distinct impression that he alone was Dareena's mate...did the elves still think that, or were they aware of their arrangement?

"It's Princess Basilla," the visitor called. "I'm coming to check on your patient."

"Come in," Lucyan said, snatching the amulet from Alistair's hand and putting it in his coat pocket. He turned to greet the princess just in time to see the look of pleased surprise on her face as she beheld Alistair.

"You are looking much improved," she said to Alistair as she stopped at the foot of the bed. "How are you feeling?"

"Like a new man, thanks to the doctor," Alistair said. "I am grateful to you for hiring him."

"It was the least I could do after the way my horrid brother treated you," Basilla said. She turned her gaze to Lucyan. "Unfortunately, my father has said that once Alistair is nursed back to health, you must leave the building. His policy about not letting outsiders into the castle is rather strict."

"I understand," Lucyan said, inclining his head. "Before I go, could I have a chance to speak to my patient and his... friend...alone? I need to give them instructions on how to administer the potions I will be leaving behind."

"Of course." Princess Basilla glanced between them, and Lucyan could have sworn he caught a glimmer of skepticism in her eyes. But she left, and Lucyan made a big show of rummaging through his doctor's bag within view of the guards before she closed her door.

"You can't leave now," Dareena whispered, clutching at Lucyan's arm. "You only just got here, and we haven't come up with a good plan yet!"

"I have no choice," Lucyan whispered back. "There is no way to smuggle either of you out with the guards watching. I will see if there is a way to sneak you out from the outside, but if not, you must find a way on your own."

"I'm sure the two of us can manage something, now that Arolas is no longer a thorn in our side," Alistair said. "We should set a rendezvous point."

"I'll be waiting at the Whistling Willow for you," Lucyan said. "Go there and ask for Ramsey, the tinkerer's apprentice."

"Tinkerer's apprentice?" Alistair frowned.

Lucyan rolled his eyes. "It's a long story. I'll be waiting with provisions, and some fast horses." It would be easier to avoid detection if they left on horseback—he could always shift later, once they were out of view. "Stay safe in the meantime," he said.

"We will," Alistair promised, giving Lucyan a fierce hug. Lucyan hugged him back, then gave Dareena a quick kiss to tide him over. She clung to him, clearly not wanting to let him go.

"I'll see you soon," he murmured, drying the tears falling from her lashes. His heart ached to see her so distraught, but he had to leave now before the guards grew suspicious.

"I know you will." She put on a brave smile for him, then pushed him toward the door. "Go now."

He did, and though his heart was heavy, for the first time in a long while, it was also filled with hope.

"What do you mean, he's not awake yet?" Drystan growled. The fork bent in his clenched grip. He was half-tempted to wad it up into a ball and shove it down the warlock's throat. Maybe that would bring him back to consciousness.

Catriona scowled. "I meant exactly what I said. He's not awake yet. The sleeping potion we doused him with must have been stronger than I thought."

"I may have given him an extra dose," Taldren said sheepishly.

"You *what?*" Catriona twisted in her seat to face him. The three of them were gathered around the table in the royal suite, eating breakfast. "Are you daft, cousin? That much could have killed him!"

"And so what if it did?" Taldren said defensively. "After what that bastard did, he deserves to die."

Drystan groaned. "As much as I agree with that sentiment,

we need him alive to question him," he said, scrubbing a hand over his beard. "You'd better hope he wakes up soon, Taldren. If he dies, I'll have you busted down to stable boy."

"Great," Taldren muttered. "Mucking out stalls again. Just what I was hoping for."

"Mucking out stalls will be the least of our worries if we don't get to the bottom of this," Catriona said. "We need to find out what the warlocks are up to, or we'll never be free of their constant meddling."

Drystan scooped a forkful of sausage into his mouth, considering the situation. Would the oracle imposter tell them anything? Drystan had no idea what he was capable of—for all he knew, by the time they went down there the bastard could have melted off his shackles and escaped despite the twenty-four-hour watch Drystan had posted. He wished Lucyan were here—out of everyone in their family, he was the only one who dabbled with warlock-enchanted items and the like. It was quite likely he would know of a way to keep the warlock restrained. Luckily, Shadley was still around; he would seek out the spymaster after breakfast and ask him if anything could be done to secure the warlock's cell against magical meddling.

"Your Highness!" A messenger bustled in, clutching a scroll. "A message has come from the elves."

Drystan's heart jumped in his chest. "Let's see it," he demanded, holding out his hand. Taldren and Catriona gathered around him as he unrolled the scroll, and Drystan clenched his jaw as he read it. The message was unsigned, but the snooty tone told him it was likely from Arolas—if he did not pay up in a week's time, one of the hostages would be executed.

"Enough of this," Drystan growled, slapping the scroll onto the table. "We cannot afford to wait for the scouts to find Father's lair."

"What are you going to do?" Catriona asked as he shoved to his feet. For once, she actually looked alarmed. "You can't be thinking about running off to the Black Mountains, can you?"

"That's exactly what I'm going to do." Drystan strode to the coat rack by the door and grabbed his cloak. "Catriona, you're in charge while I'm gone, and Taldren, you're second in command. I'll be back by nightfall. Try not to let the place fall apart until then."

Ignoring their sputtering protests, Drystan stalked out the door. Several nobles tried to waylay him, but he ignored them, stopping only to tell his steward that he would be out for the day. As soon as he was free of the castle walls, he shifted into dragon form, then launched himself off the cliffside and into the air.

He'd snatched an hour or two of free time here and there to practice flying, and to his relief, he had acclimated to his wings far faster than anticipated. Despite the dire circumstances spurring his flight, Drystan found his fears and worries dropping away as he soared higher—the feel of the wind on his face, the sight of the clouds around him and the ground so far below, all of it filled him with an exhilaration that could not be matched by any experience, not even riding a horse at full speed. He suddenly understood why his father had always been in a good mood after returning from a hunt. How could anyone not be after this?

He only hoped his father would be in a more agreeable

mood if and when he ran into him in the forest. It was likely he was getting in quite a bit of flying now that he was on his own and forced to hunt on a regular basis. With any luck, he was hunting animals, not Dragon Force soldiers. Drystan felt bad enough about sending those soldiers into danger on a regular basis—he would feel terrible if his father had killed them.

Even though Drystan was in his own territory, he made sure to stay above the clouds to draw as little attention as possible. Even so, about halfway to his destination, he spotted a caravan of traders being accosted by what looked like bandits. Part of him was tempted to keep flying—after all, from this distance they seemed like nothing more than insignificant ants—but the ruler in him could not abide the idea of bandits roaming free on his lands.

Angling his body toward the ground, he swooped down, then blasted a few of the bandits with fire, careful not to get too close to the caravan. Screams and the smell of roasting flesh filled the air, simultaneously exciting and horrific—his human and dragon halves were not reconciled on the issues. Three of the bandits were killed instantly, thrown by their horses and landing on their heads, and two more were merely singed badly. The rest took one look at him and bolted, running or riding as fast as they could manage. Drystan felt a bit sorry for the animals, which did not deserve to be scorched or frightened. But then again, the caravan did not deserve to be robbed.

The caravan's horses were spooked, so he took off with another flap of his wings. *Bloody bandits,* he grumbled to himself. The fact they roamed freely was only more evidence that Dragonfell was slipping—he must do something about these outlaws as soon as he had a spare moment.

As the Black Mountains loomed closer, Drystan banked left, heading where the scouts had reported sighting a large dragon several times. He spotted several scouts with his keen eyes as he passed, and wished that he could communicate with them—hopefully the sight of him would warn them to stay back. The last thing he wanted was any of them getting in the way in a confrontation with his father.

He landed on the side of one of the mountaintops to give his wings a rest. As he sat there, breathing in the fresh, chilly air, the wind shifted, and he caught the metallic tang of a familiar scent.

Gold.

Excitement rushed through Drystan's veins, and he craned his neck, nostrils flaring wide. The scent seemed to be coming from the east, so he took off again, gliding on the currents as he followed it. The scent grew stronger with each mountain peak he passed, and just when he felt like he was right on top of it, he spied a cave several hundred feet below.

Tucking his wings into his sides, Drystan dove, his snout pointed straight toward the valley below. The wind whistled shrilly in his ears as he plummeted, his heart galloping, and a few seconds later, he snapped his wings out. Muscles and tendons burned with strain as they caught the updraft, and he coasted toward the ledge just outside the cave. From this distance, he could smell his father quite clearly, though he wasn't certain if he was in the cave or had left recently.

Drystan landed on the ledge as softly as he could manage.

Nevertheless, his claws dislodged some of the rocks, and he stiffened as they went clattering down the mountainside. Tense, he approached the mouth of the cave, his senses on high alert. But Dragomir did not seem to be about—if he was, he would have attacked already.

By the gods, Drystan thought as he crept farther into the cave. His eyes adjusted slowly to the dimmer light, allowing him to see the mountains of gold and jewels piled inside, arranged around a small clearing scattered with animal bones where Dragomir likely slept. Chests and trunks peeked out between the piles, no doubt filled with valuables, and Drystan wondered if he could manage to smuggle one or two out. It wouldn't be enough to pay off the elves, but perhaps he could offer them to the council to mollify them. Maybe if they had something shiny to fill their coffers, they would be less miffed about the tax break he'd given to the soldiers and more inclined to back his next proposal.

Drystan was just deciding which trunk to pick when the whoosh of flapping wings gripped him in fear. He whirled about as his father approached, a dead sheep clutched in his claws. He grabbed one of the trunks and rushed for the entrance, hoping to clear it before Dragomir landed, but his father roared, filling the entire cavern with flames. Drystan's hide was fireproof, but the blast stunned and blinded him before he could make the jump. The ground thudded as Dragomir landed, and he roared again, the sound filled with rage. Drystan's heart sank as their eyes met —there was absolutely no recognition in them, no hint of the man who had raised him.

Father? he tried, pushing the thought toward him. He'd

learned from a young age that dragons could speak to each other telepathically when in dragon form if they were in close proximity—Tariana and his sisters did so often, and the skill was invaluable during battle. *Father, please! It's Drystan.*

Dragomir merely thrashed his tail, a warning for Drystan to drop the trunk. Drystan only clutched it tighter—he refused to leave empty-handed. He gathered his legs beneath him, preparing to jump over his father's left shoulder and make a break for the exit, but Dragomir tossed the sheep aside and sprang at him, his maw wide open. Drystan dodged to the side, but his father's claws raked his underbelly, sending fiery trails of pain through him. Blood spewed through the air as Drystan twisted away, but maneuverability was hard in the small space that was barely large enough to hold one dragon, let alone two.

The sight and smell of blood only seemed to egg Dragomir on—he roared again as he tackled Drystan, and this time he clamped his jaw around Drystan's throat. Drystan roared in agony as Dragomir's fangs dug deep—this part of his hide was well protected, but if he let his father hold on any longer, he would puncture a hole in Drystan's throat. Desperate, Drystan kicked forward with both hind legs, planting them in Dragomir's mid-section. It wasn't enough to propel the larger dragon back, but it did get him to open his mouth, and Drystan quickly took advantage of the moment and shoved the trunk down his throat.

Dragomir reared back, choking. More fire spewed from his throat as he attempted to incinerate the blockage, and Drystan scrambled from the mouth of the cave, then launched himself into the air. He didn't dare make a grab for any more of the gold

—he might have delayed his father for a few moments, but he would come after Drystan with fury if he took even a single gold coin.

Bloody dragon sickness, Drystan fumed as he flew away. It was a disease of the mind, and made dragons greedy, unable to part with a single piece of their hoard. If Drystan wanted to wrest the treasure back from his father, he was going to need a much better plan.

Hurry back, Lucyan, he said as he headed back to the castle. Perhaps if his brothers returned and all three of them could shift, they stood a chance of bringing down their father together. That had been the original plan, and though Drystan did not want to harm their father, he was beginning to worry that patricide might be the only option if they were to regain control over their kingdom.

TWENTY-SEVEN

"Come on," Dareena muttered under her breath as she summoned more energy to her fingertips. "You can do it!"

Sparks snapped and popped around her hand as she willed the magic to take the shape in her mind's eye. The glowing white energy unfurled, and her heart jumped in excitement as it elongated into a whip. Flicking her wrist, she made it snake through the air before coiling back to wrap around her wrist. Though the energy didn't hurt her, she knew from the scorch marks in her bedroom that they could burn, which was why she'd found an empty storage room to practice.

Dareena flicked the whip back and forth a dozen times before it flickered, the power failing. She extinguished the magic, then wiped the sweat from her brow, feeling satisfied. Each time she summoned the whip, she could wield it for longer and longer periods. No, she might not be able to kill a guard with it, especially not an armored one, but she could certainly hurt and stun them if needed. After Lucyan had left, Dareena had gone to the library to find a book on offensive magic. She had discovered a wide variety of techniques one could use to hurt, maim, or kill enemies. Most of them were beyond Dareena's skill level, but there was one called "exploding eardrums" that she longed to try. The theory seemed simple enough, though of course she wouldn't know how easy it was without an enemy to try it out on, and she didn't dare practice on the guards.

Worn out, Dareena returned to her room to freshen up before lunch. She had planned on eating with Alistair today, but a messenger arrived as she was about to go look in on him, informing her that Princess Basilla had invited her to have lunch in her private sitting room. Dareena wasn't entirely certain she was up for it, but she could not refuse after Basilla had given her so much help and support. She followed the messenger to the princess's suite.

"How is Alistair doing?" Basilla asked as they repasted on fish soup with thick brown bread and butter. "I imagine you've been snuggling with him to keep his strength up?" she added with a saucy smile.

Dareena laughed a little. "You've got us all figured out," she said. "He is doing much better after that healing."

"Good." Basilla swallowed a spoonful of soup. "Count Kianor has departed for Shadowhaven, thank the goddess. I expected him to be in a sour mood, but I'm told he left in great haste, almost as if he was excited about something. I can't imagine why he would be in any great hurry to tell his king that I've refused the match with his son."

"It may have nothing to do with your rejection," Dareena said. If the warlocks were truly behind this war, anything that made them happy could not be good for either Dragonfell or Elvenhame. "My mates and I suspect the warlocks were responsible for killing their mother, my predecessor. We found a warlock spell that induces death in an eerily similar manner to the way she passed."

"Really?" Basilla's eyes widened. "Does anyone else know about this?"

"My mates brought it to the council, but even though King Dragomir did not dismiss the possibility, he also refused to give up on his assault against your country." Dareena sighed. "From the way it looks, both the scroll and the fact that the warlocks have been arming your country against ours, it seems that they have a stake in seeing us at each other's throats."

"I wish I could say I was surprised, but our alliance with the warlocks has long been suspicious," Basilla said. "Father seems much more himself now that Count Kianor is gone, and in light of what you just said, I can't help but wonder if the count was responsible for his change in behavior. It started not long after he arrived, and I must say I am quite glad to be rid of him."

"As am I," Dareena said. Privately, she wondered if Arolas knew about the count's meddling—he certainly had no issue taking advantage of his father's mental state. "What's going to happen to Arolas?" she asked. "Is he going to be charged with a crime?"

Basilla sighed. "I'm not certain, and neither are Father or the council. They are split—some believe he should be punished, while others think that his time spent in the oubliette, and being stripped of his rank as general, is punishment enough. My brother may be a foul individual, but he is smart, and has made friends in high places."

Dareena's heart sank. "I really hope he doesn't get out anytime soon," she said. "I don't like the way he looks at me."

Basilla nodded. "I fear what will happen to Ryolas once he is released," she said. "I was going to pay him a visit after our meal. Would you like to come with me?"

"Yes, please." She was anxious to meet the foreign prince who, in concert with Tariana, had done so much for her country.

The two women finished their meal quickly, then went to visit Ryolas. His rooms were just up the hall from Basilla's, with two guards posted outside. Dareena was relieved when they let them pass without question—it saddened her that Ryolas was under house arrest when he had done nothing wrong, but at least he wasn't barred from visitors.

"Good afternoon, sister," Ryolas said with a smile, sitting up as they entered his bedroom. He was a striking elf, so similar in coloring and features to his sister that Dareena wondered if they were twins. He looked a bit ill, his skin and hair lackluster, his eyes shadowed with fatigue, but otherwise not bad for a man who had just recently been a prisoner. "Who is your friend?"

"This is Dareena, the Dragon's Gift," Basilla said as they stopped by his bedside. "I thought you might like to meet her in person."

Ryolas's eyes widened. "I would indeed!" He pushed back the covers and attempted to leave the bed. "It is an honor to make your acquaintance," he began, then gripped the wall when he stumbled.

"Please, Prince Ryolas, there is no need to stand on my account," Dareena said, holding up her hands. "I'm sure after spending all that time chained up, your body needs a bit more rest." She eyed his wrists, which were an angry red color—from what she understood, he'd been shackled for quite some time, which was cruel for an elf.

"Very well," Ryolas relented, allowing Basilla to help him back to bed. "How is Prince Alistair faring? Basilla told me all about that nasty business with his arm." His eyes darkened with anger. "Throwing Arolas into the dungeon is far too paltry a punishment. He should have something chopped off in return."

Dareena cocked her head. "Your brother seems quite different from the two of you," she said. "Why is that?"

"He was the only child of our father's first wife," Basilla explained, "so he is really our half-brother. The king has been unlucky with his wives—Arolas's mother died in childbirth, and ours died soon after she brought me into the world."

"I'm sorry," Dareena said, feeling a pang of pity as sadness crossed the princess's face. "I too have lost my parents, and I was old enough to remember them when they were gone. So I know your pain."

Basilla put an arm around her, a show of solidarity and sisterhood that warmed Dareena's heart.

"Has Father come to see you yet?" Basilla asked her brother.

Ryolas shook his head. "I sent word to him asking for an audience, but he hasn't responded yet," he said. "I imagine he is not ready to face me yet, even knowing that the elven goddess still holds me in her favor." His lips twitched. "I must say, Basilla, I am surprised to hear that. I would have thought she would be angry with me for consorting with a dragon princess."

"Perhaps Shalia is just as eager for this terrible feud to be over as we are," Basilla suggested. "She was very displeased with Arolas's actions, and I sensed she was not very happy about Count Kianor's presence either." A troubled look crossed Basilla's face. "Dareena thinks that the warlocks have been pitting us against the dragons, and vice versa, and I am inclined to believe it."

Ryolas nodded. "I have had my suspicions about that as well," he said. "It was why I arranged to meet with the dragon brothers. I wanted to plant the idea in their minds and force them to dig deeper into the matter of their mother's death. Since we did not kill her, and the dragons would not have done such a thing themselves, the warlocks are the logical suspect. I will speak to Father about this, once I manage to convince him I am not the enemy."

Basilla checked the clock on the wall. "I cannot stay much longer," she said, taking Ryolas's hand, "but please, Ryo, be careful. Sleep with a knife under your pillow. Maybe even bring one of the dogs in to watch over you. Arolas may not be out of prison yet, but he is not powerless. He has supporters and friends who are more than happy to further his agenda."

"Believe me, sister," Ryolas said grimly, "now that I am free, the last thing I intend is to end up under Arolas's thumb again. I will take the necessary precautions."

"Good."

They stayed a few minutes longer before bidding Ryolas

goodbye. Ryolas told Dareena to let Alistair know he'd asked after him—apparently, the two of them had bonded a bit while stuck in the oubliette together. Dareena wondered if perhaps Lucyan had been premature in his decision that the younger elven prince was out of danger. She prayed to the gods, dragon and otherwise, that Ryolas would come out of this on top, and that Arolas would get what he deserved. But somehow, in her heart, she had a feeling that the gods had other plans she would not like once they came to pass.

Later that night, as Alistair curled his body around Dareena and inhaled her sweet scent, he wished he could leave the confines of his room. Try as he might, he could not sleep—his mind was too busy chewing on questions, and after spending so much time in bed, his body was not tired. Lucyan's amulet had really done the trick—he'd felt good as new when he'd given it back, and as Dareena had spent most of her time cuddling with him, he barely felt the effects of the anti-dragon spell.

He should be doing something useful. Figuring out a way to escape, not lying about as if he were on holiday. For fuck's sake, he was trapped in enemy territory, and his brother was holed up in an inn waiting for them so they could go home and fix their kingdom!

Alistair lifted his right arm to wrap it around Dareena's waist, then cursed when he remembered it was no longer there. Gritting his teeth, he looked down at the remaining limb—he had to give it to Arolas, the elf had damn fine swordsmanship. The cut was clean, sliced off neatly at the elbow joint. He could almost admire it if it hadn't been his arm.

He hoped Lucyan was right, that he would be able to heal this fully once he shifted for the first time. Otherwise, Alistair would likely have to give up swordsmanship.

"Your thoughts are so loud I can hear them in my sleep," Dareena murmured, turning in his embrace.

Her sleepy gaze searched his face, and Alistair couldn't help smiling at her. Whatever his circumstances, he was damn lucky to have her by his side.

"I'm sorry," Alistair murmured. He cupped the side of her face, stroking her soft cheek with his thumb. She was his to love, his to protect...but so far, he had not done a very good job on either account. "I wish I could relax, but I've been idle too long. If there is a way to escape this place, we should do it now while I still have my strength."

"Agreed," Dareena said. "But how?"

"I've been wondering if Princess Basilla might be willing to help us," Alistair said. "She seems sympathetic, and quite fond of you. If she could at least get us some disguises, perhaps some servants' clothing, we might be able to sneak out of here."

Dareena shook her head. "I won't put her in that position," she said, "and we don't have to. I took the liberty of filching some items from the laundry room."

"Really?" Alistair grinned at the devilish sparkle in Dareena's eyes. "And when were you going to tell me about that?"

"When the time came for us to make our great escape, of

course." She gave him a teasing smile. "With me as the brains and you as the brawn, we might just be able to make this work."

"Do you think you can do something about the guard outside?" Alistair asked. "I could take care of him with my brawn, but that might draw attention to us."

"I do believe I can."

"Wait a minute," Alistair protested as Dareena rose from the bed. "You're going to do it *now*? We're not even dressed."

"Something we're going to remedy right now." Dareena donned her dressing robe. "Go into my room and search the trunk. You'll find the clothing I stashed away."

Bemused, Alistair did as she asked, using the adjoining door. While he rummaged through the trunk, he heard Dareena open the door and call to the guard at the end of the hall.

"Excuse me, sir? Can you please fetch some water? Alistair's fever is going back up."

"Can't it wait until morning?" the guard said gruffly. His voice was gritty with tiredness; he was not their usual guard, and Alistair gathered he had just been put on night shift. "I won't be relieved from my post for another few hours."

"Not unless you want to explain to the princess why Alistair is sick again," Dareena said in a severe tone. "I imagine she'll be very displeased after all the money she spent on that doctor."

The guard heaved a sigh. "I'll send for some. Don't try anything funny while I'm gone. I *will* track you down if you try to escape."

"Of course," Dareena said sweetly.

Alistair pulled out a maid's outfit that looked to be Dareena's size. Frowning, he searched the trunk for male clothing, but came up with nothing. Had Dareena forgotten an outfit for him? He couldn't very well go running about in his own clothes.

Alistair was nearly about to return to his room to ask Dareena about it when his hand closed around something hard and metallic. Grinning, he pulled a long, sheathed dagger that he knew Dareena had not taken from Dragonfell—they had not been allowed any weapons, and besides, this one was forged from mithril.

"I see you've found my surprise," Dareena said, hurrying into the room. "Quickly now. The guard will be back any minute."

"That's all well and good," Alistair said as he handed Dareena her outfit, "but what am I to wear? I imagine running about the castle naked will attract just as much attention as wearing my own clothes."

Dareena chuckled. "As amusing as that would be, I have no plans to let you run amok with your twig and berries hanging out for everyone to see," she said. "You'll take the guard's clothing, of course."

"Of course." Why hadn't Alistair thought of that? Perhaps he wasn't as fully recovered as he thought.

Alistair helped Dareena into her clothing, then double-checked both rooms to make sure they weren't leaving anything important behind. Unfortunately, there wasn't much of anything small enough for them to take. Dareena slipped her elven magic primer into her skirt pocket, and at least Alistair would have the dagger. He might be feeling better, but he still couldn't breathe fire—he'd tried it more than once.

A few minutes later, Alistair tensed as the guard's footsteps came closer. At a signal from Dareena, he hung back while she waited just behind the door. "I've got your water, Miss," the guard called through the door, sounding more than a little grumpy. Alistair rolled his eyes; he'd never encountered such a whiny guard in his life. Clearly this one was either new, or the captain of the guard was not training his subordinates very well.

"Oh, thank the gods," Dareena said. She opened the door, and the guard shoved the jug into her hands. Alistair watched closely as Dareena wrapped her fingers around his wrist, and he felt that strange hum in the air. The guard's eyes widened, then fluttered shut, and Dareena moved out of the way as he toppled over.

"Damn!" Alistair darted forward and caught the guard before he crashed onto the floor. "How did you do that?" he asked, pressing two fingers to the man's neck. His pulse was faint, but steady, as if the guard were merely sleeping.

"I siphoned his life energy, and gave myself a boost in the process," Dareena said, closing the door. She looked simultaneously pleased and relieved. "I'm glad I didn't take too much—I've never tried this on anyone before so I had no idea if it would kill him or not. Is he all right?"

"I'm sure he'll be even grumpier when he wakes up," Alistair said as he stripped off the guard's clothing, "but unless you damaged something internally, he should be fine."

"Good. Let's get going then."

Alistair donned the guard's clothing, fastening the elf's sword to his left hip along with the dagger. He'd practiced some with his left hand, and though he knew he wouldn't be winning any duels, he could use the dagger to great effect in close quarters, or distract a guard with the sword until Dareena could move in to steal his life energy. With any luck, nobody would notice his dangling sleeve.

Once Alistair finished with the guard, he shoved him beneath the covers, then ushered Dareena behind him as he opened the door. He looked both ways, listening for any approaching footsteps. Once he was satisfied the coast was clear, he took Dareena's hand and crept down the hall.

"Squeeze once to go right and twice to go left," he whispered as quietly as he could. Since Alistair had been confined to either the bedroom or the dungeon, he didn't know the castle well enough. "We need to go out through a side entrance, preferably one used by servants."

Dareena nodded. She had him take a right, then two lefts, sticking to the shadows and listening for any signs of someone approaching. They were just about to make another turn when Alistair caught the scent of blood.

Blast it! He immediately flattened himself against the wall, pulling Dareena with him. Sure enough, footsteps, so faint as to nearly be undetectable, approached. Who else would be sneaking around at night, and wounded, besides that? His nostrils flared as he sniffed deeper, and his eyes widened as he recognized the scents.

"Ryolas?" he hissed, poking his head around the wall. "Basilla?"

The siblings stopped in their tracks, eyes wide. "We were just about to come and find you!" Basilla said in a hushed voice. Eerily, she was dressed in a maid's outfit, and Ryolas also wore a guard's uniform. "Arolas sent one of the guards into Ryolas's room, and he was nearly assassinated!"

"It's a damn good thing I took your advice and had one of the dogs sleep with me," Ryolas growled. "He would have slit my throat if the barking hadn't woken me up. Bastard killed the dog before I could get to him." He shook his head in disgust. "If Arolas can manipulate our guards and servants even from behind bars, I am not safe here, and neither are you. We must leave, tonight."

"And you?" Alistair demanded of Basilla. "Are you really willing to leave your home and family?"

"Until I am certain Arolas is no longer a threat, yes," Basilla said firmly. "Come quickly now—we cannot afford to loiter. There is a secret passage that was built so our family could escape if ever there was an invasion. If we get to it now, we can slip out before any alarm is sounded."

TWENTY-NINE

Lucyan stared at the ceiling, wide awake as he listened to the tinkerer snore in the bed next to his. He would have given almost anything to have a room of his own, but unfortunately the inn was almost completely booked up—they'd only managed to get this room because of the tinkerer's popularity.

Of course, he probably wouldn't have been able to sleep even if he had quarters of his own. Lucyan had been plagued with anxiety since the moment he'd left Castle Whitestone. Alistair was doing much better now that he'd had time to heal, but how long until he succumbed to the anti-dragon spell again, even with Dareena by his side to draw strength from? If the two of them didn't find a way out of the castle before Alistair fell ill again, Lucyan would have to resort to drastic measures that could very well get them all killed. Horrific scenarios played out in his mind of all the things that could go wrong, nearly driving him mad with fear.

"Bloody hell," he muttered, throwing off the covers. What was the point in lying abed if he couldn't sleep? Careful not to wake the tinkerer—although how the man could hear anything above his own racket, Lucyan did not know—Lucyan pulled on his clothes, then slipped downstairs to the pub. It was close to two in the morning, and there weren't nearly as many people seated at the bar and tables as there had been when Lucyan had returned. He found a table easily enough, then signaled a waitress for a mug of ale and a plate of chicken.

As he started on his third ale, two royal guards strolled in, a pair of beautiful women on their arms. Lucyan nearly choked on his brew—the woman closest to him had her hair hidden under a cap, but he would recognize those emerald eyes anywhere. And the man whose arm she was on...

"Hello," Alistair said, grinning at him from beneath his cap. He'd angled it carefully to shield his amber eyes. "Are you Ramsey, the tinkerer's apprentice? We were told to seek you out if we wanted to have a good time in this town."

"You dog!" Lucyan cried, jumping up from the table. He embraced Alistair as if he were a long-lost friend—and indeed, he was much more than that. He ached to hug Dareena as well, but that would have been wildly inappropriate, so he kept his hands to himself. "It's been far too long. Come, have a drink, and introduce me to your friends!"

They did so, and the waitress brought more drinks for the rest of them. "How did you get out?" Lucyan whispered as the four of them leaned in close. "And what are you two doing here?" he demanded of Ryolas and Basilla.

"Helping you escape," Basilla said coolly, 'and coming along for the ride."

Lucyan scowled. "Why would you want to come with us? Your place is at Castle Whitestone."

"Please, Lucyan." Dareena squeezed his hand beneath the table, sending a current of warmth up his arm. "Arolas tried to have Ryolas killed tonight. He and Basilla are not safe here. Didn't you promise Tariana you would rescue him if you could?"

"I did," Lucyan said grudgingly, eyeing the elven prince. There was no reason not to trust him, Lucyan decided. "But I did not bring enough horses for all of us."

"That shouldn't be a problem if you can shift," Ryolas said. "We'll double up on the horses for now, and once we're out of sight, you can take dragon form and carry Dareena."

"We don't have much time to debate this," Alistair reminded him. "Every hour I remain in these lands weakens me. And we only have until morning before the guards discover we're missing."

"You make a good point." Lucyan drained his glass. "I'm going to leave a note with my traveling companion to tell him I'm taking off," he said, standing up. "Meet me in the stables— I'll be down in a jiff."

Agreed, the four of them parted ways. Lucyan hurried up the stairs and packed his scant belongings, then left a note by the tinkerer's bedside table informing him that he had "collected the package and was returning home." Ambiguous enough that someone else would not suspect the truth without leaving any doubt in the tinkerer's mind as to what he meant. For a moment,

Lucyan felt a pang of regret that he could not say farewell face-to-face, but he shook it off; the tinkerer would come to Dragonfell in the near future, and Lucyan would be able to thank him then.

By the time he got to the stables, the horses Lucyan had purchased were saddled and ready to go. "It was easy enough to pick which ones were yours," Alistair said while Lucyan fastened his bag to the saddle. "They all have your scent on them."

Lucyan smirked. "What can I say? I'm a cuddler." He ignored Alistair's rolling eyes as he tossed a shirt at him, and another one at Ryolas. "Put these on," he ordered. "The last thing we need is for the guards to think you two are deserters."

The two men did as he said, hiding their uniform shirts beneath piles of hay. Ryolas helped his sister mount their horse while Lucyan assisted Alistair—he could tell that his brother wasn't thrilled about his help from the way his jaw was clenched, but he was still getting used to maneuvering with only one hand.

With any luck, he wouldn't *have* to get used to it for much longer.

"Would that I could cuddle with you," Lucyan said, circling Dareena's waist with his hands, "but I think you'd be better served helping my brother with the reins."

"We'll have plenty of time to cuddle once we're out of danger," Dareena said, leaning up to kiss him. Lucyan held her a little tighter as their lips met, and even though they'd slept together last night, it felt like an eon ago. Under different circumstances, he would be carrying her to the back of the stables for a roll in the hay, but...

"I'm not an invalid, you know," Alistair grumbled, breaking the spell. "I can manage the reins with one hand."

"No one is calling your masculinity into question," Dareena said gently as Lucyan helped her up. She settled between Alistair's legs and patted his thigh. "I'd simply feel better if I stayed close to you for now."

Lucyan hid a smirk as he mounted his own horse—the annoyance had melted from Alistair's features the moment Dareena had touched him. None of them could withstand her charms. "Are you ready?" he asked the elven siblings.

Ryolas nodded. "As ready as one can be when fleeing one's ancestral home."

Lucyan felt a pang of sympathy for the prince. Just a few weeks ago, he had been an esteemed general, heir to his father's kingdom. Now, he was about to become a refugee. "You'll be back here before you know it," he said, spurring his horse into a trot.

The others followed him out of the stables, and together, they made their way to the southern gate. The sleepy guards waved them through with barely a glance—their job was to police those entering, not those trying to leave. The moment they cleared the gate, Lucyan was struck with the urge to whoop and cheer, but they were hardly out of the woods yet. Leaning into his horse, he urged the animal into a canter and headed for the hills.

"All right," he said once they were a safe distance away. "Princess Basilla, you can take my horse. I'm going to shift now."

"Are you sure?" Basilla asked. Her keen eyes scanned their surroundings, hunting for enemies though Lucyan had already checked for them. "You may want to conserve your strength."

Lucyan shook his head as he dismounted. "It will be easier on the horses if we're not doubled up, and I can spot any enemies headed our way from above." He helped Basilla off Ryolas's horse and onto his own. "You and Ryolas will be our eyes and ears on the ground. I will be our eyes in the sky."

"And I will come with you," Dareena said, taking his hand. Lucyan blinked—he hadn't seen her dismount. "As you said," she reminded him when he opened his mouth to protest, "it will be easier if we are not doubled up."

Lucyan looked her up and down. "Are you sure you will be all right?" he asked. "It is colder in the sky."

Dareena smiled. "You will keep me warm."

Lucyan chuckled, then climbed one of the hills to put some distance between himself and the horses. Closing his eyes, he summoned the anger and protective urges that had helped him to change the first time, and let the emotions run wild through him. The same pain from before ripped through him as his body morphed, and he could smell the horse's fear as it whinnied nervously, the scent ten times stronger thanks to his heightening senses. The primal urge to give chase gripped him, and Lucyan dug his claws into the dirt to keep himself from attacking the horses. He opened his eyes and focused on the one person he knew could center him.

Dareena.

"Oh, you are magnificent," she breathed, her eyes shining with wonder. Slowly, she approached, her lips parted, her hand outstretched. Lucyan made a sound in his throat that was vaguely reminiscent of a purr as she stroked his snout, running her warm hand over his scales. Her touch soothed the bloodlust in him, and he closed his eyes to savor it. He imagined that if he let her pet him long enough, he might fall asleep.

"Excuse me," Ryolas said, sounding both amused and annoyed. "I hate to interrupt what is obviously such a special moment, but we really must be going."

Lucyan huffed. He lowered his belly to the ground, then unfurled his wings so Dareena could climb onto his back. The sensation of her walking across his wings felt strange, almost ticklish, and Lucyan had to resist the urge to roll onto his back to alleviate the sensation. Thankfully, it dissipated, and Dareena settled onto his back.

Meeting Alistair's wide eyes—which were filled with both pride and jealousy—Lucyan rustled his wings, the only signal he could give them. Flexing his back legs, he launched himself into the sky. His heart leapt into his throat as Dareena screamed, but when he twisted his neck around, she was safely nestled between the spikes on his spine, her eyes blazing with exhilaration. Shaking his head, Lucyan turned his gaze forward, then pumped his wings hard, driving them just far enough above the clouds that he could still see the others below while remaining out of sight. Not that it was likely anyone could spot him in the dark unless they were paying special attention, but still, it was best to be careful in enemy territory.

"This is wonderful!" Dareena cried. He turned his head to see her looking around, her eyes shining with delight. "I can still see the city from here," she said, twisting in her seat to look back at Enethar. "It looks like a glittering jewel."

Lucyan rumbled his agreement. He wished that he could speak with Dareena, but dragons did not have voices, not in the way humans did. Still, having her close eased the anxiety that had been gnawing at him, filling him with comfort and relief. The two of them enjoyed the flight in relative silence, broken only occasionally by Dareena exclaiming over some wonderful new sight. He understood her enthusiasm quite well—Lucyan himself had yet to get used to the incredible experience.

As they traveled, Lucyan continuously checked on Alistair and the elves to make sure they were fine. Even though they were flying slowly to keep pace with the elves, they were making good time; at this rate it would only take them another day or two to reach the border. Lucyan couldn't wait until they crossed back into dragon territory and were finally free of the spell. Then Alistair could finally attempt to shift, and hopefully regrow that arm of his.

"Lucyan," Dareena called anxiously, only two hours into their flight. "Something is wrong."

Frowning, Lucyan glanced down. He cursed inwardly—the party had slowed down. Swooping low, he saw that Alistair's horse was limping. Wonderful. Just what they needed.

"What happened?" Dareena cried as Lucyan landed. Their party halted so Alistair could dismount.

"I'm not sure," Alistair said as he checked the horse's hoof. The horse whinnied in pain as he poked at it. "I think she stepped on something sharp—she made an awful noise, then started limping. I don't believe she can carry my weight anymore."

"I could try healing her," Basilla offered. She made to dismount, but Alistair held up a hand.

"Hang on," he said. "I have a better idea. Lucyan, could I borrow the amulet?"

Lucyan cocked his head, wondering what his brother was about. He extended his clawed hand, and Alistair carefully took the necklace. Backing up, he clenched the amulet in his fist and closed his eyes, his brow furrowed in deep concentration.

"Oh!" Dareena exclaimed as his form began to blur. "He's changing!"

Ryolas and Basilla hastily backed the horses away as Alistair's form rapidly expanded. His roar of pain echoed through the night, and Lucyan winced, hoping no one else had heard it. Had he made such a sound the first time he'd shifted? If so, it was a wonder no one had come to investigate. Pride swelled in Lucyan's chest as Alistair's form solidified into a large dragon with green scales that shimmered in the moonlight. Large horns curled back from his great head, like a ram's, and his spiked tail lazily whipped back and forth. Lucyan's heart filled with joy as he looked at Alistair's front legs—both seemed intact. With any luck, his arm would be whole again when he shifted back to human form.

Looks like you're not the only one here who can shift now, Alistair teased. Lucyan started at the sound of his brother's voice in his head, then grinned in delight—finally, he had someone to talk to!

Better late than never, Lucyan teased back. *Do you think you can fly?*

Alistair gave a flap of his wings, then hurled himself into the sky. Lucyan took off after him, fully expecting his brother to fall after a moment, but to his great surprise, Alistair not only stayed aloft, but also managed to do a roll in the sky.

Show off, Lucyan grumbled. Of course Alistair would be a natural. He excelled at everything physical.

"Don't get ahead of yourself, Alistair!" Dareena called. "We can't afford to lose the others! Lucyan, can you bring us down so I can talk to them?"

Right. Lucyan and Alistair doubled back to where Ryolas and Basilla were—the two had stayed behind so Basilla could finish healing the third horse. "How is she doing?" Dareena called, pitching her voice high to be heard over the sound of Lucyan's flapping wings.

"She'll be fine," Basilla called back, patting the horse's neck. "And so will we!"

"You three go on ahead," Ryolas said. His lips curved in a knowing smile as he beheld them. "I know you are anxious to get home, and there is no point in slowing yourselves down on our account."

"Are you certain?" Dareena asked. "I hate to leave you behind." Dareena suspected that if Alistair had more experience flying, he might have tried to carry the elves. But he'd only just shifted for the first time and Dareena felt it unwise to push him.

"We're more than capable of looking after ourselves," Basilla said. "And besides, you really need to make it to the border before the anti-dragon spell forces one of you to shift back. Go on—we'll see you soon."

"Thank you," Dareena said. She bade the elves farewell, and Lucyan and Alistair took to the skies again, speeding through the starry night. At first, they attempted to outrace each other, until Dareena complained that the wind was going to tear her eyeballs out of their sockets unless they slowed down. A quick check assured them both she was fine, but even so, they slowed to a more manageable pace, keeping their eyes on the real prize ahead.

Soon, they would be reunited with their brother. Soon, they would be home.

THIRTY

For the next several hours, the brothers flew, speeding through the skies as fast as they could without dislodging their passenger. Through it all, Dareena clung to Lucyan's back, wrapping her arms around one of the spikes jutting from his spine as she gazed out at the world with wonder. Everything looked so different up here—the moon larger, the clouds thicker, the stars blazing so bright and true that Dareena almost felt as if she could reach out and pluck them from the night sky.

This high up, she should have been miserable and freezing. But with her body pressed against Lucyan's hide, soaking in the heat from his scales, she was toasty-warm. It was rather like snuggling beneath a blanket with a cup of hot cider in one's hands and a warm fire roaring in the hearth. Your nose and cheeks might be a bit cold, but that only made you savor the heat even more.

Dareena had a few such memories from her childhood,

before her parents had been taken by that horrible illness. As she rubbed the elven stone on her finger, she wondered what her parents would think if they could see her now. When she'd been a little girl, she'd dreamed of being a princess living in a castle with handsome suitors currying her favor, but those had just been that—dreams. No one could have imagined in their wildest fantasies that Dareena Sellis would become a consort to dragons, riding them wild and free in the middle of the night. If only her friends could see her now...and her enemies! How had Mr. Harrin and Lyria Hallowdale reacted when they'd learned she had become the Dragon's Gift? She would have paid good money to be a fly on the wall for *that* conversation.

Such petty thoughts are unbecoming of you, a voice in her head said—likely her conscience. She blushed a little—she *was* being a little catty, now that she thought about it. But surely she was allowed to indulge a little in the privacy of her own mind? She had come so very far...

A surge of energy rippled over Lucyan's scales, distracting Dareena from her thoughts. She looked around, trying to see what had caused it, but in the darkness, it was hard to make out the terrain. Puzzled, she turned her attention toward Lucyan and Alistair, accessing the bond between them. She'd noticed that though she couldn't speak with them in dragon form, she could sense their feelings to some extent. Right now, she felt joy and relief emanating from them—they both seemed quite peppy.

"Have we crossed the border?" she called, excitement thrumming in her veins. Lucyan rumbled something that sounded like an affirmative, and Alistair did a somersault in the air, then blew a stream of fire from his snout, lighting up the sky.

Dareena laughed, patting Lucyan's hide affectionately. They'd finally made it out of elven territory! Only a few more hours of flying, and they would be back at Dragon's Keep.

Unfortunately, Lucyan and Alistair didn't have a few more hours of flying in them. Despite the boost of energy they got from crossing the border, they began to flag only an hour later. Dareena couldn't blame them—this was their first long-distance flight. She clung tighter to Lucyan as the two dragons descended, landing in a thickly wooded vale.

"My goodness," Dareena said as she dismounted. Her legs were a little wobbly, and she braced herself against Lucyan's big body to keep from falling. "I didn't realize how taxing that flight was. My muscles are going to be sore in the morning!"

Lucyan and Alistair's forms blurred, and a few moments later, they were back in human form. "A good night of sleep and a massage will help," Lucyan said with a roguish smile. "I think Alistair and I can help you with both."

Dareena swallowed hard as she looked between both men, who were stark naked. Moonlight bathed their muscular bodies, beckoning her to close the distance so she could run her hands over each swell and crevice. The twin expressions of hunger in their gazes told her they wouldn't at all be averse to the idea, and if she looked lower...

"By the gods!" Dareena exclaimed, rushing over to Alistair so she could take his right hand in hers. "You're completely healed!" She ran her fingers up his new forearm, feeling the muscles and tendons flexing beneath.

"That I am." Alistair's eyes sparkled. He grabbed Dareena by the waist and lifted her high in the air, spinning her around and making her laugh with delight. "I worried I might never get to do this again," he said roughly, pulling her against him so he could kiss her. Dareena clung to him as he kissed her deeply, savoring his hot skin beneath her hands. His cock pressed insistently against her belly, and she could feel herself getting wet as she imagined wrapping her hands around it—no, her lips...

"Quit hogging our mate, Alistair," Lucyan growled. He pressed against her from behind, and Dareena gasped as he gently scraped his teeth along the sensitive spot on her neck. His cock ground insistently against her bottom, and she moaned as her pussy clenched in anticipation. She'd long fantasized about having more than one at a time...

"We agreed we were going to wash up together, didn't we?" Alistair asked, adjusting Dareena so that he was cradling her rather than holding her flush against his body.

"We certainly did." Lucyan's eyes gleamed. "I'll lead the way, brother."

"Wash up?" Dareena asked, shifting in Alistair's arms. "Is there a stream nearby?"

"Something like that," Alistair said, a secretive smile in his voice. Dareena craned her neck as they traveled through the forest, using a narrow but well-worn path. Leaves and branches rustled and cracked as they moved, but the noise was barely audible beneath the crickets chirping. They were so loud that it took Dareena a while to realize she was hearing another sound—rushing water.

We have to be close, she thought excitedly. The trail grew steeper, rocks jutting out of the dirt, but if the brothers noticed or found it uncomfortable, they didn't let on. Gradually, the air grew warmer, and when they stepped out of the trees and into the clearing...

"By the gods," Dareena whispered as Alistair set her on the ground. "This is incredible!"

An oasis sprawled in front of them—a collection of steaming pools cradled in a basin that seemed to have been carved out of the mountainside. Trees loomed all along the edges of the basin, providing some privacy while still remaining completely open to the elements. The air was hazy with steam rising from the hot springs, clinging to Dareena's skin and urging her to divest herself of her garments.

"Do you like it?" Lucyan asked, sliding an arm around her waist.

"I love it," Dareena breathed, still looking around. The large stones surrounding the hot springs were stacked in such a way that a person could easily lay their clothes out, or even perch comfortably while they tested the water with their toes. "How did you know this place was here?"

"The three of us found it on a hunting trip," Alistair said, smiling fondly. "We've come back a few times since, but never with anyone else." He moved closer and threaded Dareena's fingers with his own. "You're the first person we've brought here."

He tugged Dareena to the closest pool, and she followed, eager to try out the water. Alistair waded right into the steaming pool as if he'd done it a dozen times—which, apparently, he had.

Dareena was a bit more hesitant—she dipped her toe into the water, testing the heat.

"You may want to take this off first," Lucyan said, his warm breath caressing her ear. Dareena's heart jumped in her chest as he circled his arms around her from behind, then began to undo the buttons on the front of her maid's uniform. Alistair watched as his brother slowly bared her body to the elements, and Dareena's breath quickened as his hungry gaze trailed across each bit of exposed skin. Her breasts tumbled free as Lucyan popped the fourth button, her nipples already growing hard, and the way Alistair's amber eyes flared with lust filled her with an answering need.

"Gods," Lucyan growled, cupping her breasts in his hands. Dareena moaned, her head falling back against Lucyan's chest as he played with her nipples, teasing them

into stiff, aching peaks. "You're so damn tempting, Dareena. I haven't even gotten you into the water yet and all I want to do is bend you over and sink my cock into your tight little pussy." He tweaked her left nipple, pinching just a little too hard, and Dareena whimpered. "Would you like that, little minx?"

"I believe we promised our mate we would do something about her tense muscles first," Alistair said, wading closer. He slid his wet hands up Dareena's legs, pushing her skirts high as he gently dug his strong fingers into the muscles. "Ahh, there we go," he purred as she cried out, her legs going boneless. Lucyan caught her around the waist before her knees hit the ground. "Let's get you into the water."

Alistair pushed Dareena's dress higher up her body, and Lucyan tugged it off the rest of the way. The two of them made short work of her undergarments, and Alistair tugged her into the steaming hot water, Lucyan nudging her from behind.

"Ohhhh," Dareena sighed in pure bliss as she submerged herself in the pool. The heat from the water seeped beneath her skin, loosening up stiff muscles and sending waves of relief through her. "This feels *so* good."

"Then this will feel even better," Lucyan said, coming up from behind her. He pulled her flush against him so that she was sitting on his lap, then nudged her legs open with his thighs. Dareena gasped as his hand delved between her thighs, finding that sweet spot he often liked to tease with his tongue. She arched her hips, pressing firmly against his fingers, but he used his other hand to pull her hips back against him. His cock was wedged between the cheeks of her bottom, pressing against her rear entrance, and Dareena's eyes widened as she felt an unexpected bolt of pleasure.

What is this?

As Lucyan rubbed against her with his fingers and cock, Alistair moved between her legs. Dareena lifted her face to meet him as his mouth descended onto hers in a scorching kiss full of need. His left hand cupped her breast, massaging her nipple, and she moaned into his mouth, her body trembling from the combined sensations. Dareena wrapped her fingers around Alistair's cock, and this time *he* moaned into *her* mouth. Stroking him beneath the water was a bit different, but Dareena quickly grew used to the new rhythm, sliding her hand up and down, letting the water flow over her fingers as they flowed over his shaft. Lucyan's fingers seemed to move over her clit in time to her strokes, moving faster, faster, until her muscles stiffened, and she threw her head back, crying his name.

"Yes," Lucyan growled in her ear as she came. He bit down on her neck, sending her even higher. At the same time, Alistair slid his cock inside her, filling her completely. He moved his hips in slow, deep thrusts, one hand on her hip while the other still toyed with her breast.

"And now," Lucyan said, a devilish smirk in his voice, "let's try something a little different."

Dareena frowned as he removed his finger from her clit. She reached for his hand, wanting to put it back, but he slid it beneath her bottom instead, lifting her a bit higher. A startled cry sprang from her lips as his fingers teased the tight rosebud muscle of her rear entrance, and her stomach muscles fluttered in a combination of fear and anticipation.

"Dareena," Lucyan breathed in her ear. "Do you trust me?"

"Yes," she said breathlessly, even as she stared up at Alistair. The muscles in his face were tight with concentration as he pounded into her, and she focused on him, watching the way his cock slid in and out, in and out, sending pulses of pleasure and need through her.

"Good," Lucyan said. He slid a finger inside her, and Dareena let out a strangled cry, her hips instinctively driving forward. Alistair groaned as he plunged even deeper inside her, and Lucyan pushed his finger higher. Her rear muscles clenched around him as a bolt of pain-laced pleasure hit her, and she clutched at Lucyan's free arm, holding on for dear life as the sensation assaulted her.

"That's it," Lucyan crooned in her ear as she panted,

straining against him. Slowly, he withdrew his finger until it was nearly all the way out, then pushed it back in, going a little deeper. Dareena dug her nails into his flesh as the sensation lanced her again, but this time there was more pleasure than pain. Soon enough, her muscles relaxed, and she began to rock back and forth, taking them both, savoring the dual sensations as she was filled and stretched.

"Just imagine," Alistair said roughly, leaning in to tongue Dareena's earlobe. "One day, that won't be a mere finger inside you. It will be a thick, hard cock, pumping you so full you'll think you're going mad."

Dareena's eyes flew open as the image branded itself in her mind. She'd never heard Alistair say something so dirty, and though the words scalded her ears, they also pushed her over the edge, throwing her into another orgasm. Screaming, she bucked her hips harder against Alistair's, and he swore, then came inside her with a rush of heat.

"My turn," Lucyan panted, shoving Alistair away with his foot. He withdrew his finger, and Dareena moaned as he slid his cock inside her pussy, which was still pulsing from the after-shocks of her orgasm.

Alistair watched as his brother fucked her from beneath, his eyes gleaming with satisfaction while he leaned against the rocks. His cock was still hard, and he stroked it lazily as Lucyan pumped his cock in and out of her while using his free hand to play with her clit.

"I want you to scream my name when you come," Lucyan growled in Dareena's ear as his thrusts grew faster. "Scream it so loud they'll hear you all the way back in Elvenhame and know that you've been reclaimed by your mates. No one else will *ever* touch you again."

The fingers on her clit began to move faster, forcing the knot of tension deep inside her to build, build, build. Moaning helplessly, Dareena moved her hips faster, grinding herself against Lucyan, straining for the release that was just out of reach.

"Gods, yes," Lucyan groaned, his cock swelling inside her. She felt another rush of heat as he spilled his seed into her, and she came, screaming his name so loud that a flock of birds burst from a nearby tree, disturbed from their sound slumber. Dareena hardly noticed as wave after wave of bliss rushed over her, and with it, a wave of exhaustion. Coming so many times, coupled with the stress of escaping, and all this hot, lovely water...

"That was...nice..." she murmured, sinking against Lucyan's body. "Really...nice..."

"Under other circumstances, we might be offended," Alistair said, sounding amused. He slid his arms beneath her and lifted her out of the water. "Come," he said, wading to the edge of the pool. "Let's dry you off and get you to bed."

Dareena nodded, snuggling against Alistair's chest. She didn't see where they were going, but the next thing she knew, Alistair was settling her atop what felt like a warm fur. Blearily, she noted that they were in a cave, and briefly wondered how they'd managed to find it. But when Lucyan and Alistair curled their bodies around her, sandwiching Dareena between them, she found she didn't much care. Happily, she sank into their embrace and let their combined warmth and scents lull her to sleep.

THIRTY-ONE

Another day passed with no sign of the warlock resurfacing from unconsciousness. Drystan worried that Taldren had permanently damaged him, but after a thorough inspection from the healers, the oracle imposter was pronounced healthy.

"He simply needs to sleep off the effects of the sleeping draught," the healer said in a placating tone. "Giving him a double dose was not the wisest course of action, but warlocks have hardier constitutions than humans. He will survive this."

"He'd better," Drystan muttered, leveling a death glare at Taldren, who was sitting in one of the visitor chairs in Drystan's office. His cousin suddenly found the dirt under his fingernails to be of supreme interest. Drystan was tempted to strangle him —instead, he drew in a deep breath, counted to ten, then let it out.

"Thank you," he said to the healer. "You are dismissed."

The healer bowed. He opened the door, but before he could

leave, the steward came in. "Your Highness," he said, an uneasy note in his voice. "There is a messenger from Elvenhame here to see you."

Drystan stiffened. "Bring him in."

Tarius motioned with his hand, and an elven male with black hair entered the room. He stopped in front of Drystan's desk, then turned to face him, his posture ramrod straight. Drystan narrowed his eyes as he noted the wooden chest the elf was carrying—there was a strong scent of blood and rot coming from it.

"A gift, compliments of Prince Arolas," the elf said, placing the chest on Drystan's desk. His face betrayed no hint of emotion.

Taldren was instantly at Drystan's side. "Perhaps I should open that—"

"No." Drystan knocked his cousin's hand away, his gaze fixated on the small chest. An awful feeling grew in the pit of his stomach, telling him to leave the chest be, to look away. Steeling himself, he lifted the latch, then opened it.

"Oh gods," the healer choked, his face growing pale. Rage and disgust built in Drystan's chest as he stared at the severed arm, lying neatly in the wooden chest on a blood-stained pillow. The skin had taken on a greenish hue, and had burst open in several places, oozing rot and maggots. The stench was overpowering, but beneath it, Drystan could still discern the scent of the man this arm belonged to.

"The prince has instructed me to inform you that he will be sending more pieces of your brother back every week you delay paying the ransom," the elf said in that same emotionless tone while Tarius retched behind him. "And if that is not enough of an incentive, he—"

Drystan didn't let him finish the sentence. He opened his mouth, unleashing a torrent of fire. The elf was incinerated in seconds, reduced to a pile of ash, and it wasn't nearly enough. Drystan's entire body trembled with effort as he locked down his jaw to keep from torching the room and everyone in it. He wanted to give himself over to the beast, to become a dragon and rage across the lands, raining hellfire down upon anyone who might oppose him.

But the horrified expressions of the others stayed him. He recognized the look on Taldren's pale face—it was the same look he'd seen many courtiers give his father when he'd given in to one of his fits of rage.

You are not your father. You are NOT. Your. Father.

"I'm sorry," Drystan said, exhaling sharply. "I should not have destroyed the elf."

"Like hell you shouldn't have," Tarius said. True, his voice sounded a bit shaky, but the conviction blazing in his eyes seemed very real. "The elves promised our prince and Dragon's Gift protection, and this is how they repay us? For all we know, they've cut Prince Alistair to pieces already!"

Drystan snarled at the horrific image that statement conjured. "We cannot allow such an insult to stand," he said. "Tarius, bring my sisters here at once."

The steward bowed, then hurried out of the room. "What are you going to do?" Taldren demanded. "You said that you found Dragomir's lair yesterday—are we going after the treasure?"

"No," Drystan said in a clipped voice. "The elves have broken their word. I shall not give them what they ask for just so they can stab us in the back again."

A few minutes later, the door burst open, and Tariana and Catriona rushed in. "What is that gods-awful smell?" Tariana exclaimed. She'd just come back that morning from the elven lands after checking in on the troops. His eldest sister's amber eyes latched onto the open chest, and the blood drained out of her face. "Is that..."

"An arm?" Catriona finished, sounding faint. Neither of them were the kind of women who had fits, but at that moment, Drystan was certain he could have knocked either sister over with a feather.

"Not just any arm," Taldren said grimly. "Alistair's arm."

Dead silence descended upon the room.

"What does this mean?" Tariana finally asked, meeting Drystan's eyes.

"It means," Drystan said, his voice vibrating with anger, "no more stalling. No more waiting around for help or miracles. No more negotiating. I want you two to gather the Dragon Force and make them ready to march on Elvenhame. Tonight, we get our brothers and my mate back, no matter the cost."

"Yes, sir."

His sisters saluted, and under different circumstances, Drystan might have been taken aback, as it was the first time they had done so. But he was almost too angry to care.

"It will not be easy to attack in dragon form," Tariana said, "not with all that anti-dragon magic and those horrible bracelets.

But you are right—the time to act like sniveling cowards has passed. We must stand and fight."

"Exactly." Drystan rose from his seat. "Tariana, contact your lieutenants and get this in motion immediately. Catriona, Taldren—with me."

He stalked out of his office, the others following. Seething, Drystan stormed down to the dungeons and headed straight for the private, closely guarded cell where the warlock was being held.

"Let me through," Drystan ordered the guards. They opened the cell, then stepped aside to let him in. Smoke puffed out of Drystan's nostrils as he beheld the imposter, who lay on the hard bench with his eyes closed and his hands folded over his stomach. If not for the enchanted manacles around his wrist, the warlock might have resembled some sleeping princess waiting to be awoken by her long-lost love.

Well, Drystan would awaken him all right. Just not in the manner of his choosing.

"You miserable wretch," he snarled, grabbing the warlock's robe. He hefted the man, and when he merely hung limply from Drystan's arm, Drystan slammed him into the stone wall. "I know you are faking it, old man. Wake up now, or I will burn you to ashes!"

The warlock's head lolled forward in response, almost as if he were mocking Drystan. Smirking, Drystan pushed the man's head back up, then leaned in and oh-so-gently blew a stream of fire directly onto his shiny, bald head.

"AAAAIIEEEEEEEEEE!" the warlock screeched, his eyes flying open. He smacked at his head with his sleeves, thrashing against Drystan's iron grip. "What in Xaldor's name is wrong with you?"

"Ah, so you are awake." Drystan looked over his shoulder at Catriona and Taldren. His sister's expression was an interesting meld of amusement and shock, while Taldren merely looked relieved that the warlock was no longer unconscious. "I knew you were faking it."

"You can hardly blame me for trying," the warlock whined. "These manacles may prevent me from using my powers on you, but I am perfectly capable of using them on myself to affect sleep."

"So I surmised," Drystan spat. He threw the warlock at the bench, and the man cried out in pain as he smashed against the wall. "You are going to tell me who you really are, and what you're doing here, or I am going to slow-roast your testicles and feed them to the dogs."

"A-all right!" the warlock stammered, holding up his manacled hands to fend off Drystan. He trembled as Drystan opened his mouth, letting a cloud of smoke waft over the imposter. "My name is Mathias Black. I was sent here by King Walarian to spy on the dragon court!"

"To what purpose?" Catriona demanded. She and Taldren had moved in, flanking Drystan on either side. Mathias clenched his jaw, and Drystan opened his mouth wide, giving him a glimpse of the dragon fire lurking just down his throat.

"Fine, fine!" Sweat broke out across the warlock's forehead. "To weaken the kingdom and prepare it for an eventual takeover. My king had already heard about King Dragomir—he's been using magical mirrors to spy on the goings-on in Dragon's

Keep and saw your father showed signs of dragon sickness. We needed to speed up the progression of the illness, so he sent me in to get rid of his Dragon's Gift and to sow doubt and mistrust in his mind."

As the pieces of the puzzle finally clicked into place, a red haze descended over Drystan's vision. Roaring, he grabbed the warlock by the throat and slammed him into the wall again, squeezing hard.

"You...killed...my...mother," he ground out between clenched teeth. The fire raged in his chest, demanding retribution.

"P-please!" Mathias choked, his eyes bulging. "I-I-I...can help...you!"

"Drystan," Taldren said gently from behind him. "We came down here because we needed information. If you kill him now, we may not find out what we need to know."

Disgusted, Drystan released his hold and let the warlock collapse on the bench. Letting out another roar, he punched the wall just above Mathias's head. Spiderweb cracks raced across the stone as the room trembled, and the warlock whimpered. He still wore the oracle's guise, but he was a far cry from the smug, self-righteous arsehole he'd been portraying.

"You are going to tell me how to circumvent the anti-dragon spell that has been laid over Elvenhame," Drystan said in a too-soft voice. "And you are going to tell me how the elves are bringing down my dragons and forcing them to change back into human form."

"T-there is no way to circumvent the anti-dragon spell!" the warlock stammered, holding up his manacled hands to fend off

Drystan. Drystan bared his teeth, puffing a cloud of smoke at the warlock that caused him to lose control of his bladder and fill the room with the stench of piss. "Not unless I crafted warlock amulets for every member in your army, and that would take months!"

"We don't have months," Drystan snapped. "The elves have mutilated my brother and threatened further harm to him—we are marching on them *now*. Give me something to use against them, or so help me, I will tie you to a spit and let one of my sisters slow-roast you to death."

"The bracelets!" the warlock whined, his voice cracking. "The secret is the bracelets."

Catriona sucked in a sharp breath. "What do you mean?"

"We crafted special brass bracelets that force dragons to shift back to human form and prevent them from breathing fire," Mathias croaked. "That is how Arolas was able to turn the tide so quickly against you."

"Is there a way to combat the effects?" Drystan demanded.

"As I said, warding amulets," Mathias panted. "But again, it would take me months to craft enough for all of you."

"That's insane," Taldren snapped. "Lucyan has a warding amulet—he's using it right now. If he was able to get his hands on one, that means they are for sale."

Mathias laughed harshly. "Indeed, in Shadowhaven. Good luck making it to any of the market stalls there, or getting them to take a large order. It is foolish to attack the elves now. We have armed them against you. The plan was to get the two of you to weaken each other, and it has gone splendidly so far. Once the elves finish you all off, Shadowhaven can move in and annihilate what is left of Elvenhame's army. Both of your peoples will be ground into the dust, and we shall reclaim our homeland and return it to its former glory." His eyes shone with a fanatical light. "Terragaard will thrive once it is free from the influence of elves and dragons."

Drystan clenched his hand into a fist. He wanted to grind Mathias's face into the dust, or at least give him a few good punches. Neither of them were even close to what his mother's murderer deserved, but...

"Leave him, Drystan," Catriona said, laying a gentle hand on his arm. "This scum isn't worth bloodying your knuckles over. Besides, we will need his testimony for the council."

Drystan exhaled. "You are right," he said, gathering his composure. He stalked out of the cell and ordered the guards to lock it up behind him. "Let us call a meeting now. It is time to drag those useless bastards' heads from the sand and make them confront the *real* enemy."

THIRTY-TWO

Dareena woke the next morning to bright light streaming in from the cave entrance and two hard, warm male bodies pressed up against her. Smiling, she ran a hand down Alistair's muscular arm, marveling at the way it had perfectly healed. There was no scar, not even the faintest trace of a line to indicate that Arolas had severed it. Her dragon prince was good as new again.

Alistair made a pleased sound in his throat, emboldening Dareena. She slid her hand down a little farther, over his hip, to grip his hardening cock. Gently, she stroked him, savoring the feel of his hot, velvety skin sliding against the palm of her hand. His member flexed in her fist, and as Alistair moaned, Lucyan moved in closer, his lips trailing along the back of Dareena's neck.

"I must say, this is a nice way to wake up," he said, nudging his cock between her legs. Dareena gasped as he entered her from behind, her back arching, and she instinctively tightened her grip around Alistair's cock. The three of them moaned in unison, and Dareena quickened her strokes as Lucyan moved inside her.

The three of them made love, then washed off in the hot springs, where they made love again. Dareena's cheeks ached from smiling so much, and yet, there was an ache deep in her heart for Drystan. Their merry band wasn't complete without him. He was back at Dragon's Keep, probably worried sick about them all, dealing with the crushing burden of running the kingdom without any of them to help.

Alistair and Lucyan mirrored Dareena's sentiments—they did not linger after finishing their bath, but shifted back into dragons while Dareena donned her maid uniform. She climbed on Alistair's back this time, and the three of them took to the skies, determined to get home and reunite with their family.

ALISTAIR COULD STILL HARDLY BELIEVE he was flying. The wind whipped past him, clouds brushed the tips of his wings, and below, the landscape rushed by, far faster than he could ever travel on foot or even horseback. He'd thought it would take him longer to get used to flying, but he'd taken to it like a duck to water, executing flips and turns mid-air, loving the way his muscles sang as they propelled him through the sky.

He also loved the feel of his mate sitting between his shoulder blades, her curvy body pressed against his hide. Her sweet scent wafted around him, warming his blood, filling his heart with contentment. No longer was he a useless wretch stuck in bed while she took on the burden of caring for him. He was a fearsome, fire-breathing dragon, capable of protecting what was his.

And he was whole again.

Lucyan and Alistair carefully stuck to the clouds. Even though they were back in their homeland, spies were everywhere. There was no need to tip off their enemies that all three of them could shift, and lose the element of surprise. But as Alistair scanned the landscape through the cloud cover, he noticed something odd.

Lucyan, he said slowly, using mind speech to get his brother's attention. *Do you see those men down there?*

Lucyan turned his head to where Alistair was looking. *A nobleman, traveling with mercenaries. All heavily armed. What are they doing with all those mules?*

Alistair dropped lower to get a better look. Five mules all carrying empty sacks. *My guess is that he's here to collect something,* he said warily.

"Is...is that Count Kianor?" Dareena asked. Alistair twisted his head to see her looking over his shoulder, her green eyes wide. "I was told he was on his way back to Shadowhaven!"

Count Kianor? Lucyan asked.

He was a warlock envoy at Elvenhame's court, Alistair explained. *I don't see how he has any legitimate business in our realm.* That a warlock was moving freely through Dragonfell was not a good sign. *They must have used magic to sneak past the border guards.*

Lucyan growled. *Let's follow him and find out what it is he's after.*

The two of them stuck close, staying out of sight while making sure not to lose track of the warlocks. As expected, the party did not head for Paxhall, but instead headed north. The count seemed to be following directions—he had some shiny device in his hand, perhaps a sort of magical compass, and glanced at it frequently.

I believe we're headed for the Black Mountains, Alistair finally said. The mountain range loomed close, only an hour away by horseback. Either the mountains were their destination, or something that lay beyond. But what?

Isn't that where Drystan said Father went off to? Lucyan asked.

Damn, Alistair swore. *We can't bring Dareena this close to danger. One of us needs to take her back to Dragon's Keep and warn Drystan about these intruders.*

"You're not taking me back to Dragon's Keep!" Dareena cried, startling them both. Lucyan and Alistair whipped their heads around as one to look at her, and she glared back at them, defiant. "I may not be able to read your thoughts, but I know you both well enough. I want to find out what Count Kianor is up to. Perhaps I may even be of some help in stopping him."

Lucyan and Alistair exchanged looks. *She's pregnant,* Alistair protested. *She shouldn't be anywhere near Father.*

Normally I would agree with you, but she is also the only one among us who can use magic, Lucyan said reluctantly. *The least we can do is see this through, find out what is going on. If things get too hot, you'll head back to Paxhall immediately.*

Agreed, they continued, following the warlocks to the base of one of the mountains. Alistair and Lucyan hung back as they watched the warlocks begin the laborious ascent up a particularly steep one, using ropes and pitons to dig into the rock. Alistair followed the trail they were ascending and narrowed his eyes when he saw where it led to.

Do you see that cave up there? he asked Lucyan as his heart beat faster.

Lucyan followed Alistair's gaze. *The opening is quite large,* he said, echoing Alistair's thoughts. *Do you think...?*

A ferocious roar echoed from the inside of the cave, cutting off Lucyan's thought. Dareena gasped as Dragomir shot out of the cave, spewing fire from his gaping maw. Even from this distance, Alistair could feel the waves of fury rolling off his father, and he cringed inwardly, as though he were a child rather than a full-grown dragon himself.

Blast it! Lucyan swore. He shot upward, and Alistair followed, hiding behind the clouds as they watched the battle below. Two of the warlocks were incinerated instantly. The mules, waiting on a sturdy ledge far below with one of the warlocks, tried to bolt back down the mountainside, but their collars blazed with magic, and the mules stopped in their tracks. The remaining warlocks, including Count Kianor, held fast, using a blue, glowing shield to combat the worst of the fire.

Unfortunately for the warlocks, the shield couldn't withstand the onslaught—Alistair saw it flicker, and he knew Dragomir did too. Baring his teeth, the giant dragon swooped down, drawing close enough to incinerate the warlocks with one bellow of fire while remaining well away from their swords.

Before Dragomir could unleash the flames, Count Kianor raised his hands. Alistair caught the glint of brass bracelets around his wrists, and his father's form blurred. The three of them watched in horror as Dragomir shifted back into human form, plummeting toward the jagged, rocky ground. He disappeared into a crevice, and the warlocks cheered while Alistair's stomach sank.

By the gods, Lucyan said, sounding shell-shocked. *Tariana said the elves had a device that could rip dragons out of the sky, but to see it in action...* He shook his great head, disbelief in his eyes.

"We can't get any closer," Dareena said, her voice trembling. She stared down at the mountain, watching the warlocks continue their ascent with a mixture of anger and fear in her eyes. "If they see either of you, they'll take you out of the sky as well."

Lucyan leaned in and nuzzled his giant snout against Dareena, reassuring her they weren't going anywhere. She smiled, leaning into him, and Alistair felt a momentary flash of jealousy that he couldn't do the same. Staying out of sight, they watched the warlocks finish making the climb and enter the cave, carrying empty sacks in with them. Quickly, they began bringing the sacks back out, filled to the brim with gold and treasure, and lowering them back down using the ropes.

"So *that's* where the treasure is!" Dareena exclaimed. "The warlocks are taking it for themselves!"

Fucking thieves, Lucyan fumed, his eyes blazing with anger.

Go find out what happened to Father, Alistair said. *Dareena and I will take care of the warlocks. Your amulet should shield me against the effects of the bracelet, correct?*

It should, Lucyan confirmed. *But why do you get to have all the fun?*

Because, Alistair said, sticking out his tongue, *I'm the one who has the girl.*

Alistair tucked his wings in at his sides and dove out of the clouds before Lucyan could answer. Dareena shrieked, or perhaps that was the sound of the wind screaming in his ears—Alistair couldn't tell. He pointed his body directly at the cave just as two of the warlocks were coming out. Their eyes widened as Alistair opened his mouth, blasting them with fire. Their screams briefly rent the air before their lungs crumbled to ash, and the fire cleared, leaving nothing behind but charred human and plant remains. Count Kianor ran out of the cave, brandishing his bracelets, but as Lucyan had said, they had no effect. His face paled as Alistair moved closer.

"Wait!" Dareena cried. "Let me!" She jumped off Alistair's back, her whip already crackling at her fingertips. The warlock tried to jump to the side as she flung it at him, but the whip coiled around his legs and brought him tumbling down. He screamed and writhed in pain, his body shaking uncontrollably. Dareena yanked on the whip, tightening it around him, and the warlock loosed a cry of such agony, it sent a shiver through Alistair.

"Go and get the last one," Dareena said, meeting Alistair's gaze calmly. "Before he gets away with the treasure."

Alistair dove toward the ledge below, where the remaining warlock was busy ushering the mules down the mountainside. He'd been forced to leave several sacks of gold behind, but there were still three on the mules' backs. Snarling, Alistair grabbed the warlock and flung him away, sending him tumbling into the vale below. The mules brayed in terror, frantically trying to get away, but Alistair used his bulk to block them while he ripped the sacks from their backs. Once they'd been unburdened, he let them flee, then flew back to Dareena.

"I didn't want you to accidentally melt these," she said, holding up the count's bracelets. He lay on the ground behind her, passed out. "I think this is what the warlocks have been using to force the dragons to shift back to human form."

Alistair rumbled his agreement. He landed on the ledge so Dareena could climb onto his back, then grabbed two sacks of the treasure and flew back down the mountainside to meet Lucyan. Even with the amulet to shield him, he could sense the *wrongness* emanating from those bracelets; if Lucyan tried to fly up here, he would be incapacitated immediately.

Lucyan was already on the ground waiting, still in dragon form. Their father was laid out at his feet, and Alistair's heart clenched at the sight of Dragomir's broken, bloodied body. As he moved in for a landing, Lucyan's form blurred, the bracelets Dareena held forcing him to change back.

"Bloody hell," Lucyan growled, a scowl planted on his face. Alistair shifted back into human form so the three of them could talk. It was a bit strange for them to be standing around naked, with his father naked on the ground between them, while Dareena remained fully clothed, but there was little they could do about it unless they found clothing up in the treasure hoard.

"Is he still alive?" Dareena asked, staring down at their father. She looked like she was torn between wanting to approach and wanting to get as far away from him as possible.

Alistair couldn't blame her—his father had threatened and demeaned her, and even tried to rape her once. The man who had raised them had turned into a truly despicable being.

"I think so," Alistair said softly, crouching next to the body. He felt for a pulse and found one beating at his father's neck, faint but present.

"I think his back is broken," Lucyan said roughly, folding his arms across his naked chest. "His leg is at an odd angle, too, and I wouldn't be surprised if he has broken ribs. It will take him quite some time to heal, and the bones will need to be set."

Alistair sighed. "I know he's done terrible things, but we cannot leave him like this," he said. "He's our father, Lucyan."

Lucyan nodded tightly. "We cannot bring him back into the Keep, though," he said. "It would be impossible to hold him in a cell or put him under house arrest."

"Not necessarily," Dareena said thoughtfully. She held the bracelets out to Lucyan, who backed away hastily. "These will keep Dragomir confined to his human form. It likely also hampers his ability to breathe fire and heal, which means that he is effectively rendered mortal so long as these are nearby."

"And so are we," Lucyan complained, his face screwed up in disgust. "Just what is the range on those blasted things anyway? Alistair was still a ways up when I was forced to shift."

Dareena smiled. "Let's test it then, shall we?" She slid the bracelets onto her wrists, then backed away. "Let me know when you stop feeling the effects."

Alistair dropped the amulet into the dirt so he could participate. The moment he did, he felt something squeeze him tight, as if a band were wrapped around his chest, except the feeling was *inside* him. A shiver of revulsion rippled through him, and suddenly he understood Lucyan's reaction when Dareena had held those bracelets out to him. He would not have wanted anything to do with them either.

Thankfully, the farther Dareena walked, the looser the band around Alistair got. When she was around a hundred yards away, it disappeared completely, and he and Lucyan let out twin breaths of relief. Looking down at their father, they noticed that the scrapes on his body were healing, a large gash on his inner thigh almost completely closed already.

"Stop there!" Alistair called. "That's the radius!"

"Excellent." Dareena beamed as she strolled back to them. "I don't think there is an easy way for us to transport your father and the treasure back ourselves, so one of us needs to go back to Dragon's Keep and get help. Lucyan, why don't you go? I'll wait here with Alistair." She slipped her hand in Alistair's after he placed the amulet back around his neck.

"Are you sure?" Lucyan asked. "You wouldn't rather come back to the Keep with me?"

Dareena dropped the bracelets onto the ground, then came over to Lucyan and wrapped her arms around his neck. "As much as I love spending time with you, I'd hate to leave Alistair here all alone," she said, leaning up on her tiptoes to kiss Lucyan. She brushed her lips against his, and Lucyan tightened his arms, pressing her against his naked body. Alistair didn't miss the way his brother's cock had hardened, and his own twitched in response, as if it were feeling left out and wanted to join the party. "Hurry back," she murmured against his mouth. "Don't keep me waiting."

"I don't plan to." Lucyan grinned, then turned around and walked away. Alistair snorted, noting the way Dareena's gaze was glued to his brother's arse. He wrapped his arms around Dareena from behind as Lucyan shifted into a dragon and propelled himself into the sky.

"If my father weren't here, I would suggest all kinds of ways to keep ourselves entertained," he said, nibbling her earlobe.

Dareena giggled and turned in his arms. "I don't think we can afford to drop our guard while we're out in the open," she said with a mischievous smile. "But," she added as she pressed her lips against his, "there is no reason we can't kiss and cuddle while we wait."

THIRTY-THREE

As Drystan stood over the map in the war room, going over strategy, the urge to tear his hair out struck him. The war wagons were being readied, the troops rallied...and yet, Drystan knew it wouldn't be enough. Not if those elven bastards were wielding those infernal bracelets, and not once they crossed into the heartland of Elvenhame and ran headlong into the anti-dragon wards.

"We've managed to gather twenty warding amulets," Shadley said, placing a wooden box the size of a medium dog on the table. "That will be enough to protect you and your lieutenants," he said to Tariana.

"And me," Drystan added. He was not going to cower behind the battlements while his sisters went off to war again. He was a dragon now, and he would use every ounce of strength and power available to get his mate and brothers back.

"That still leaves the rest of the Dragon Force unprotected," Tariana said tersely. Her jaw was clenched tight, her eyes burning with frustration. "The moment we come up against the anti-dragon wards, they'll be reduced to the same fighting capacity as humans."

"Which is still better than nothing," Drystan pointed out. "And even if the Dragon Force must fight like humans, they will still have us to back them up. We will just have to fight harder to make up for it."

"It would be nice if we had *all* the dragons at our disposal," Tariana said, folding her arms. "Where the bloody hell is Lucyan? Have you heard from him since he set off for Enethar?"

"No," Drystan admitted. He scrubbed a hand over his beard, briefly glancing out the window. Outside, soldiers and servants ran about, loading up the war wagons, saddling horses, packing supplies, and so on. "You were the last one to speak to him."

A troubled look crossed Tariana's face. "It's possible he tried to infiltrate the castle and failed. He could be held prisoner even now."

"My spies have reported no such thing," Shadley said, "but it has been impossible to plant anyone in the castle itself since they found my last informant, so my information could be out of date."

"Your Highness!" The door banged open, and a page rushed in. His face was flushed, his wide eyes bright with excitement. "There is a dragon approaching the Keep!"

Drystan jumped out of his chair. "Is it my father?" he demanded, though he didn't know why the page would be so happy about that. It wasn't as if anyone missed Dragomir. Or could it be...?

"I don't think so," the page said. "He's smaller, though still bigger than your sisters, and has red scales. Come quick—I think he's headed for the courtyard!"

Drystan, Shadley, and Tariana sprinted from the war room, following the page to the balcony overlooking the courtyard. Sure enough, a dragon was coming in, his brilliant red hide glinting in the afternoon light. He let out a roar that shook the battlements as he landed, frightening the servants half to death. The soldiers gripped their weapons, an instinctive reaction to the predator before them even though they had to know the dragon was on their side.

Or was he?

The dragon landed in the middle of the courtyard, crushing a wooden cart that had not been moved aside fast enough. He furled his wings in, then lowered his head as his form blurred.

"Lucyan!" Tariana gasped, her eyes shining with joy and relief. Before Drystan could so much as blink, she vaulted over the balcony. His sister landed the thirty feet below in a crouch, then sprang up and engulfed their brother in what looked to be a bone-crushing hug.

"If you don't mind," Shadley said, an amused look on his face, "I think I'll take the long way down."

Drystan grinned, then followed after Tariana, jumping the railing. "I was beginning to worry about you!" he said, coming in for a hug of his own. On his way, he snagged a cloak from one of the guards to wrap around Lucyan's body. "What the bloody hell happened? Did you ever reach Enethar?"

"I did," Lucyan said, grinning from ear to ear. "And Dareena and Alistair are both safe."

"They are?" Drystan exclaimed, exchanging surprised glances with Tariana.

"We received a box this morning with Alistair's severed arm in it," Tariana explained when Lucyan gave him a quizzical look. "*And* a threat to send more pieces if we did not pay the ransom."

A dark look crossed Lucyan's face. "Yes, that was a horrific ordeal. Alistair was on death's door when I arrived, but with the help of the amulet, he recovered. Thankfully," he said, a grin banishing the shadows from his face, "the both of us have learned how to shift, and Alistair regrew his arm."

"That is excellent news!" Drystan cried, feeling incredibly relieved. All the weight seemed to sluice off his shoulders, making him so light he felt as if a stiff wind might topple him. "I assume this means Alistair was able to fly back with you?" Where is he now? And Dareena?"

"They are waiting for us outside our father's lair," Lucyan said. "Along with the treasure."

"The treasure?" Tariana sounded as stunned as Lucyan felt. "What were you doing at Father's lair?"

"And how were you able to get the treasure from him?" Drystan demanded. "I was there myself not that long ago, trying to reason with him. He did not recognize me at all, and nearly tore me to pieces."

Lucyan gave them a smug smile. "That's because you don't know how to let others do your dirty work for you."

Inside, over mugs of hot mead, Lucyan told Drystan, Tariana, Shadley, Catriona, and Taldren all about how they'd followed a group of warlocks to the Black Mountains, then watched as they incapacitated their father using the brass bracelets the oracle imposter had told them about. Lucyan had retrieved their father from the crevice he'd fallen in while Alistair and Dareena took care of the warlocks, and they had agreed to remain behind while Lucyan flew back to Dragon's Keep for help.

"Is Father all right?" Tariana asked in a worried voice. Drystan felt a pang of sympathy for her—she knew better than anyone else how terrible their father was, and yet, as his eldest child, she shared a bond with him that none of their other siblings had.

"His body will heal," Lucyan said. "His mind is another matter entirely. Dareena is using the warlock bracelets to keep him subdued while they wait for us."

"If the warlocks have truly been using mirrors to spy on us," Shadley said, "then they will have learned of this development. We must retrieve the treasure, and our friends, before they send someone else out to take it again. They will know all three of you can shift now, and will adjust their plans accordingly."

"Agreed," Drystan said, rising from his chair. "Enough sitting around. Let us go."

Since Drystan and Tariana had already been preparing to march on Elvenhame, it did not take long to gather a squadron of Dragon Force soldiers. Tariana ordered them to take some of the war wagons and head for the base of the mountain—

Taldren, who had been briefed on the location, would lead them.

In the meantime, Drystan took flight with Lucyan and Catriona, while Tariana flew in the opposite direction. She would stop by Solara's encampment to brief the others on what was happening, then go to meet Ryolas and Basilla at the border. Lucyan had told them how the royal elven siblings had helped Dareena and Alistair escape, and Drystan was more than happy to offer them refuge, especially after everything Ryolas had done for them. He strongly suspected that if he had refused, Tariana would have ripped his balls off and fed them to the dogs—she'd been hardly able to contain herself when Lucyan had informed her that her beloved was on his way here.

Drystan understood how she felt. His entire body hummed with excitement as he approached the Black Mountains. Even the thrill of soaring through the air with his siblings was not as exhilarating as the thought of being reunited with Dareena. It had been less than two weeks since she'd been taken, and yet somehow it felt like months, perhaps even years, since he'd last seen her. Would she still taste and feel the same when he embraced her again? Or had being exposed to elven magic changed her?

Slow down, Lucyan warned as Dareena and Alistair came into view. They were sitting at the base of the mountains next to a prone form Drystan assumed was their father. *If we get too close, the bracelets will force us to change back.*

Right. A chill went through Drystan at the thought of shifting back into human form while he was thousands of feet up in the sky. The three of them slowed, then gradually came in for a landing a good five hundred yards away. Dareena and Alistair jumped to their feet at the sight of them, and Drystan shifted back, eager to have his beloved in his arms again.

"Drystan!" Dareena cried, running toward him. He met her halfway and caught her in his arms, swinging her around. "Oh, I've missed you so terribly!"

"Not as much as I've missed you," Drystan said roughly as he pulled her against him. He kissed her hard, one hand in her hair while the other clung to her shapely waist. He was naked as the day he was born, his cock growing hard as her curves pressed against him, but he couldn't bring himself to care that the others were watching. He was just thrilled to have his mate back.

"If we were alone," he panted against her lips, "I would tear your clothes off and take you right here in the grass."

"Unfortunately, you are *not* alone, and I would prefer if you refrained for now," Catriona said in an acid voice. She threw a set of clothes at Drystan—they'd each packed a bag and carried it around their necks as they flew—and he caught them with one hand while he continued to kiss Dareena. "You might want to put those on before the others get here."

"That won't be for a few hours," Drystan pointed out, more to heckle Catriona than anything else. But he released Dareena and pulled on his clothes while his siblings dressed as well.

"Thank you for the clothes, brother," Alistair said, clapping Drystan on the back. "I was getting a bit itchy, sitting nude in the grass."

Drystan laughed as he embraced his youngest brother.

"Itchiness is the least you've had to endure," he said. "I nearly lost my mind when I received your arm in a box today."

Alistair looked horrified. "I'd forgotten all about Arolas's promise to send it on. That must have been terrible for you!"

Drystan snorted. "Typical of you to worry about how *I* would feel," he said, shaking his head. "You are the one who had a limb severed and was forced to live with that horrible spell for so long. I can't imagine how traumatic the experience was."

"It was awful," Alistair admitted, "but having Dareena with me made it bearable." He put an arm around their mate and kissed the top of her forehead. "Without her power as the Dragon's Gift, I might not have survived. Did you know she's learned to heal, and fight, with her elven magic?"

"I heard," Drystan said, grinning down at Dareena. "You've become quite formidable, haven't you?"

"Not as formidable as my three dragons," Dareena said, smiling.

Catriona glanced over Dareena's shoulder, back to where their father was lying. "We should cover him up," she said, pulling a cloak out of her bag. "It seems undignified to leave him there like that."

The mood of their party sobered instantly. The three of them approached their father's prone form, and as they got closer, a tightness squeezed inside Drystan's chest. Unpleasant tingles spread across his skin, and he could only imagine this was the influence of those horrible bracelets.

"It seems cruel to subject him to these," Alistair said softly as Catriona draped the cloak across their father. "And yet, if we do not, he will simply shift back and try to kill us all."

Drystan sighed. "Perhaps we should do some research and see if anything can be done about his mental state," he said. "Has anyone ever heard of dragon sickness being cured?"

"No," Catriona said sorrowfully. "But perhaps there might be some bit of magic that can help."

"The elves specialize in healing," Dareena said thoughtfully. "I didn't think to look and see if there were any books on treating dragons, though, and when Alistair grew ill, the elves didn't seem to know what to do. I can ask Basilla about it when she arrives."

"The warlocks have the largest library of the three kingdoms," Lucyan pointed out. "If we can conquer them, we might be able to find answers there."

Drystan laughed harshly. "That is no mean feat," he said. "The warlocks are the strongest kingdom right now—they have not suffered casualties from the war like we have, or the elves."

"Perhaps the elves will be willing to band together with us," Dareena suggested. "Basilla seems to think the warlock envoy— who is lying unconscious outside Dragomir's lair, by the way— was using some kind of spell to addle the elven king and make him more susceptible to suggestion. Now that he is free, and his children have made their position clear, he may be open to considering an alliance."

"Either way, we must do something about those bastards," Lucyan growled, "including finding a way to shield ourselves from their magical spying."

Drystan and Lucyan shifted back into dragon form and took Dareena back up the mountain while Catriona stayed behind to guard their father. As promised, the warlock still lay there, unconscious, surrounded by several bags of treasure. The brothers shifted back to human form, and the three of them entered the cave to take stock of their recovered wealth.

"By the gods," Lucyan said, his eyes shining with awe as they beheld the mountains of gold and valuables. "This is far more than we anticipated. We could have easily paid the elves their ransom and had five years' worth of taxes left over."

"I have a feeling this hoard has been around a lot longer than Father," Drystan said as he hefted a giant ruby in the palm of his hand. "Our predecessors must have been hiding gold here for years, and Father decided to bring the rest over here." He shook his head. "With these funds, we could hire a mercenary army from across the sea to wipe out our enemies."

"If the people find out about all this gold, they will be furious about the tax increases," Dareena pointed out.

Lucyan snorted. "We are not going to tell them about this," he said. "Hell, they don't even know that the treasure has gone missing in the first place. If they had, Drystan might have lost his head, dragon or not. There would have been an uprising."

"It's going to be very difficult to hide the truth about this now," Dareena countered. "People are bound to notice when they see a group of soldiers carting back sacks full of gold, and the soldiers won't keep silent. I think we ought to give something back to the people of Dragonfell, especially since there *is* still so much unrest," Dareena said. "I think a two-year tax holiday should do the trick."

Drystan winced. "The council will have an apoplexy if I suggest it," he said. "They nearly mutinied against me when I gave a tax break to the soldiers."

Dareena shrugged. "If we truly have as much gold as you say we do, you should be able to give them a token of your appreciation to mollify them."

Lucyan nodded. "She's right. A sack or two of gold for each council member will barely put a dent in our coffers."

"It *is* a good idea," Drystan said. Hooves approached in the distance, and he knew the squadron of soldiers he'd sent out were not far off. "Let's get this treasure back to the Keep," he said, picking up one of the empty sacks the warlocks had left behind. "The sooner we finish up here, the sooner we can get back."

"And celebrate," Dareena said, winking at him. She bent to pick up a sack of her own, giving Drystan a fantastic view of her luscious rear. Drystan's blood heated, and he and Alistair turned to one of the piles of gold and began shoveling it into the bags. If *that* wasn't a good enough motivator for them to get this done as fast as possible, he didn't know *what* was.

THIRTY-FOUR

In the end, Catriona came up with a solution to handle Dragomir. While Taldren returned to Dragon's Keep with the soldiers, the warlock prisoner, and the treasure, Dareena and the other dragons flew to Blackmore Manor, a small estate in the countryside the royal family sometimes used as a retreat.

Dareena and Lucyan flew ahead, while the others stayed well back, away from the warlock bracelets. Lucyan's amulet allowed him to keep his dragon form as he carried Dragomir in his claws and Dareena on his back.

She leaned over and stared at the former king as he lay limp in Lucyan's grip. She'd used a spell she'd found in the primer to keep him unconscious while she and Alistair had waited, and now for this journey. If he had been awake, he would be screaming in agony right now.

Even though the sight of Dragomir still gave Dareena the shivers, she couldn't help but pity him. Once, he had been a great dragon king, ruler of a vast kingdom that was powerful despite the curse that had crippled its royal line. Now, he seemed a frail, broken man, a slave to his avarices, his will no longer his own.

Unless they somehow found a cure for him, Dragomir would never see his sons sit on the throne. He would never meet the babe growing in Dareena's belly, or see the return of the dragons once the curse was broken. Smiling, Dareena placed a hand on her belly. Her pregnancy was just starting to show, though no one who did not know her intimately would be able to tell. She couldn't wait to see her mates' reaction when she showed them tonight.

The servants were surprised when they arrived, but once the four of them introduced themselves, they were delighted. Apparently, none of the royals had visited since the war had started. They were especially pleased to finally meet the Dragon's Gift and assured Dareena they had never believed the nasty rumors about her.

The housekeeper immediately readied a bed for Dragomir, and Dareena took the bracelets away for an hour to give him a chance to heal a bit. They'd found two additional sets amongst the dead warlocks and had spread them about the manor, putting one in the bedroom drawer, one in the dining area, one in the kitchen, and so on. As long as Dragomir was within a hundred yards of any of the bracelets, he would not be able to shift or use his abilities. Even with the hour reprieve they'd given him, it would take many months for Dragomir to heal from his extensive injuries—Tariana promised she would bring a healer to see him and also check on him weekly to make sure he remained under control.

By the time the five of them finally returned to Dragon's Keep, it was well past sunset. "I'm starving," Alistair complained as they walked up the steps. "I don't think we've eaten since this morning, Lucyan."

"I admit to feeling a bit faint," Dareena said, passing a hand over her forehead. "I'm not used to going without food for so long anymore."

"Damn," Drystan swore, putting his arm around Dareena's waist. He searched her face, his gaze round with concern. "Of course, you need to be eating more—the babe needs nourishment!"

The brothers all gathered around Dareena like mother hens, practically carrying her to the dining room despite her protests that she was fine, just hungry and tired. Catriona ordered dinner brought up to them, and soon enough, they sat around the table, stuffing themselves with roasted duck, spiced rice, and vegetables. Dareena's strength quickly returned, and though she was a bit envious that the others were enjoying their wine, overall she was just happy they were all together again.

Halfway through their meal, the door opened, and the steward brought Tariana in, along with the elven siblings.

"Ryolas! Basilla!" Dareena cried, jumping out of her chair. She hurried around the table to hug all three of them. "I'm so glad you've arrived. Did you run into trouble on the way?"

"Only this one," Ryolas said, his eyes twinkling. Smiling broadly, he wrapped his arm around Tariana's waist and drew her close. "As soon as she stopped scolding me for scaring her half to death, she demanded I marry her."

"Is that right?" Drystan lifted a brow. "Without consulting me first?"

Tariana tossed her bright red hair over her shoulder. "*Especially* without consulting you first," she said, and everyone laughed.

"I am very much looking forward to planning your wedding," Dareena said, grinning so hard that her cheeks hurt. There was so much happiness in the room, she felt as though she overflowed with it.

"Their wedding?" Basilla asked, sounding amused. "What about *your* wedding?"

Dareena and the brothers shared a glance. "I suppose we haven't quite figured out how to have a wedding amongst the four of us," Alistair confessed.

Tariana snorted. "It's just a matter of rewriting the vows a bit," she said. "As the dragon god has truly blessed your union, he won't mind."

"Half the nation will be scandalized," Lucyan said wryly, "but we'd best get it done soon, so they can get used to it. The dragon god said that the four of us are needed to break the curse. I have no intention of disappointing him."

"Neither do I," Drystan said with a smile. He came up behind Dareena and put his arms around her. "But we can worry about the wedding later. Right now, you need to take it easy. You've been through quite an ordeal, *and* you're pregnant."

Tariana and the elves joined the rest of them at the table,

and they finished their meal in peace, trading stories, making jokes, and enjoying the easy camaraderie between them. Ryolas and Tariana were glowing, and Taldren and Basilla looked like they were getting on quite well together. He looked quite smitten with the princess already, and Dareena wondered if Basilla already had another suitor on her hands.

"We heard that the delegation my father sent had arrived ahead of us, and we spoke with them before coming here," Basilla said as they worked on polishing off the chocolate torte the cook had brought out.

"Oh?" Lucyan asked. "Were they shocked to see you?"

"Very," Ryolas said with a wry smile.

"We had a bit of a talk with them, and they've agreed to return home and speak to father personally on your behalf," Basilla said. "With any luck, this next set of negotiations will go well, and we will finally be at peace."

"Good," Drystan said. "It's about time we put aside this silly feud and deal with the real threat."

Dareena smiled at Basilla and Ryolas. "I am so glad you two came with us," she said. "There is real hope for our future, now that we are all working together."

Ryolas lifted his glass to her. "*That* is something I can drink to."

After the meal, Dareena expected to return to her quarters, but the brothers led her in the opposite direction, up a flight of stairs and toward a tower at the end of the west wing.

"What is this place?" Dareena asked as Drystan unlocked the heavy wooden door.

"The royal suite." He opened the door to reveal a tastefully decorated salon in shades of red, gold, and white—the house colors. There was a seating area in front of the fireplace, a fully stocked bar, and a large dining table. Several other rooms branched off from this one, though with the doors closed, Dareena couldn't tell what they were. "Father lived here, of course, but we've had it redone to suit our collective tastes. We'll be living here together."

"Together?" Dareena asked as Alistair led her across the room. Lucyan opened one of the doors, and she gasped—there was a giant bed, big enough to sleep six people comfortably, and the room was done in shades of green, her favorite color.

"Yes, together," Lucyan said, a smile in his voice as he nudged her toward the bed.

"We've converted two of the other rooms into bedrooms for nights we may not all want to sleep together," Drystan added, "and the third into a nursery."

"A nursery?" Dareena gasped, her hand flying to her belly. She hadn't even thought that far ahead. "I can't believe you had time to do this!" She threw her arms around Drystan and hugged him fiercely. *I am the luckiest woman in the world,* she thought as she buried her face in his chest, inhaling his sexy, masculine scent.

"I didn't, but that's what servants are for," Drystan said, laughing. He scooped her up and carried her to the bed. Dareena's blood heated as he stripped off her clothes, and she reached for the brothers as they climbed into bed with her in nothing but their underclothes. She stroked Drystan's chest, then ran her hand down Alistair's arm, but the feel of the soft bed beneath her made her sleepy...

"Don't worry," Lucyan said, pulling her back against his chest. His hard cock pressed against her rear, but he merely draped a hand over her belly while Drystan stroked her face, lying on his side so he was facing her. "There will be plenty of time for love play later. For now, we'll rest."

Dareena smiled, then put her arm around Drystan. Alistair, who was on Drystan's other side, laced his fingers in hers, and together, they slipped off into a deep, dreamless sleep.

THIRTY-FIVE

The next morning, Dareena and her mates rose with the sun, then gathered around the dining table in the royal suite to enjoy a leisurely breakfast. The four of them had slept soundly last night. As Dareena feasted on poached eggs, bacon, fried tomatoes, and buttered toast, she had a hard time remembering the last time she felt this well-rested and content.

Home truly is where the heart is, she thought. A smile tugged at her lips as she watched her mates tease and joke with each other. The four of them fit so perfectly together, like a real family, something she hadn't had in so long. Dareena couldn't wait until she finally brought their babe into the world. She had a feeling it would bring them even closer together, and if the dragon god was correct, finally break the curse.

"Now that we have some food in our bellies," Drystan said, "we really ought to talk about our warlock problem."

"Do you mean the warlocks in our dungeon?" Lucyan asked. "Or the warlocks in general?"

Drystan raised his eyebrows. "It can't be both?"

"We must do something about their surveillance magic," Alistair growled, his eyes sparking with annoyance. "I don't like that they can spy on us at any time, especially since there is no way of knowing when they are listening."

"Perhaps either the count or the imposter can fashion a spell to block them out," Lucyan said thoughtfully. "I assume they value their lives, though I'm happy to start with their toenails first." He mimed pulling them out with a pair of pliers.

Dareena shuddered at the mental image that conveyed. "I think relying on the warlocks is very risky," she said. "There is no way to test whether or not whatever magic they do works, and they could just as easily try to sabotage us."

"Dareena is right," Drystan said grimly. "We cannot trust any of the warlocks not to betray us, even the trader you do business with at the market."

"Well, well." Lucyan raised his eyebrows. "Spying, are we, brother?"

Drystan smirked. "You aren't the only observant one around here."

A knock came at the door, and Tariana entered, Ryolas close behind her. "I figured the four of you were already up and eating," Tariana declared as she took a seat next to Alistair. She and Ryolas looked very relaxed, Dareena noted with some amusement. "Are you discussing anything useful?"

"We're trying to figure out how to get the warlocks off our

backs," Drystan said. "Now that they have proven themselves to be the true enemy, we must confront them."

"I've heard that Arolas has been released from the dungeons," Ryolas said darkly. "Count Kianor's influence may have lessened when he left Elvenhame, but it clearly has not diminished completely. We need to remind my father of the elven goddess's decree and have him return control of the armies to me."

"The elven goddess's decree?" Lucyan asked.

"The day Arolas cut Alistair's arm off, the elven goddess took control of Basilla and spoke through her," Dareena said. Chills still ran through her whenever she recalled that day. "She said that Arolas had brought dishonor upon his house and forsworn his family against the dragons. She also made it very clear that the king should choose either Basilla or Ryolas to be his heir, and that Arolas should be punished."

"That must be what the dragon god was talking about," Lucyan muttered, a speculative look in his eyes. "Were there any witnesses other than you and the royal family?"

"Count Kianor and Duchess Valenhall," Dareena said. "The former is unreliable, but the latter might be willing to testify. And, of course, there is Princess Basilla herself."

"Where is Basilla?" Alistair asked, looking around the table. "Was she not hungry this morning?"

"I knocked on her door, but she was still asleep," Ryolas said. "I must admit I found that a little unusual, but we did have a hard ride yesterday. I assume she's exhausted."

"That's only natural," Drystan said, and the others returned to their food. But something niggled at the back of Dareena's mind, and she was not hungry anymore.

"I'm going to go check on Basilla," she said, standing up.

The brothers immediately rose from the table. "We'll come with you," Drystan said.

"There is no need," Dareena protested. "I know you're all still hungry, and Tariana and Ryolas just sat down. Please, enjoy yourselves. I'm only going down the hall—it's perfectly safe for you to let me walk about on my own."

"Not when you're carrying our child," Drystan said firmly. He pushed his chair in, motioning for his brothers to sit back down. "At least allow me to accompany you."

Dareena sighed, glancing down at her belly. The brothers were already overprotective, and this baby was making them doubly so. But she had just been stolen away for two weeks, so she could hardly blame them.

"All right," she said, slipping her hand into Drystan's. "But just you."

They walked down the hall and headed toward the guest rooms, where Dareena had spent her first few weeks at the Keep, first as one of the Chosen, and then as the Dragon's Gift while the brothers vied for her favor. Thinking about that time summoned a wave of nostalgia—while she was happy that she and the brothers had ended up together, she also missed those simpler times, when all she had to worry about was whom she would marry.

"Do you remember the first night we met?" Dareena squeezed Drystan's hand.

"How could I forget?" Drystan smiled fondly at her. "You

were like a vision, standing in the garden, the moonlight shining in your lovely green eyes. I think you had flower petals in your hair." He reached out to brush his hand along the fine black strands, and the tender look in his eyes gave way to laughter. "You were perfect, and I acted like a total brute."

Dareena grinned. "You acted like a fearsome dragon defending his castle," she corrected. "And you have done a splendid job of it."

Drystan's smile faded a little. "I could not have done half as well without you," he said. "You gave us the strength to drive our father out, and your clever mind has finally set us on the path to destroying this curse once and for all."

"And that is why we are a team," Dareena said as they stopped outside Basilla's door. She leaned up to peck Drystan's cheek, then rapped on the door. "Basilla?" she called. "Are you awake?"

No answer.

"Basilla?" She knocked a little harder, then tried the door knob. It gave easily. "I'm coming in," she warned, pushing open the door.

Dareena gasped in horror.

"Fuck!" Drystan swore. The bed was empty, the room had been destroyed, and a trail of blood led from the middle of the room to the open window. Drystan and Dareena rushed to the window together, batting the billowing curtains aside. It was a sheer drop to the bottom, a good hundred feet. Not possible without climbing gear.

Or magic.

"Guards!" Drystan bellowed, his voice full of rage and guilt.

Four of them came running, stunned looks on their faces as they surveyed the room. "The Princess Basilla has been taken from her chamber. We must find her at once!"

The castle was put on full alert, and a full search of the Keep was conducted. The brothers tried to get Dareena to wait in her room, but she refused, choosing to help with the search instead. As she went from room to room, with Lucyan at her side, anxiety rose within her, along with incredible guilt. Ryolas had looked absolutely stricken when he'd been told the news. He'd assumed his sister would be safe in the Keep, and why wouldn't he? If the princess could be taken from her bed in the middle of the night, were any of them truly safe?

"Hang on," Lucyan growled as he and Dareena rushed down a stairwell. "I smell blood."

Dareena froze. Now that she was paying attention, she smelled it too—a coppery tang that made her shoulders tense with nerves. "Is someone injured?" she asked as she followed Lucyan down the stairs, keeping her body behind his.

"No!" Lucyan roared, an agonized cry that tore at Dareena's soul. He traversed the rest of the stairs in one giant leap, landing in a large pool of blood at the bottom. Dareena's stomach twisted at the sight of Taldren lying there, staring straight at her with blank eyes. His throat had been slit, and his guard's uniform was drenched in blood that was already turning brown.

"He...he's been there for a while," Dareena said, her voice trembling. Tears blurred her vision as she braced a hand against the wall for support. How long ago had Basilla been taken? Why hadn't Taldren's body been found before?

Lucyan yelled for help, and the guards came running, along

with Drystan, Alistair, Tariana, and Ryolas. Their faces turned white at the sight of Taldren's body, and Ryolas passed a hand over his face, looking like he wanted to break something.

"This is just bloody great," he snarled. "On top of everything else."

"What do you mean 'everything else?'" Lucyan demanded, twisting around to face the others. He'd dropped to his knees next to Taldren to check for a pulse, and his trousers were stained with his cousin's blood. "What else has happened?"

"Both the count and the imposter have broken out of their cells," Drystan answered, his voice filled with barely leashed rage. A vein throbbed in his temple, and he looked even angrier than Ryolas, if that were possible. "They must have found some way to circumvent those manacles."

Footsteps pounding against the stone floor drew their attention, and they turned to see Shadley rushing toward them. "They used the catacombs to escape," he said, his face flushed with exertion. "The captain of the Guard and I just confirmed it."

"That means they had inside help," Tariana snapped. "Only the royal family and a trusted few retainers even know of the catacombs."

"So, there is a traitor in our midst," Alistair said softly. Outwardly, he appeared the calmest, but Dareena knew that Taldren's death had to be hitting him just as hard. His eyes filled with grief as he looked down at his cousin, and he crouched to close those dead, unseeing eyes. "And because we were too blind to see it, Taldren paid with his life."

Grief swelled in Dareena's throat, choking off her airway.

Wasn't it just last night that he'd sat at the table, his eyes bright and his cheeks flushed with color? She'd wondered if he and Basilla might develop a courtship. Instead, he lay here, bled out, while the princess was being spirited off to gods knew where.

"There's more," Shadley said, his tone dire. He pulled a sheaf of parchment from inside his sleeve and handed it to Drystan. "We found this sitting on the throne."

Drystan's jaw clenched as he looked at the paper. "Enjoy what little time you have left together," he read aloud in a flat, emotionless tone. "Your dynasty will soon come to an end, and I will come back to claim what I have left behind."

"What does that mean?" Ryolas asked, his voice cracking. "What more could they want? And why have they taken my sister?"

"They are obviously not pleased that Basilla rejected Prince Mordan's marriage proposal," Alistair said. "Perhaps they mean to force the issue by planting a warlock babe in her belly."

Dareena shuddered, placing a hand on her own belly. It was becoming a habit, one she couldn't quite help even though she knew her hand didn't keep him any safer. "If our dynasty is under threat," she said slowly, dread filling her heart, "they must mean to target our child."

The brothers' eyes flared bright red. "We will never let that happen," they snarled as one.

"It is time to take the fight to Shadowhaven," Tariana said in a hard voice. She placed her hand on Ryolas's shoulder and gave it a gentle squeeze. "We will rescue your sister and vanquish the warlocks once and for all. The time has come for the dragons to rise again, and we shall not let these insidious liver-eaters stand in our way."

Tariana's fierce declaration banished some of the fear in Dareena's heart. Taking a deep breath, she met each of the brother's eyes in turn, exchanging a silent vow with them. She didn't know how, but the four of them would find a way to penetrate Shadowhaven's indomitable defenses and strike at the heart of their empire.

The gods help anyone who stood in their way.

To be continued...

Dareena's story continues in DRAGON'S CURSE, Book 3 of The Dragon's Gift trilogy. Make sure to join the mailing list so you can be notified of future release dates, and to receive special updates, freebies and giveaways!

CLICK HERE TO JOIN

Did you enjoy this book? Please consider leaving a review. Reviews help us authors sell books so we can afford to write more of them. Writing a review is the best way to ensure that the author writes the next one as it lets them know readers are enjoying their work and want more. Plus, it makes the author feel warm and fuzzy inside, and who doesn't want that? ;)

ABOUT THE AUTHOR

JASMINE WALT. She a NYT bestseller who is obsessed with books, chocolate, and sharp objects. Somehow those three things melded together in her head and transformed into a desire to write, usually fantastical stuff with a healthy dose of action and romance. Her characters are a little (okay, a lot) on the snarky side, and they swear, but they mean well. Even the villains sometimes.

When she isn't chained to her keyboard, you can find her practicing her triangle choke on the jujitsu mat, spending time with her family, or binge-watching superhero shows on Netflix.

Want to check out Jasmine's other books? You can do so at www.jasminewalt.com. She loves hearing from her readers, so drop her a line anytime at jasmine@jasminewalt.com.

Fugitive by Magic

Claimed by Magic

Saved by Magic

Taken by Magic

Tested by Magic (Novella)

Forsaken by Magic (Novella)

Called by Magic (Novella)

Her Dark Protectors

Written with Emily Goodwin

Cursed by Night

Kissed by Night

Hidden by Night

Broken by Night

www.ingramcontent.com/pod-product-compliance
Lightning Source LLC
Chambersburg PA
CBHW050603190726
48283CB00007B/2261